Deception and Redemption

A Quay Thompson Novel

Gail Lee Cowdin

ISBN-13: 978-1976564017
ISBN-10: 1976564018

**Library of Congress Control Number: 2014919766
CreateSpace Independent Publishing Platform, North
Charleston, SC**

This is a work of fiction. Names, characters, places, and
incidents either are the product of the author's
imagination or are used fictitiously, and any resemblance
to actual persons, living or dead, business
establishments, events or locales is entirely coincidental.

This book is dedicated to my grandchildren in hopes that my footprints will lead them to a love of reading and writing.

Chapter 1
The Press Conference

Karen Thompson stood unsettled but ready behind the podium. She was anxious, not because her life was about to end—she had no idea that a sniper was setting his sights on her—but because of the import of her announcement. The glass façade of the Cameron BioTech building reflected Karen Thompson's poised stance. She gave the appearance of confidence as she scanned her prepared speech one more time. Her words would be world changing. Cameron BioTech's latest research would reveal a nearly futuristic advancement into genome studies and stem cell growth and regeneration. Karen was certain people's lives would never be the same.

Karen watched as security guards settled into their positions at each side of the plaza. Tension arced through the air. She expected the left- and right-wing pundits to pounce on this. The portent of this momentous announcement was not lost on Loren Michelson either, the president of Cameron BioTech. The members of Cameron's board took seats next to Michelson on the dais behind and to the side of Karen at the podium. The sniper aimed carefully while aligning with Karen through the scope.

Karen scanned the crowd. She spotted her husband, Quay Thompson, near the back. He stood tall, hands dug into his jeans pockets, a blue crew-neck sweater fit snugly over his broad chest. He broke into a grin and winked at her as she caught his eye. Surprised and pleased that he had come, she acknowledged his wink with a slight nod and smile. Then she spied the small group of protestors banded together not far from Quay. Her smile faded.

She laid her notes on the podium, smoothed her suit jacket, and brushed a stray lock of blond hair from her eyes, securing it behind her ear. The popcorn snapping of the cameras and the buzz of the video cams echoed across the plaza as the press maneuvered for positions. Media members pushed microphones toward the dais. Karen refocused on the protestors' placards bobbing and waving. They were certainly not Cameron BioTech well-wishers. They just wanted their minute in the limelight. They had no idea what they were doing. Karen's apprehension intensified.

As if on signal, the activists began shouting. Their shouts built slowly, rising to a fevered pitch of raucous demands.

"How can you justify telling lies to the world?" a voice in the crowd began.

Another called out, "Cameron BioTech isn't about saving lives. It's about destroying lives! You're all liars!"

"Baby killers!"

Clearly, the intent was to grab the attention of the media. The taunts escalated.

"You think we don't understand where those stem cells came from? Humans! Real, live humans. You're condemning thousands of babies just to use their cells."

"Nazis!" a man's voice boomed out above the rest. "You're all going to be condemned to hell!"

The voices became a chorus of shrill shrieks.

Karen heard each voice. Her resolve intensified. Her job was to help them understand. They were wrong.

"What does Cameron have to gain besides money? You're ruining your own lives and ours. What happened to biblical morality?"

Another voice shouted from the midst of the crowd, "Cameron is destroying the moral fiber of America. Cameron is abusing everyone."

Murmurs of agreement rose from one side. Heads bobbed in unison with the placards.

"You're not telling the world the truth. You're murderers," a young woman shouted.

"You're just creating a Brave New World in there. We don't want your future of using embryos for stem-cell research!" a man's deep voice boomed out over the shouts of the crowd. "We don't want Cameron's future of clones and murder. We want the truth," he continued. "We want our own future. We won't accept Cameron's world control!"

The voice came from a man who was clearly the leader of the protesters. The crowd of objectors tightened around the man, protecting their leader.

As a security officer edged closer to the man, a chant began near the back and seemed to roll over the heads of the crowd up to the dais. "Cameron lies! Babies die! Cameron lies! Babies die! Cameron lies! Babies die!"

Karen cleared her throat, settling herself to begin. The press jockeyed for positions while pushing the protestors aside. The protestors would get their moment of fame on camera later. The cameras focused on Karen now. Sensing the moment was right, she leaned toward the microphone.

"Good afternoon," she said firmly and loudly, and then paused for the crowd to quiet. She took a deep breath and continued.

"My name is Karen Thompson. On behalf of Cameron BioTech, I'd like to thank all of you for joining us for this important announcement."

She surveyed the group and continued, "And I do mean all of you." She paused and smiled toward the protestors. Gathering strength, she continued, "Today, Cameron BioTech leads America into the exploration of a new frontier. The world is watching. Americans will once again stand out as leaders in scientific advancement in the world. Cameron BioTech is proud to announce today a major discovery made here, which will lead to exciting improvements for all of our lives tomorrow. I am pleased to ..."

The red dot moved down her forehead and rested under her right eye. Quay Thompson watched in horrific recognition as the dot moved across his wife's face. He sprang forward, toppling people to each side like bowling pins as he rushed to his wife.

Crack!

The retort brought everyone's eyes toward the side of the building. The sound echoed from one side of the plaza to the other, bouncing off the retaining walls at each side and reverberating against the glass wall of the entry.

Someone in the crowd screamed, "She's down! Look! Look at Thompson!"

Confused murmurs became screams.

"Oh my God, she's been shot!"

"Somebody help her."

Quay reached the dais, bellowing, "Call 911! Now!"

All eyes shifted to Karen Thompson, who had slumped over the dark oak podium. The audience watched in frozen horror as Quay reached for her. She slid to the side, almost collapsing onto the ground. Quay pulled his wife's crumpled body toward him, murmuring in her ear. The back of her blond hair was coated with deep crimson that slowly trickled forward and down into her unseeing eyes. Rivulets of her blood stained the gray cement of the plaza.

Security guards who had been positioned on each side of the plaza raced to Karen and Quay, guns pulled and ready, too late. They scanned the area, searching the perimeter for a shooter. Loren Michelson knelt next to Karen. He whispered in her ear, looked at Quay and mouthed, "I'm so sorry." Others surveyed the crowd. Others held their cell phones to their ears, talking, pleading for help. People yelled and pointed in every of direction with confusion about where the shot had originated. It was clear the echoing in the plaza had distorted the sound.

In the mayhem, no one noticed the single shadowed figure ducking behind the mirrored façade of the building.

Chapter 2
One Year Later: The Present

Minnesotans take pride in withstanding the record-low, subzero temperatures set each year in Embarrass or International Falls. They will inform you that they are a hardy lot. Snow and cold won't stop them from enjoying the great outdoors. And probably most important to the Minnesota state coffers, the Minnesota sportsman finds his Valhalla in the winters of the North Shore and the Boundary Waters Canoe Area, or BWCA, where an avid sportsman can ski, go ice fishing, take part in the Iditarod dog race, or play a brisk game of hockey on outdoor ice.

But the BWCA is popular in summers, too; tourists flock to the North Country where back country resorts offer a bit of peace and tranquility on one of the ten thousand lakes. Never mind the mosquitoes, commonly referred to as the Minnesota state bird. If a Minnesotan is tough enough to withstand the winters, this pesky insect isn't going to deter him or her from enjoying the great outdoors during other seasons.

This was the land where Quay Thompson came to escape and perhaps finally recover from the loss of his wife.

Quay struggled to wakefulness. Fingers of sunlight crept over the treetops and through the blinds into the log-walled room. He rolled over, reaching once again for Karen.

And once again, just as he had so many mornings since Karen's death, he left his dream sleep to face the emptiness in his gut. Although it had been little more than a year now, he still found himself caught in the grip of old habits. The hollowness had since become a routine part of his life. Above all, guilt dominated his life. He had never found the sniper. Karen's murder remained an unsolved case. As the lead investigator for the Minnesota Bureau of Criminal Apprehension, he believed he should have been able to figure it out. But he had run into barriers at every turn.

Her murder had been caught live on the local TV's Breaking News and then had been quickly picked up by the national networks. The grisly attack had shut down the work that Cameron BioTech had intended to announce. Protests and murder were not the kind of news Cameron BioTech wanted or needed. Nor was the media attention what Quay Thompson had wanted or expected.

Quay had relived the nightmare ceaselessly, trying to sort through each event of that day. Cameron executives had no answers, or at least none that they would voice. Quay originally posited that since Cameron BioTech remained mute about the announcement they had planned to make that day, there might be a connection between that announcement and Karen's murder. He even reasoned that it may have sealed some sort of blackmail threat. The company had closed their doors to the public and shut down media access. And in the entire last year, no one had been able to discover just how, or even if, Karen Thompson's murder and the BioTech announcement were at all connected.

Cameron BioTech simply pled innocence. Loren Michelson and his executive board swore they had not received any murder threats. They claimed they knew of no reason Karen would have been singled out. The company announced that it had decided to hold off on any research announcements until they'd further completed more decisive research. At least that's what they'd called it. Nothing more had come of it.

Quay lay in bed, barely awake in a gray fog while reliving that day again, grasping for any clues. Quay remembered it had been a bright, cool autumn morning in Maple Grove, Minnesota, a northern suburb of Minneapolis. She'd stood poised and beautiful in front of the microphone. He had been so proud of her. Then he had seen the sniper's dot, heard the "pop," and watched her collapse in a slow-motion slide down the side of dais.

Now, here he was a year later, still certain her death could have been prevented. It was his fault. He had missed the signs. He should have seen it coming. He should have been more aware of the dangerous atmosphere escalating at Cameron. He should have warned her. He should have alerted Cameron. He should have ... should have ... After all, crime, murder, and mayhem were his areas of expertise. He was part of the Minnesota Bureau of Criminal Apprehension, the BCA.

He still believed there was a piece to the puzzle he had never been able to put in place. The thought nagged at him constantly. Why would anyone, even a crazy fanatic, single out Karen and take her down like that? She was the messenger. People weren't supposed to shoot the messenger. But then, maybe they hadn't. Maybe there was another message in her murder. A message everyone had missed.

And now here he was in this isolated resort near the North Shore, trying to pull his life together. Trying to get over his wife's death. And still remembering their life together.

They say big men fall hard. Had he ever. They'd had a good life—a great life together. He had to either let it go—or solve it.

Quay grunted, yawned, and forced himself to roll out of bed. He needed to get out on the lake. He needed to fish. That would help.

His small fishing boat trolled along next to the shore, creeping through the heavy morning mist that hovered over the lake in the early hour. The haunting call of a nearby loon echoed a minute later from the other side of the lake. Quay trailed his line in the water, hoping to catch a bass or walleye for his meal. There was nothing like fresh fish fried over a flame in the outdoors. Being on the lake calmed and comforted him. Here he found himself reminiscing.

Karen had loved coming up here, too. The North Shore had been a frequent escape for them. But it took a while for them to discover their mutual interests.

Their love hadn't been love at first sight. More like interest at first sight. He had been a confirmed bachelor when he'd met her. He'd dated and done the singles scene, but without much enthusiasm. It had been merely a form of recreation for him. Nothing more. Then Karen had come along and taken him by surprise.

He remembered their first encounter at a fundraiser sponsored by the local police association. He didn't like those formal events with everyone wearing their best penguin suits. Denims and flannel shirts were more his style. So after the dinner that night, he had slipped out for quick smoke. That brisk January night air had cut into his lungs as he inhaled.

She'd come up quietly behind him.

"I take it this isn't your type of event. You seemed rather uncomfortable in there," she'd said, smiling at him. She had moved next to him, pulling a light jacket around her. He'd turned to look at the most striking woman he'd ever seen. With heels on, she was eye level with him. She had beautiful, blue eyes fringed with dark, feathered lashes. Her porcelain complexion and ash-blond hair completed the look of Scandinavian heritage so common to Minnesotans. She wasn't cute. She was classy.

She'd admitted to him later that she had seen him in the crowd, and she had decided right then that he was a man she needed to meet.

"Well," he'd said, "I just thought I'd take a quick break before they begin the heavy-duty lobbying for funds. I'm supposed to get up to say a few words."

"Yes, I heard that. So am I. I've worked with the police department in the past and also the BCA in the capacity of field expert on DNA forensics. Right now I'm the PR person for Cameron BioTech. I guess that qualifies me as someone who can explain why the police association needs more funds. Helping find cures for children's diseases is a worthwhile cause. It's good PR to have the police supporting kids," Karen had explained.

They'd spent the rest of the evening discussing their viewpoints about the future of law enforcement, the judiciary, civil rights, and scientific advancements that could change many people's lives. Karen's initial work as a research scientist and DNA expert and then as the PR head for Cameron BioTech had made her a well-known figure in the Twin Cities. She was outspoken about the future she wanted to see. She saw Cameron's current work as being directed toward helping the disabled, the paralyzed, and those plagued by disease. She was passionate about it.

Karen had seldom spoken to Quay about the specific research at Cameron, explaining that it was top secret. But with rapid-fire enthusiasm, she'd told him, "We're just a minute away from discovering the causes of diseases like cancer, or finding the key to regenerating nerves for those who've been paralyzed or incapacitated by an accident or disease. We can do so many things if we have the money and freedom to develop the techniques. We can create a *Star Wars* future if we just can have approval to use these special stem cells and this gene replication research. These are major advancements that could affect everyone's daily lives in a very positive way.

"My current job is to ensure that no one feels threatened by Cameron's research. We don't want the public to have any misunderstandings about the purpose of the research Cameron's doing. I know Cameron's being very responsible in their genome research. I need to impress upon anyone who will listen that Cameron's promise is to continue to bring all future, exciting advances to the public in a responsible manner.

"I must emphasize not only the need for this scientific research, but also make potential sponsoring groups aware of what we hope to accomplish and explain how they can also contribute. Anytime we can get some positive press, the better. There are so many misconceptions about Cameron BioTech research. If people only knew what we can do."

Once she'd gotten started, there was no turning her off. It was a highly competitive field of research, she had said. Speed was of the essence. They had been close, very close. To ... what? He didn't know.

14

The press conference, her final press conference, had been scheduled to make that critical announcement about Cameron's newest advancements. That's all he knew.

She had always had a fervent desire to find cures for the helpless and the hopeless. That was part of what Quay had loved about her instantly. She truly believed they could change the future and make the world a better place. She exuded classy, sexy intelligence with a loyalty and commitment to this cause. He realized now that he'd fallen in love with her that first night.

After that evening, they'd begun dating regularly. Then their relationship had accelerated into a wildly passionate rollercoaster affair. Within six months, they were engaged and planning an August wedding. They'd both agreed that a small, private wedding would be best, especially given their public personas. Karen's sister Susan had been her attendant, and Quay had asked his brother John to be his best man. Both sets of parents had come down to the wedding at the small Catholic church outside of St. Bonifacius. Everyone was happy.

And they'd had two years of blissful marriage, celebrating their second anniversary in August with a quiet dinner at the Porter Club, an upscale restaurant downtown. Their work schedules had been so hectic they'd savored every minute they'd had with each other. That anniversary evening had been a different kind of special, Quay remembered. They'd talked about starting a family. He wanted a boy or a girl or both, he'd told her. She'd decided even twins would be great.

Not quite a month after that anniversary evening, the sniper had murdered her. Quay had not been able to get his footing since then. His future had been destroyed in a single moment. He'd lost his purpose.

But at least now, he admitted ruefully to himself, he was finally able to go for longer periods of time without feeling that powerful, disabling punch in the gut. Yet, it always caught him off guard when the grief came rolling in like a smothering fog. There were times in the past year he'd been so incapacitated with grief that he hadn't been able to function. He'd been riding that rollercoaster for months now. He wondered if it would ever stop and let him off.

His brother John had very bluntly told him that he was worried that Quay wasn't going to pull out of this. But at this point, Quay guessed it didn't matter what his brother thought. Nothing seemed to be worthwhile anymore. He just missed Karen. And he still believed he should have done something to prevent her murder. He just couldn't figure out what.

John wouldn't give up on Quay. This past Saturday, at John's suggestion, Quay had made the five-hour drive up 35W to Duluth and on up Highway 61 to his brother's new home in Lutsen.

Quay had steadfastly insisted on staying at one of the local lodges instead of at his brother's home. He'd explained that he really wanted the time alone to "sort things out" and to use the time up north as a getaway. He'd brought his boat and had planned to do a little fishing.

He wondered if maybe he should have stayed with John, Sharon, and the kids. The kids were great. He loved his little niece, Alli, and nephew, Adam. John was three years younger, his little brother. He was also the youngest sheriff ever in Northern Minnesota's Cook County.

Now, Quay sat in his bass boat trolling next to the shore of the small inland lake. It was still and early. And he was trying to put it together.

The sun had reached over the silhouetted pines. He flicked his line into the water, pulled it out, and flicked it in again. The boat rocked slightly as it glided quietly through the water. The trolling motor made a muted hum. He could just make out the shape of the loon he'd heard earlier swimming toward the middle of the lake with a little one on its back.

Despite the calm of the lake and the fishing that he loved, Quay couldn't stop thinking about what was and what could have been. This time, he had a week's vacation. A week to come to terms. A little fishing, sitting in the boat out in the Boundary Waters—on Bearskin Lake where he was now—or maybe head up at the end of the Gunflint Trail on Gunflint Lake. Watch the sunrise and sunset, admire the families of loons. Maybe he'd be lucky again and spy a moose and her calf as they ambled down to the water's edge for a drink. He'd seen it all before, but it never ceased to put him in awe. Enjoy the quiet, drink a few beers, absorb the peace in the scenery. That's what would help.

"Reminisce. Come to grips," John had suggested. He'd pictured it. It had sounded okay at the time.

The Getaway Lodge down the road had seemed the perfect place for him right now. But now, thinking about his arrival yesterday, he wondered why he had visited so freely with the girl at the desk when he checked in. That had been his first mistake. She'd started asking questions right away.

17

"Here for a little vacation?" she'd asked.

"Yeah, I decided I needed to get out of the Cities for a while and get back to real life."

She'd laughed. "I just couldn't get into city living myself. I tried. I really loved the Mall of America and all that stuff, but the traffic and the hectic pace just drove me wild. It always seemed like you had to be somewhere five minutes ago."

"Yeah, I know what you mean," Quay said. "I've worked with the BCA for a few years now. Everyone's always in a rush to find someone or something. Used to work homicide for the Minneapolis Police Department before, and that was even worse. Had me running all over the Cities, doing overtime, taking calls. I was never home. Wanted to slow down when I got married. But I guess the slowdown never really happened. So I grabbed the job working for the BCA. It's just as crazy as homicide was in the Cities."

"Wow. That sounds like really interesting, exciting stuff."

"Yeah, maybe, but it gets to you. That's why I'm here for a break."

At least he hadn't given the girl at the desk his whole life story. He'd probably get the sympathetic looks the rest of the time he was there.

The cell phone in his pocket vibrated, jarring Quay out of his musing.

"Yeah," he answered. His voice echoed over the water.

"Mornin', Quay. You awake?" his brother asked. His tone was urgent.

"Yeah, I'm fishing."

"Well, that's good, I guess. I hate to do this, but I was wondering if you could give me a hand this morning. Can you spare some time?"

"Oh, I suppose I could fit something into my busy schedule." Quay yawned aloud. "Whatcha got?"

"Well, we've got a body over by Spruce Falls Beach. I know you planned on fishing today. But I thought you might like to look at this with me. Looks like a young girl's been murdered. Since you're the BCA guy, I thought I'd ask you to come over and take a peek. Give your expertise, so to speak."

Quay began reeling in his line while pulling himself out of his half-reverie and back to reality. *Huh*, he thought to himself. *Some vacation this is. What on earth is John up to?*

"Yeah, I suppose I could," he said. "I can be back at the lodge in twenty minutes or so."

"Okay, big bro. I really appreciate it. You'll be back out on the lake in no time; I promise." He gave Quay directions and promised to meet him at the site. He hung up before Quay could respond.

So much for the getaway, he thought. *Damn!*

Earlier that morning, the call had come in to the sheriff's office about a body found up near Pedagogue's Road north of Lutsen. John admired Quay's talents, and he and Quay worked well together. In the past, when they got a case, they would bounce ideas around until something hit home. Since they had split into different parts of the state and different agencies, Quay had begun to carve a reputation for himself in the Cities and beyond. He had become "the guy to call," the go-to guy for difficult cases.

19

After the call came in about the body, John realized it might be good to get Quay's perspective as long as he was already here. It was a perfect opportunity. They could bounce things around like old times. And maybe with this case, Quay would be able to return to his old self.

Originally, he'd thought Quay might want to spend some time in the outdoors, do some hiking, maybe some hunting or fishing. The brothers were outdoors guys, and there was no place on earth as peaceful and refreshing as the North Shore Country. John and his wife had hoped that maybe they could reminisce like old times. They would encourage Quay to talk a little about Karen. It might help Quay if they could get into his head about what he was feeling these days.

On the other hand, John was glad that he had been able to reach Quay on the cell this morning. He hoped he could convince his brother to get involved in this case enough to stay. Quay could keep busy with a new investigation up here. It would help out both of them. It was like killing two birds with one stone, so to speak. Quay was on his way. It'd be great to work together again.

Chapter 3

John turned onto Pedagogue's Road off Highway 61. Pedagogue's Road ran parallel to Highway 61 for several miles. It followed along the North Shore of Lake Superior and was populated by about fifty small cabins and year-round homes as well as one small resort. Spruce Falls, and the creek leading from it, actually bubbled through the small resort down to Lake Superior.

Lutsen, a small town and a popular ski resort, was south about four miles. Grand Marais was the next largest town, about thirty miles north. Highway 61 was the usual thoroughfare to bring city people up for getaway weekends at the cabins. Lake Superior provided their needed therapy and sanctuary. Weekenders also frequently brought guests to enjoy their special hideaways.

As he waited for Quay, John's mind returned to the body that had been discovered behind one of the cabins. The North Shore territory was a tourists' Mecca. It was unlikely that someone would have recognized a new person in this area of the shore. It might be difficult to ID the body if it was indeed a stranger.

But to be sure, within the next twenty-four hours, just to be thorough, John and Quay would make sure each of the residents was interviewed. That meant getting the names and permanent addresses of each person living here. Some cabin owners may not have come up north this particular weekend. That meant they would still have to be contacted and interviewed to find out if they had offered their cabins to friends.

This investigation would require cooperation between the sheriffs' departments of Cook County and those in Hennepin and

21

Ramsey Counties located in the Twin Cities. That's where Quay would be helpful. What a break it was that Quay was already there.

The Lutsen CSI crew (meaning Craig and Bernie from the sheriff's department) was taking pictures of the body when John arrived. After they were finished, four men would have to carry the body up the rocky path in a tarp hammock. Only after laboriously winding up through the cedar and pine trees to the road would they be able to lift the body onto a gurney and slide it into the ambulance. But the ambulance crew hadn't even arrived yet. They were due shortly.

It was close to nine by the time Quay arrived. His breath formed white puffs as he climbed out of his truck. The cool night air still hung close to the shore. September twenty-ninth. The leaves had just begun to turn, and the sun was dappling the yellows and oranges with bright splashes of light. The lake air still had a brisk cut to it. The last weekend in September was truly the last getaway for many of the cabin people. Many would be there to enjoy the lake before closing up the cabins for the winter.

A small group of onlookers gathered near the top of the property at the driveway's sandy entrance. Trying to see through the trees, people craned and bobbed their heads one way and another in hopes of seeing something as exotic as injuries or even murder. Even more exciting was watching the CSI crew and the sheriff in action.

"It's just like the TV show," murmured one young man to a friend as Quay pushed through the group.

Homeowner Arlene Carlisle remained huddled in her cabin. She had called 911 at seven that morning.

Distraught and wheezing with fear, she had described the scene that had met her as she'd wound her way from her cabin down to the rocks near the shore in the early morning haze. She had just completed her morning ritual of soaking in the sights and sounds of the lake. She loved to sit on a boulder closer to shore while listening to the waves crashing against the rocks and sipping her morning cup of coffee.

The fragments of her cup lay on the rock where she'd dropped it when she first realized that the object below her was a body. The body had been lying in a water-filled crater in the rocks. Dashing back to the cabin, she had placed the frantic call without bothering to look back. The gruesome picture was etched into her memory. Pacing nervously in her kitchen, she'd waited for the sheriff to arrive.

She didn't look out toward the lake again. She hoped she'd made a mistake. Wait until she told her husband, Rick. He'd left at five that morning to go fishing with a buddy up on one of the inland lakes. Maybe the body had already been there when he left. Maybe it really wasn't a body. Maybe it was just a bag of something that someone had tossed into the lake. Maybe it was an animal that had fallen into the lake and washed up onto the rocks. She'd hoped. But she knew what she'd truly seen.

Chapter 4

Gitchigumi translated to Big-Sea-Water. That was what the Ojibwas and later Longfellow called Lake Superior. The Great Lake could be a beautiful and equally treacherous lake. Huge, gray lava boulders often lined the shore of the lake. A stone bowl had been etched into the top of one of the boulders. Now the crashing waves spouted gray plumes of icy spray onto a small twisted body resting in the bowl.

The Ojibwa name for the lake said it best, Quay thought. Big-Sea-Water was powerful, eternal, and in this case, an unforgiving body of water. The silver water rhythmically reached out, flicking fingers of water at the ensnared body in seemingly vain attempts to pull it into the deep, dark water. It seemed the action was becoming increasingly stronger and fiercer. Superior was relentless, but the massive wall of shoreline boulders resisted, cradling the girl's body securely.

Quay Thompson looked down at the girl's brittle form. His expression was impassive, but he was making mental notes. She appeared to be in her late teens or even early twenties; the ME would have to make the final determination. His experience told him the girl would not be easily identified. He hoped the medical examiner was good.

Whoever she was, she was badly bruised, especially about her face. The distortion and swelling in her cheek contours and additional bruising on her forehead may have been caused by the battering of the rocks and the frigid spray of Lake Superior. But that was unlikely.

Quay also noticed what appeared to be bruising and swelling on the neck

24

of the girl. From where he was standing, it was difficult to be sure what caused her death. But he could make a good guess. He began to form a picture of what had happened here.

John made his way down the path and over the boulder up to the crater by Quay.

"What do you think?" he asked Quay.

"I think this little girl met someone who wanted her to disappear."

"Yeah," agreed John.

"Did you see the marks on her neck? She must have been choked, and then her body was dumped."

"Do you think she was dead when she was dumped?" asked John.

"Hard to say. We'll let the ME take a good look. I wonder if the intention was to leave her here or to hope the lake would wash her away and sweep the body up shore. What do you think?"

"Could be a botched cover-up."

"Yeah," mused Quay. He was still working it out in his mind.

Icy, dark curls surrounded the girl's round, ebony face. The dark brown eyes had probably sparkled in life, but now water crystals clustered on her eyelashes, providing an unnatural sparkle in her lifeless eyes.

"Must have been a pretty girl," Quay mused out loud.

John nodded and nudged Quay into movement back up the path to the cabin.

As Quay looked up, scanning the rest of the area, he noticed several local officers talking quietly as they stood a short distance away. They looked away when he looked up. He suspected they were talking about him.

"Did you tell the guys who I was?" asked Quay.

John followed Quay's gaze. "No, not yet. I'm sure some may remember you from other times you've visited, though."

A wad of bubblegum bulged in Quay's cheek, replacing the smokes he'd given up a couple months earlier at the doctor's insistence. The bubblegum helped a little. He still felt urges for the nicotine fix at the most inopportune moments. He ignored the local guys as they covertly observed him. He slid the gum around in his mouth and purposefully blew a large pink bubble, drew it back in, and popped it. John slid up next to him, pretending not to notice the giant bubble. Quay knew he'd seen it. Quay looked at John and gave him his best innocent smile. John looked down, grunted, shook his head, and gave Quay a slight shove.

They didn't look at all like brothers. John was the dark-haired one with the dark brown eyes. Quay had ended up with blond hair and blue-gray eyes. He was two inches taller, and his features were more chiseled than John's. When Quay got dressed in his hunting gear and let his beard grow out, he'd been told he became a brawny Paul Bunyan look-alike.

John and Quay had been close growing up. They had even worked together in the same police district in Minneapolis after college. That was before Quay had been called in to coordinate with the Bureau of Criminal Apprehension guys on a local case in the Twin Cities. Quay had stayed on at the BCA. At that time, John had stayed with the Minneapolis Police. It was later that he got the call to head north to work as county sheriff.

At six foot four, Quay Thompson wasn't easily ignored. He stood out from other men not only in size, but also in attitude. Quay exuded self-assurance. Some might have assumed he was even arrogant. Of course, there were those who thought investigators who worked in the BCA had an abundance of ego. He'd seen that ego in some of his fellow investigators. But that wasn't how he operated. He wanted John's team to know that. The bubble he'd just popped might have told the real story.

Just messin' with ya, boys, he thought, grinning at them as he blew and popped another bubble.

Quay saw his purpose as support for the local group. First, he wanted to make his own observations and form his own opinions. He didn't want his observations to be tainted by others. Not yet.

Quay realized John's invitation to this murder site had now evolved into a dual purpose. John wanted him to give up thinking about Karen and her murder. That was a given. But John also respected his brother's investigative expertise. Quay suddenly understood this suspicious death had provided John with just the opportunity he'd wanted to draw Quay back from the edges of his grief.

John had once told Quay, "You're as dead inside as Karen is dead in the ground. You need to get busy. You're still living. You need to get on with your life." Now here he was, getting busy.

John had been right to call him this morning. He needed something that wasn't mundane to shake him out of this lethargy.

Quay walked back again to the edge of the boulders and looked down several feet at the waves as they thundered against the rocks. Gulls screeched while gliding and circling above. He inhaled the crisp lake air that mixed with other smells of fish, pine, and leaves. All

27

together, it made the moment nearly hypnotic. He looked out into the distance, watched a barge move across the lake, and began to drift again into his past.

Quay didn't associate with any of their extended family or old friends anymore. Too many memories. He couldn't handle it.

Now here was this young girl. Life cut too short. What had happened? Where was her family? Had she distanced from them? Why? He needed to make sense out of this one.

"John," Quay turned to look beyond his brother, "we need to find out who she is. Let's get a picture of this girl released to all the media outlets as soon as possible. I can get the Bureau to do an artist pic if we need to. Something might pop up. We need to find out who she is and alert her family."

"On it," John agreed. He moved on up the path past the cabin and the crowd.

Quay turned back to the lake. Such a beautiful setting for such a cruel ending.

Another gull screeched directly overhead, wrenching Quay out of his reverie. John had walked partway up the hill. He was huddled with his men, giving out the orders. He was probably covering procedures before they began their sweep of the area, Quay thought.

He shuffled the bubblegum around in his cheek and scanned the scene once more. He blew another bubble and popped it, thinking about the dead girl. It initially occurred to him that the girl's body had probably been left there by someone who'd hoped the lake would carry her away. But she had ended up in this kettle depression. The lake didn't get her. There was more to it.

28

Now he wondered why this particular spot had been chosen. Quay moved up to join John and the men up ahead on the path.

Quay nodded at each of the guys as John introduced him. After the handshakes and initial background was finished, Quay began sharing his thoughts.

"I've been wondering why the killer didn't just toss her body into the lake farther up the shoreline? It seems like it would have been easier to carry a body down to the shore up that way. It also makes sense that if the body was dropped at another location, the lake might have carried the body away more easily to another more concealed cove. Don't you think?"

John nodded. One of the men, Ron, Quay thought his name was, added, "I live not too far up toward Grand Marais. It would have been unlikely that the lake would have tossed the body this high up onto the shore. The water isn't high enough right now. The waves haven't been that high here lately."

"So there were plenty of better places to stop and drop, right?" Quay asked. "That could mean that whoever killed this girl really didn't know the shoreline that well. This spot was a matter of convenience."

The men picked up Quay's line of thinking.

Bill added, "But then, perhaps it was a matter of the perp being in a hurry!"

John joined in, "Or then again, maybe that was too calculating. The guy might have known the area up here and decided this would be a place far enough away from the kill spot to go undetected for a while."

Quay agreed. "The girl probably wasn't killed here. That would have presented too many problems.

Too much noise. Difficult walking at night. There are lots of possibilities. Now we have to begin sifting through the evidence we have. Let's get going, guys. Go over the site with a fine-tooth comb. Let me know if you see anything we can use."

The tall, white pines and cedar trees were thick here. They created dark shadows while at the same time shedding mounds of needles. It would be hard to find clues in the pine mulch. The path to the lake was covered with at least a half-inch blanket of dried pine needles. Quay looked at the nearby mattress of moss stretching under lacy arms of ferns, multihued wildflowers, and emerald shrubs under the dappled shade of leafy limbs. Footprint clues would be unreadable in this groundcover. If someone had skirted the pine needle path, they probably would have used the rounded, gray rock formations leading back fifty feet from the lake. He laughed to himself. They'd need the equivalent of an Indian scout to find any clues here.

Quay looked up toward the road. He wondered if John's guys might find something up on the dirt driveway. The driveway led fifty feet winding up to the dirt and gravel road at the top of the hill. John had told him the locals called it Pedagogue's Road. By now, he guessed, even the clues left in the fine dirt at the top of the drive would have been destroyed by the group of curious residents gathering there.

He tensed and shivered as the wind pushed through the trees after picking up the cold, damp air from the lake. Something about this girl's body, this place, this day, brought a quickening sensation of release. It was almost like he had a premonition. Maybe this would be the light at the end of his tunnel. Could it all come together with this girl's death and this case? He shivered again.

Quay watched as the emergency squad arrived at the top of the drive with the ambulance. Their arrival elicited more of the usual curiosity and excitement in the growing crowd up and down the road. Too bad the crime crew in this quiet area was not quick enough to have cordoned off the area immediately.

It really wasn't their fault, he mused. Most of the crimes up here involved break-ins and theft, not murder. He could hear the murmured chatter among the residents. They were probably registering their disbelief that something like this could happen in their area.

The waves continued to thunder, spewing a fine, ice-cold mist over everyone and everything at the scene. This late in September, everything was brisk and cold.

John's investigating group huddled together in the familiar Minnesota Hunch—their rigid bodies curled inward with rounded shoulders, backs to the lake winds. To a man, they wore black knit caps pulled down tight on their heads, covering their ears. Their necks were tucked down into pulled-up collars. The overall effect made the group look like hulking predators. Four other deputies from the sheriff's department stood to one side and talked in hushed tones as they wiped the spray away from their eyes. Quay strode back up the path, overhearing muffled pieces of their conversation on the way.

"What's that guy's name again?"

"Who?"

"You know, that guy who was down there with John checking over the scene. Looks like he's sizing things   up."

31

"I think his name's Cay or Kway or something like that," the other man said. "Don't think I've really met him before. One of the other guys said he's John's brother. Up here from the Cities. Heard he's BCA or something like that. He's got connections, anyway. Guess he was up here visiting with the John and his family. Since he was already up here, John asked him to come along to check out this scene with him."

Quay eavesdropped on their discussion without acknowledging the men. His name was unusual, he had to admit. Almost everyone he'd met in his life had asked about it. It was his mother's fault. She'd been enough of a feminist not to want to give up her maiden name, but old-fashioned enough to take her husband's name when she'd married. As a result, when her first son was born thirty-four years ago, she had insisted on giving him her maiden name. "Kway" was the way it was supposed to be pronounced. She thought it sounded strong and manly—a good name for a son—and it had pleased her that she'd been able to pass along her family name to her child.

Chapter 5

Minutes later, Quay was fighting off another feeling of déjà vu. John placed a fine gold chain in his hands. Quay eyed the small charm attached to the chain and felt a tight clenching from the depths of his chest. He couldn't believe his eyes.

The necklace John had placed in his hands had been found on the girl. The girl's body had been found wearing only a light blue Old Navy sweater and tan cargo pants. She'd had no identification on her. However, in one of her frozen hands, she'd been clutching this broken gold-chain necklace. The necklace had a medusa head etched on a charm. The investigator brought it to John, who in turn took it to Quay.

Quay took the charm, examined it, and turned it over and read the single word SPARTA engraved on the back. Quay looked up at John and then back at the charm. He stared at John, nodded, and smiled grimly.

"This is our lead, John. This just might be it. Let me go with it?"

John nodded. "You've got it, Quay. We'll go for it together this time."

Quay tried to control his emotions. It was too much to hope for. But the capital letters on the necklace had reached out to Quay.

The hundreds of data files he'd read on SPARTA flashed through his mind. He had catalogued every bit of SPARTA's history when Karen was killed by the sniper. He could recite names, dates, and places without effort. SPARTA was the group connected to so many protests at Cameron BioTech. They had been actively protesting at the press conference when Karen was gunned down.

Of course this explained his feeling, his déjà vu about this girl's death. This was it. With a new spark of hope, he thought this was the opening he'd been looking for. If he could follow up on this murder investigation with SPARTA, it just might give him the answers he was looking for in this girl's death and ultimately Karen's death. He had always believed SPARTA was behind her death. He just hadn't been able to find the link. Now he had it.

That is, if they'd allow him to take this case. He'd go after SPARTA. John would back him. John understood he needed validation. John knew he needed closure. This could be it.

He had to start clean. He wanted to have another set of eyes take a look at this. He needed someone who had more knowledge of Karen's case and of the SPARTA group. Someone who had been in on the other investigation of SPARTA. Still clutching the necklace in his hand, Quay turned to John.

"Would it be all right with you if I called for some support? I think Sam might be a good eye on this."

John stared at Quay for a long moment before nodding. "Do what you need to do," he said.

Quay drew in a breath, squared his shoulders, turned, and took long, quick strides in his climb to the road. He needed to get a clear signal on his cell phone. He placed the long-distance call to Sam.

They were an odd couple of sorts, he and Sam. Samantha Atwood had been assigned as Quay's partner about three months after Karen's death. He hadn't been ready for any more changes, but his former partner had been reassigned to Washington.

34

The longer they worked together, the more Quay came to appreciate how her abilities filled in voids in his areas of expertise. At first their reluctance to accept each other's talents led to a bit of a rivalry. Their grudging acceptance of each other had finally led to an understanding and mutual respect.

Samantha Atwood knew more about SPARTA than anyone. She'd spent hours sitting in computer chat rooms, following as SPARTA fanatics sounded off. He had to admit this case needed her input.

She answered after the third ring.

"Sam! Thank God I caught you. I've got something. It's going to be big. I need your help!"

"Really? You sound different. Where are you?"

"I'm up visiting my brother by Lutsen."

"Yeah, yeah, I know that. I mean where are you calling from? There's a lot of noise there."

"I'm on the shore of Lake Superior. We've got a murder."

"Oh, wow! I thought you were on vacation."

"I was. John called me in on this one. It's something you're not going to believe. This one has a SPARTA connection."

There was a pause before Sam spoke again.

"Quay, are you sure?"

"Absolutely! And I need you up here like an hour ago," he demanded.

"Okay, but I'll have to get clearance. We need to get the boss in on this. Okay?"

"Sure, just explain that there are more than local connections with this one. This murder has far-reaching tentacles. I think we can finally get SPARTA!"

By the time Sam pulled up behind Quay's Tahoe a little over four hours later, it was midafternoon. Quay had left the scene for a short time to grab a cup of coffee and some lunch. Then he had returned to the site to wait for Sam. He heard her car pull up and turned to watch Sam as she climbed down the path to the rock embankment where he sat waiting.

She could have been a model, he supposed. She was tall, limber, and lithe, a woman in her midthirties with chiseled, high cheekbones and wide, green eyes laced with thick lashes. Her long, amber hair fell in loose curls about her face. She was not a remarkable beauty, Quay thought, but she certainly had a look about her that radiated sensuality. All in all, he thought as he watched her, she was a very attractive woman. He thought Karen would have agreed with him. In fact, Karen would have liked Sam.

Today, Sam was wearing jeans, Doc Martin boots, and a long, green corduroy shirt over a turtleneck. The shirt swayed around her hips as she walked. She hadn't worn a coat or hat, but she had pulled on gloves. The pine needles crunched with each step she took until she reached the boulders and clambered over them to stand next to him.

"Hey, Thompson. What's up?" Sam didn't bother with a polite hello or courteous small talk. She and Quay didn't need the small talk.

"You sounded like an excited, little kid on the phone. This must be good." She was curious to know what had finally excited Quay so much.

She asked to see the site firsthand before fully discussing Quay's theories with him. From their conversation on the phone, she'd understood there were aspects to this situation that suggested to Quay that there was more here than a simple local homicide. He had indicated a possible link to Karen's murder. She was here to help Quay determine if that was an illusion or reality.

She pulled up her shirt collar and pulled her shirt close to her to ward off the spray of the lake and its accompanying chill. Turning her back to Quay, she surveyed the shoreline and waited for him to begin.

"You made good time, Sam. Thanks for coming up," he said.

He moved in next to her, and they huddled shoulder to shoulder for a moment, listening to the waves crash against the rocks. Quay reached into his pocket and pulled out the pictures taken by John's crew. He handed them to her.

"This is what we found."

"How long do they think she'd been lying there? I see there was a pool of water around her," Sam said as she shuffled through the stack of pictures. "That must be the 'kettle' you spoke of in the rocks there." She pointed to an area to the side of them.

"Yeah, that's where we found her. We're not really sure how long she'd been there. Best guess is about six to seven hours. Lividity was just beginning. The ME will let us know as soon as he gets the autopsy done," answered Quay.

"Any idea who she was?"

"No, but best guess is that she's probably not from around here. So far none of the neighbors we questioned saw or know about any young black woman in the area. The residents are suggesting she may be a tourist who snuck down here, got too close to the edge, and slipped, hit her head and died from exposure. They've all had trespassers on their property, people trying to get a good view of the lake.

"But she couldn't have fallen. There was no head trauma, and no one's called in a missing person report. And what we know that they don't is that there was bruising on her neck. It was broken." Quay was filling her in rapidly. His excitement barely contained, he continued.

"Somebody strangled her and broke her neck in the process. This is definitely a homicide. I don't think she was killed here. What we don't know is how far the body may have been brought after her death. She was probably dumped sometime in the middle of the night. We'll have to check the lake currents and wind direction to see if someone could have come up from the lake and dropped off the body." Quay paused as he moved the bubblegum around in his cheek, blew out a small bubble, and popped it.

Sam turned to him and smiled. Quay was definitely in his investigator mode. He was working the bubblegum hard. Quay popped more bubbles as he launched deeper into thought.

"What's the matter?" He looked at her almost defiantly.

"Oh nothing," Sam answered, trying to smother her smile.

He shifted away from her and then turned back. "Remember I told you she had a SPARTA necklace in her hand? The chain was broken."

"Yeah. So? You think she tore it off? Or did someone place it in her hand after she died?"

"I don't think it was placed in her hand. She wouldn't have held it so tightly. It sounds like she had it in a death grip."

"I haven't checked on SPARTA recently. If this is related to SPARTA, it looks like there's a possibility that there may be a little trouble brewing in SPARTA ranks."

"You think so?" Quay asked, his voice rising sarcastically. "A *little* trouble? I was hoping you might have some new information about that group."

He pulled the wad of gum from his mouth, tossed it into the water, and reached into his pocket to pull out another piece. He unwrapped the chunk, tucked the wrapper back in his pocket, and popped the pink bubblegum into his mouth. She could see he was doing his best to avoid giving in to another fix. That nicotine had gotten a hold on him. This case wasn't helping. She could sense his tension building.

There was something here. Sam watched him, understanding.

"Quay, I don't—"

Quay interrupted her before she could finish. "Let's let them finish their work out here—the crew is coming back out. We'll go back to John's office and gather up all the interview sheets. I want to check on the last meeting location for the SPARTA group. Maybe they've been gathering up forces in this area. You can always find some hermits in the backwoods who want to stop the world and get off." He turned, leading the way back up the path to the road.

"After we get that stuff," he called over his shoulder, "maybe we can head back to the Cities and start checking on the SPARTA action there. We've always known they were a dangerous group of kooks. We just

39

couldn't get anything on them. We can always count on John to keep us filled in on any other info that crops up here. He's a good man and a great sheriff. You'll like him when you meet him. He'll do the legwork here while we chase down news back home."

"That works for me. But aren't you on vacation?" Sam was attempting to slow him down. "I thought maybe you'd like to finish out your week here. It's a great area to get away and relax."

"No. I think I'm done with that for now. I'll come back to finish my vacation later—after we've solved this case. I have a feeling about this one. I want to follow up on it while I've got the chance."

It was obvious to Sam that Quay had once again become the gritty investigator. When he was like this, she knew there was no stopping him.

"Okay, if you're sure that's what you want. I'd like to meet your brother."

She was trying to match his strides, half running to keep up with him.

"We can check in with him at his office, like you said, and then I'll start running the backgrounds on the current SPARTA members when we get back. We'll need to get names and recent locations for the top people in the organization. Maybe we can get an ID and some background information on this girl from some of them. I'm betting they don't want to make the news with this. Maybe we can use that angle to pry a little information out of them. I think we—"

Quay suddenly stopped, turned, looked at her, and then gave Sam one of his lazy grins. "Samantha Atwood, I can see you're on board, and you are already on a roll."

She pulled up short behind him, stopped midsentence, looked at him, and returned the grin. It was nice to see this side of Quay.

Chapter 6

Tight pods of students jostled through the crowded halls of the suburban high school. A few intentionally jabbed sharp elbows into others as they passed by. Much of the bumping, jabbing, and pushing was in fun—friends engaging in horseplay. Occasionally, the play escalated into malevolent bullying. The youngest bore the brunt of it.

As a general rule, seniors believed the little freshmen needed to be taught the same lesson they had learned upon entering high school. There was a pecking order, with seniors at the top.

The freshmen entered the doors of the high school each fall feeling no small amount of fear and trepidation. The standard words of advice were passed down from their older, more experienced brothers and sisters.

"Don't try to talk to or join in with the juniors and seniors. Just stay out of their way. And whatever you do, don't ask upper classmen for directions. They'll tell you to take the elevator at the end of the hall to the third floor, or worse, that the pool is on the third floor."

Of course there was no elevator or even a third floor for that matter. The naïve freshmen ended up as the jeering butt of laughter and jokes as they arrived late to class. Juniors and seniors felt it was their duty to initiate the freshman into the high school routine. After all, they had each gone through the same initiation ritual. It was a part of high school life. Everybody had to go through it.

Ernie Elson, the senior chemistry teacher, knew about high school life. He was an experienced teacher. He knew how to establish his rank in the pecking order. He was on top! He began

42

each year sitting on a lab stool in the hallway next to his classroom door before school and during passing time. He'd smile at the students as they passed by. He'd observe the action between the upper classmen and the poor little freshmen. And then he'd make a point of singling out one of the senior jocks. He could always bring them down to size with a quick reminder of school rules, including his own interpretation. They got the message.

More than anything, he was always ready to share his strategies and lessons with first-year teachers.

"Someone has to be out there," he explained to one young teacher. "Who knows what these kids will do to one another? We have rules. We make sure they follow them. You have to get them at the beginning of the year. Catch the slightest infraction and enforce it. Then you don't have any problems.

"You know, I always have a bucket next to me for their gum when I sit in the hall," he continued. "That's the rule. No gum! I enforce it. If I see one of them with gum, I make that kid stop and tell him or her to deposit it in the bucket. It embarrasses them in front of their friends, and it lets them know the rule will be enforced. That also makes them a little more wary when they walk by me. They know I'm there to enforce those rules. It's a start, and it's enough to keep them on their toes. I can tell you it's a lot more than a lot of teachers here do. If everyone made these kids follow the rules, we wouldn't have so many problems."

In the teachers' lounge, Ernie complained, "It's a dog-eat-dog world out there. And it's the same in the halls of the high school. In reality, this place is just a microcosm of the real world out there. They might as well learn now."

As soon as they realized Ernie was fueling up for his soapbox, someone would cut him off.

"Yeah, right on, Ernie."

"You go ahead and keep 'em in line. They'll respect all of us more for it."

There would be a few knowing smiles passed between the veteran teachers, and the conversation would change to sports or politics, or anything to divert him.

Ernie Elson considered this his private war, and he wouldn't give up. A few teachers supported Ernie with comments about the futility of trying to discipline unruly kids in this day and age, but most of the staff seldom gave more than lip service.

"Yeah, well, Ernie will do enough for all of us," George Harrison, a fellow science teacher told his colleagues.

At forty-five years old, Ernie had covered a lot of ground in his life. He already had the beginnings of an older man's hunch. His head was forever bent over a magazine or stack of papers as he walked down the halls, making his five foot nine inch frame look like five seven. He avoided eye contact with students when he wasn't perched on his stool. He saw no reason to fraternize with more than a few exceptional students.

It was Ernie's appearance that presented the oxymoron. For all his ranting about rules and being respected, Ernie looked like a hippy from the sixties. His shoulder-length, dark hair was streaked with gray and hung loosely about his face. It fell in waves down around his neck. His beard had also begun to sprout flecks of gray.

Teachers who had known him for a while remembered when his hair used to be short and neatly trimmed. He'd had no beard. Then about three years ago, they had noticed that he'd begun to let his hair grow longer. And longer. He didn't get haircuts. He didn't shave. His personal hygiene took on an entirely new identity. As Ernie's hair grew longer, his rage and ranting at the government seemed to increase.

George and the rest of the Science Department began to worry about Ernie. They talked about Ernie's downslide when he wasn't around, but no one really wanted to confront Ernie. Who knew how he would react? He was unpredictable. He was becoming a powder keg.

They all understood Ernie had a tough life at home. Ernie had been open about his problems with his mentally ill wife. He said he lived in fear of her and for her. When he joined the guys occasionally for a Friday night happy hour at the local bar, he seemed to be hoping for a counseling session. Who could help him?

As Ernie told it, his life had had many twists and turns. He was sure no one on their staff could match the heartache, adventure, and torment he'd experienced. What a life he'd had.

As Ernie told it, his father had been abusive. Ernie could never meet his father's unrealistic expectations no matter how hard he tried. His father had used a fist or a strap to teach his son proper behavior. His mother usually got the same lessons right after his father was done with him. Any excuse would set him off.

After each "lesson," his father left for the local bar. His mother did her drinking at home after his father left. During those times, neither parent was aware of Ernie or what he was doing.

Despite his home life, Ernie had been a studious boy. He'd been shy and didn't make friends easily. Regardless, he'd loved school, especially science. Science opened an entirely new world for him. With science, the answers were always clear. There was no room for guessing. It was also easy for him. Everything was so clear cut, black and white. It was just the way Ernie liked it.

Surprisingly, Ernie also loved church. He'd discovered the love of God after meeting Father Flannery. At church, he held lively discussions and arguments about creation and the higher power with Father Flannery. His neighborhood church soon became his sanctuary. He'd said that was the only really good thing his mother had done for him; she had made it a rule that he attend Mass regularly.

As he neared the end of high school, Ernie had begun to think the church was the place for him rather than the science lab. Even with his love of science, he'd decided that faith in God had a more important place in his life. So he entered the seminary directly after high school.

Then the war came along. Vietnam. Ernie felt a new calling and left the seminary. He said he felt it was God's will. He must fight for his country. He must be a soldier for God. He enlisted in 1967 before he was drafted. He trained as a medic instead of a chaplain. It was there, he explained, that he felt he could use his love of science and feel like he was serving a higher purpose at the same time. He put the seminary on hold.

As Ernie told the story, things were just beginning to turn really ugly in Vietnam at that time. According to Ernie, he saw it all. He heard the cries of young boys calling for their sweethearts and their mothers as they died horrible deaths. He prayed over their mangled bodies as they suffered. And he began to wonder about the real meanings of patriotism and religion.

Why were we killing one another in the name of God and country? Did God really intend for us to fight and kill for our country? Then a grenade fragment slammed into Ernie as he bent over a young soldier who was breathing his last prayer. The fragment entered Ernie's shoulder, tearing into the ligaments and making his arm useless. As he was evacuated by helicopter to the nearest medical hospital, Ernie actually smiled.

"I'm going home, fellas. I'm going home." Vietnam had changed his life. He went home, recovered from his injuries, and left the church.

Three years later, using a Vet's education scholarship, Ernie completed his degree in education with a major in chemistry. His experience in Vietnam had taught him that science and religion were miles apart.

"You can't teach intelligent design and scientific theory," he orated. "They don't go together. Evolution is a scientific fact. This world with science is ordered, and all things are explained with real data. There can be no chaos and living on faith alone if one understands the science of creation."

He was sure he knew what the world was really like. God had been absent when Ernie Elson had needed him most.

Ernie relished reliving and sharing the stories of Vietnam with other vets who were teachers with him. George and Rick and many of the men on the staff were vets, too. Some were "weekend warriors" now—part of the Reserve. They told and retold their war stories over drinks on Friday nights. They commiserated about the state of affairs in their beloved country, talked politics, and discussed how the left-wing do-gooders ought to have been in Vietnam instead of at home protesting.

But in the last year or two, George and the boys began to feel that Ernie enjoyed the stories in a different way than they did. Ernie had an unleashed anger buried beneath his armor.

More and more frequently, Ernie railed against the "liberals in government who are selling out the future of our young people." Ernie's conversation began to sound almost radical. That was also about the same time Ernie's appearance began to deteriorate.

His fellow teachers began to distance themselves from him. They were hesitant to voice their concerns for fear that he'd really come unglued. Everyone knew Ernie needed his job. His wife had medical bills. Questions about his own emotional stability might make things even worse for him.

It was Tuesday, and the students ran for the classroom door as the last tones of the bell faded. Mr. Elson was just closing the door. His classroom policy was to close his door as the bell finished ringing. If a student arrived after the door was closed, it was too bad. The student was late if the door was closed, and he or she must go to the office for a pass. Ernie took pride in the fact that his students always made it to class on time.

Rules were necessary if you wanted order.

Once class began, the kids loved to get Mr. Elson riled up about his favorite topic—genetic research. They knew he could use up an entire hour ranting about the evils of the people who were misusing the good name of science and destroying the future for the world's youth. That meant no homework for the day.

"Hey, Mr. Elson. What do you think about that protest they held this weekend on using animals for experimentation?"

"I can tell you this," he said, "they're using animals for their experiments now, but in the future, it could be your brother or sister!"

Now he had his opportunity to teach them all something important.

"Imagine a little rabbit in a cage waiting to be cut open, then having cells implanted for new organ growth or being impregnated with combined eggs of various animals. Imagine the possible results of gross tumorous growths and disfigured creatures. Can you imagine the future for those animals that are developed as a new species? I can't. I won't. As responsible citizens, you and I can't stand by and allow it."

Ernie knew he was treading on thin ice in these classroom "discussions." The district curriculum didn't support him; so neither would the school board or parents. But he felt he needed to excite the students. This was the best way to get them involved in science. He wanted them to become active participants in their world, not apathetic followers. So he continued preaching the moral sermons as extensions of science class.

"Do you believe that this is morally acceptable? Do you want to live in a world like that? Do you want to raise children in a world where new species can be developed by man, not by God?"

"But, Mr. Elson," a smirking boy interrupted, "just think of all the possibilities and the creative geniuses we could develop. Think about the possibilities of combining monkeys and humans. We could fly through the trees by our tails, still work a computer, and all we'd need to eat would be bananas. We could help increase the world food supply." The class laughed at the picture he'd created.

"And then think of the Einsteins we could develop," added another student, joining in the mockery. "What about the world of geniuses we could create?"

This kind of talk always agitated Elson. His students knew it.

"Yes and what about the evil geniuses who could unleash more harm than Hitler even began to imagine? What about those who decided that only a specific kind of human was good enough to exist? What about the evil genius who decided that all of you weren't worth taking up air on our planet and, because of that, plotted to destroy all of you?" he responded.

The room was momentarily silenced until one of the school heroes in the back of the room said, "Yeah, right, Mr. Elson. And where would you fit in?"

The class erupted in laughter. Ernie had lost them once again. He knew the kids thought it was great to get him going. But he felt he had to teach them these important things.

Regardless of the other students' feelings, Annie Bell liked Mr. Elson a lot. She realized the majority of students thought Mr. Elson was just plain weird. Not Annie. Annie Bell wasn't laughing. She was enthralled. Mr. Elson inspired her. He got her thinking. Annie Bell understood Mr. Elson. Although Annie was perhaps one of the quietest students in the class, she always listened intently and nodded in agreement. She found his lectures stimulating.

Ernie took notice of her response. She would be a good prospect, he thought. Her color wasn't a factor. It didn't matter that Annie was an African American. What was important was her intelligence. She always earned As and actually seemed to enjoy writing in-depth essays on the history and future direction of genetic research.

Elson enjoyed reading Annie's essays. He realized that none of the other students were even capable of understanding what Annie Bell was talking about. She was so far above them. She would be a perfect candidate for his group.

Unfortunately, Annie's fascination with Ernie and his praise for her turned Annie into an outsider with the other students. She had no close friends. She kept to herself. Her closest relationships were with adults and especially her teachers. She seldom spoke up in class, but she would stay after to ask questions. She stayed to talk with Mr. Elson most frequently. The other students took note. Annie Bell had a thing for weird Mr. Elson.

After class, at the lockers, she tried to ignore their torments. They called her names like "that black brain buster" and "teacher's pet" and worst of all, "Elson's ebony clone." She pretended not to hear them or even care. It really didn't matter to her. Most of those kids were so self-involved and tuned in to their own private cliques that they really didn't get it anyway. Of course, they didn't give her any credit. They didn't believe a shy, little black girl would ever amount to anything.

But Annie was determined she was going to amount to something. She had set her goals. She did hours upon hours of research online and at the library. She used her intellect and ambition to develop and determine her direction.

Her studies had taught her that Linus Pauling, the scientist who'd provided much of the foundation for modern genetic studies, had won the Nobel Prize for chemistry in 1954, as well as the Nobel Peace Prize in 1962 for his campaign against warfare used to solve conflicts. He was also concerned about the direction biochemical research and modern ethics were taking. He'd even made speeches about his fears. She'd read each of them with interest. She believed she understood Pauling's concerns. Mr. Elson agreed, too.

Annie had another reason to be interested in the ethics involved in genetic research. Annie had hoped that some of the genetic studies in process at this moment might bring about discoveries that could help her brother. Two years ago, her brother, Danny, had become a quadriplegic as the result of a car accident. A drunk driver had broadsided his car just as Danny left the school parking lot for his first day at an after-school job. Danny had been trapped in his vehicle for two hours while the fire department used the Jaws of Life to pry him out. His doctors told their parents that Danny would never be able to walk or move about independently again.

Since then, her parents had devoted every waking minute to Danny. She loved her brother. But she wanted her life to be normal again. She wished her parents would at least remember that she existed, too. They weren't even aware of what she did as long as it didn't interfere with their care for Danny.

So Annie was even more determined to help Danny, if only to restore her family to some normalcy. According to all the information she'd gleaned from books at the library as well as the Internet research she'd conducted, current scientific studies in genetics indicated there may be a way to regenerate a spinal cord. Danny's crushed spinal cord could be re-grown. He might be able to walk again. That was an amazing thought for Annie.

But therein lay the problem. She'd wished for help and maybe even a cure for Danny, but at what cost? That was her dilemma. She didn't want those cures to come at the expense of all the other evils that Mr. Elson talked about. Those were the evils that would be released by advancements in genetic research. Mr. Elson had explained about that cost. Evils like mutated animals, cloned humans, a society of perfect geniuses. A "brave new world" Mr. Elson had called it. Annie believed Mr. Elson was right.

And when she had stayed after class to ask more questions, Mr. Elson had taken the time to explain to her about how the genetic research labs were lying about their capabilities. He said they weren't really working to help people like her brother. He said they had different agendas. He was sure that it was all about money. The large research labs did not care about people. They just wanted to make millions at the people's expense.

Most of all, she wondered how companies like Cameron BioTech right here in Minneapolis could continue research that could and probably would, according to Mr. Elson, lead to a cross-contamination of species or, even worse, the extinction of some species.

She did her research and wrote term papers about the use and misuse of animals in experimental labs. She wrote about the future of genetics and the Nazi-like possible misuse of genetics to determine the sex, eye color, and intelligence of future children. As she wrote, she developed a set of beliefs. She was processing everything she'd learned.

We could be headed for a new world society created by scientists who are producing genetically enhanced criminals and possibly even cloned Hitlers, she wrote.

Mr. Elson loved it. He raved about her insight and intelligence. His coworkers began to wonder if he was developing a love for more than her intellect.

But Annie could not stop thinking about her brother, either. What if Cameron BioTech could develop a way to help him and other quadriplegics? What if the research was being conducted by honest people with real morals, who wanted only the best for our future? What if Mr. Elson was wrong? She didn't mention those conflicted feelings she had about genetic research to Mr. Elson.

Ernie Elson continued to sing praises nonstop in the staff lounge about Annie's sophisticated capabilities and mature thinking. In fact, considering how often he raved about the fantastic research she'd done to support her work, his teaching partners began to question Ernie's true interests. She was his star, no doubt about it.

"After all," he raved, "where is the scientific process in education anymore?" he would ask. "Look what this girl does. There are only small percentages of students who really get it anymore and are willing to do real research like Annie does. Most kids these days are just plain lazy. Our system just lets them slide by. We don't teach kids to think or how to use deductive reasoning. Or how to apply their research using valid experiments. Kids like Annie don't happen very often. She really works to learn by using true scientific methods!"

"Yeah, Ernie. We get it. She's great," groaned George. "You know, we teach, too. You could keep that in mind."

Ernie continued to ramble on, oblivious to the disdain of his fellow teachers. When they wouldn't listen anymore, he expanded his audience and complained to anyone who would listen about how American education was coddling kids. He bragged that he was one of the few who had set the bar high enough by inspiring complex thinking. Annie Bell was the proof that kids could reach the bar.

What Ernie didn't admit to anyone was that he was using Annie. Annie's adoration of him was very useful. No one at school knew about his other life after work. He knew that while he was helping Annie become a star pupil, she would also be an excellent addition to SPARTA. She was just the kind of activist he needed. Annie was a follower.

After school, Annie was doing more than just hitting the books. At Elson's encouragement, she began spending hours with him after school. Then there were the times she visited him at his home for extra "help." Ernie's wife gladly hid in the bedroom when Annie visited.

55

Finally, Annie got the courage to ask about Mrs. Elson. She said she thought it was odd that she had never seen her. Did Mrs. Elson really exist?

Ernie finally shared his secret of his wife's ailments with Annie. He explained carefully that his wife was a paranoid schizophrenic. He told Annie he was even afraid of her at times, but he said his wife also needed him to be there to help her. Annie listened to the stories he told her about his wife's crazy behavior and bought into his sympathy plea.

According to Mr. Elson, one of the most unusual things about his wife was that she demanded that he let his hair grow long. He could get a haircut only when she decided it was time. Then she was the one to cut it. That explained why he always had shoulder-length hair except for the once-a-year haircut.

He confided in Annie that his wife had even attacked him in a crazy rage with a knife. Since then, he had slept in another room with a lock on the door. However, despite all that, he told Annie he couldn't leave his wife. He told her he believed his wife really needed him. He explained that it was for exactly that reason he wouldn't have her committed, or even put her on medication. That would just be another way of giving in to the control of the medical quacks. His wife would find a way to recover with his help. She didn't want or need medication.

Annie devoured everything Mr. Elson said. Elson's stories drew her closer to him, just as he intended. She listened intently. She loved that he treated her like an equal. She loved how he really appreciated and noticed her.

Finally, Annie Bell had someone who recognized and admired her for her intelligence! He didn't treat her like a child, like her parents did. He didn't ignore her, like her parents did. He also didn't treat her differently because of her color. He respected her as a human being. The fact that she was an African American girl who'd been adopted into a white family had no effect on him. He told her she was an intelligent person who deserved respect. Her color didn't matter to him.

Ernie lavished her with that special kind of attention he knew she wasn't getting at home. Frequently, he initiated what he called thought-provoking discussions. Their discussions and their relationship grew. He sometimes focused upon what he called the mistake of Vietnam and his experiences in the service. He told Annie how the government had conceived of and completed a major cover-up in the use of biological weapons in Vietnam.

He told her, "Saddam didn't even have a corner on the market when it came to biological weapons. Our own government has him beat all to hell. Excuse me for my language."

"Excused," Annie said, smiling.

"You know, Saddam Hussein was accused of using biological weapons on his own people. But the US did similar things to our people long before Saddam Hussein. Consider the use of Agent Orange in Vietnam. I saw how it affected the soldiers. My buddies, my foxhole brothers, have never been the same. I believe our government even did other experiments on our soldiers during World War II.

"We were the victims of our own government's tests. And that wasn't even the first time. There were those times in the later forties and early fifties when soldiers were also used as guinea pigs. You must remember," he urged Annie, "never trust the government. That's most important of all. They'll lie every time. You have to dig through all the shit to find out what's really happening. Go on the Internet and talk to the real people in the trenches."

"Where should I look?" Annie asked.

"You could begin with a group called SPARTA. They're protecting us from our government's secret activities. They're committed, and they're good people."

"How do you know? Do you know the people in that group?"

"I not only know them, I *am* them. I'm the leader of SPARTA."

Annie's mouth formed a small O. She needed to find out more. Ernie had set the hook.

Annie listened, surfed the Internet, and learned. There were others out there with similar concerns and beliefs. But SPARTA seemed to be the most organized. She loved the fact that she knew Ernie as the president of SPARTA. She filled her brain with all sorts of exciting information from the online chat discussions.

Meanwhile, her parents had no idea who their daughter was becoming.

By the time Annie neared the end of her senior year in high school, she had become a junior member of SPARTA. She was proud to be a dissident against the US government, a government she now perceived as one presenting a warped campaign of disinformation to the American people.

Foremost in her study of SPARTA was the information they had on the use of genetic testing at

58

Cameron BioTech. She was now convinced that Cameron must be stopped. However, at the same time, a small voice in the back of her head reminded her of her quadriplegic brother's need for a real life. A constant prickle of doubt plagued her.

Despite her skepticism, her ego won out, as did her pleasure at finally being a part of a group. It was the first time in her life she'd had so many friends. Because of Ernie, they respected her. Through Ernie Elson, she'd met and joined others who understood the truth about their country just as she now did. They applauded and valued her opinions. They respected her and listened to her views. She finally had the attention she so desperately craved. Ernie was proud of his young progeny.

Before Annie became a member of the group calling itself SPARTA, she learned about the group through the chat rooms Ernie had directed her to. They told her Ernie was on the brink of uncovering a major disinformation campaign being waged by the US government. The work at Cameron BioTech, she was told, was not just the study of DNA and individual genetic blueprints.

According to the group at SPARTA, Cameron's research was also a planned operation sponsored by the government to extract and rekindle the DNA of heroes from the past and cross match that same DNA with modern humans to provide a strong line of humans who would go on to lead the world. It was Hitler's world with the perfect human specimen all over again.

The SPARTA chat room had been buzzing for several weeks. Annie hadn't learned the final purpose of creating this new superhuman, but Ernie had hinted that there was an evil purpose behind the experimentation being done at Cameron BioTech right there in Minneapolis. She could only imagine the DNA of Jack the Ripper, Adolf Hitler, Ivan the Terrible, and Genghis Khan being surreptitiously slipped into a lab. The results would prove disastrous.

Annie was sure SPARTA had done its homework. They knew what was real and what wasn't. More than any other group, they understood the vulnerability of the country today. People needed to be warned. She wanted and planned to be involved in making history by being a part of SPARTA when they began warning America. She would make a name for herself by being a hero for her country.

SPARTA was an apt name for their organization, she thought. The ancient civilization of Sparta was known for its military organization and discipline. Its people were courageous and valorous against all odds. She, too, would be undaunted against this threat to her country and the world. It was up to their small group at SPARTA to expose the scientists' work at Cameron BioTech to the world. Like most teens her age, the fact that she might be endangering herself and others in the process was not of concern. Nothing was going to happen to her. What was most important was the fact that she was accomplishing something significant for her world and the future of that world.

Annie graduated with high honors that spring, and in September she began classes at the university. She moved out of her parents' home and found a small townhouse near the college that she could afford to rent. She'd gotten a full scholarship to attend the University of

Minnesota, and then she found a job at a local doctor's office as a receptionist. The doctors were willing to work around her class schedule, so she was able to make enough to live on her own while attending college. Her life couldn't have been better.

That is, except for her life with her family. Her parents were still fully involved with Danny. They didn't even seem to care that she was gone. In fact, she was sure they didn't care. So, she turned more and more to her other family: SPARTA. She'd make *them* notice her. They cared. She'd make that family proud.

That was when Ernie called to tell her there was going to be a SPARTA conference. They were actually going to get together and begin to formulate their plans. Ernie had organized this conference in a place called Castle Danger up in Northern Minnesota. Ernie told her it was a time for the members to come together and share their views and ideas.

Castle Danger was a perfect out-of-the-way location, Ernie said. Even more importantly, it would give him and Annie some time to get away together. He's explained they could forget about all the family issues they both had.

There would be at least fifty people attending from all over the United States and even some people from Sweden, Denmark, Great Britain, and India. Ernie Elson had made a name for himself with this group. SPARTA had become his family, too.

SPARTA members understood about the degeneration of the world. They trusted in Ernie's leadership. They also believed they could make a difference in the future of their world with the leadership of a man like Ernie Elson.

Annie felt the same way. She was excited about the conference. But, at the same time, she didn't think her family would understand. Her parents had never liked Ernie Elson. They said he was a crackpot. Her father had actually forbidden her to visit him after school last year. He'd said Mr. Elson was just some kind of "kook" who would do nothing but cause trouble.

So when the planned weekend finally arrived, Annie left for the conference at the North Shore without telling her parents. They wouldn't even know she was gone, she told herself. She was living away from home, and they'd think she was in her townhouse studying all weekend.

Ernie greeted every member personally as they arrived at the lodge in Castle Danger. The conference began with opening remarks by SPARTA President Ernie Elson.

After a few welcoming remarks, Ernie said, "We will lead people into the future with a full understanding of what's happening. We'll show Americans and the world a clear view of what a future with technology and scientific exploration can do to the world.

"We can and will become the guiding force as we enter this new century. That's why we're here this weekend. We will plan. We will secure the future. We will make a difference."

The group began to applaud. When the applause died down, Ernie continued.

"Most recently, I have found support for us inside the walls of Cameron BioTech. We will begin with Cameron. We will move on to other genome research corporations. We will make a difference."

Louder applause greeted his words. Ernie raised his voice above the sound.

"The world will look to those of us in SPARTA for guidance. People will understand the value of human dignity, life. The pursuit of information in a formal study using the true scientific methods of inquiry developed by the fathers of science—Aristotle, Hippocrates, Newton, Einstein, Werner Von Braun, and more recently Linus Pauling—will be the guide for our future. We cannot deny the foundations developed by these great men. We must continue on the paths set before us. We cannot allow giant corporations and governments to dictate the direction of our future. We must act now!"

He sat to a standing ovation. All forty-eight of them. Ernie didn't notice the two who remained seated in back.

Chapter 7

By ten thirty Sunday evening, Ernie Elson was back in his room packing his suitcase. The SPARTA conference had broken up at five thirty that afternoon, and it had been nearly seven o'clock before the last of the group had headed out. That was just the beginning.

He'd been so exhilarated. This first SPARTA conference had proven that their numbers were growing. Fifty people had attended. Fifty! The breakout discussions that afternoon had covered the gamut of topics from genetic experimentation, gene splicing, and mutations to animal testing. His people were even more informed and motivated. Everyone agreed that some action had to be taken. Ernie knew just was to be done. SPARTA was ready to forge ahead. He had done his job well!

Most importantly, Ernie's boss would be very happy with him. He'd been told there would be an extra reward for him when all this was finished. He'd never actually met his boss. All his instructions and information came via e-mail. The address of the sender was an alias. He'd checked. Still, he was confident that his reward would be great.

He'd never been able to trace the e-mail to the sender. But then, he hadn't really tried. For some reason, he didn't want to know who he was working for. It made him nervous. He thought it might be better if he could claim innocence if anything went wrong.

Besides, Ernie had what he wanted. He was doing something he felt was important. He believed in the need for SPARTA activism. And most importantly, there had been that packet of money on his doorstep the morning after each agreement was made and each job was completed. The money would buy him his freedom. True freedom. His little SPARTA slaves were just a means to an end.

He would finally be free! It wouldn't be long before he could live his life the way he wanted. Free from his wife, free from this crazy government, and most importantly, free from that worthless job where he was considered to be nothing but a freak. He chuckled to himself. Wouldn't they be surprised when he up and left it all? Wouldn't they be surprised?

"No more school, no more books, no more students' dirty looks," he softly chanted to himself as he finished packing his bag, with a smug smile emerging on his face.

There had been several small jobs assigned to Ernie by his anonymous boss prior to this first conference for SPARTA. The most recent job had been this very weekend. It was a bigger job. It was a perfect setup, having the job go down while SPARTA was out of town. His orders had been to do a break-in at Cameron BioTech. He'd gotten word after the conference that the break-in had gone extremely well.

He'd assigned two of his best men to find a way into Cameron while the rest of his group was at the conference. That way, if they were caught, he had plausible deniability. He was up here at the conference. He couldn't have known about any break-in. This wasn't the first break-in they'd managed. There had been other similar jobs. Each time the order was to break in but to leave things undisturbed. Nothing was taken. Each break-in had been successful.

This time it was different. His men were supposed to locate the research files and photocopy specific sections. The goal was to determine the progress Cameron was making in gene splicing.

The boss had always provided the information they needed to make a clean break-in. He knew that it was no easy task to put that together. The Cameron research facility was a fortress. He'd love to know who this guy was! He figured him for an insider.

His men were talented. They followed directions to the letter and managed to pull it off early in the afternoon. They reported that the files they found appeared to indicate that Cameron was on the verge of another breakthrough with genetics. They were processing the photos from the digital cameras they used. They'd even used the Cameron computers to e-mail some of the research files out to a free Hotmail account. They cleaned up their trail on the Cameron computers afterwards. He'd see everything tomorrow and deliver it.

The men said it sounded as if Cameron labs had identified specific gene strands in the human DNA. That was important. The men said it looked like the scientists had begun working almost day and night on connected research. The information they got this weekend would be key to indicating the direction Cameron was heading and how far along they were. The competition was as fierce as it had been when they discovered how to sequence the genes in the genome strands.

Ernie had studied the history behind this research. The Genome Project had been huge. In 1990, Congress had authorized a human genome project. The vote came after James Watson testified. Watson, one of the original scientists who identified DNA, gave specific testimony about the myriad benefits mankind would reap from this research. Congress anted up the money, and the race began.

Then one of the original scientists had broken away from the group. A man named Craig Venter had believed that the research under government control was entirely too slow. So he'd gone to another lab, organized a private company he called Celera, and began to compete with the government project organized by Watson.

Watson became incensed and made a trip back to Congress to demand more money. President Clinton stepped in at some point along the way and convinced the groups to work together for the common good.

Their ultimate goal had been to discover how many genes in a human being formed the human "operating system." Finally, they were able to map the human genome. Venter and Watson announced their success to the world together. It was an incredible feat that had been originally projected to take thirty years and cost billions of dollars. They had completed the project in less than ten years. No one really knew how many government and private dollars had been used. As a result of that research, scientists were able to move on into what they generically called incredible new frontiers.

But the possible outcome could also be problematic. This was Ernie's fear. This was the area that the current labs weren't thinking about. He believed most of them were just in it for the money. And the winner in this race could be worth billions. He could imagine himself being a part of that. Only his role would be a bit different.

Ernie truly believed that, before long, human organs would be developed in test tubes in labs all over the country. New clones of geniuses, both the good and the bad, could be developed. He didn't know if they would be developed, but they could be. Especially if those government Nazis were taking charge. He hated government control in anything.

The giant in the national research labs was Cameron. If they won this race, they could conceivably take control over everyone and everything. Ernie had learned that they were on the verge of a power sweep. The person who was paying him had helped him get the information. Ernie had been told that with this information, Cameron could name their price for just about anything. It would amount to worldwide blackmail. He wanted to stop them. He needed to stop them. He could be a hero and as a side benefit get rich in the process.

Ernie's motives were never totally altruistic. Once he had been contacted, he realized that he would be able to cash in on all of it. This would definitely be more lucrative than teaching. He'd be free and rich—really wealthy. And he'd be able to make a statement about Cameron at the same time. As far as he was concerned, it didn't get any better.

As he packed the last of his clothes, he emerged from his musings and flashed back to the incident this evening. Annie. Damn! Why had Annie turned on him? She had been such a bright girl. He had been so sure she bought into the whole program. She'd idolized him. He'd encouraged it. She'd had such a bright future with SPARTA. He thought she'd understood what this was all about. He had even considered taking her with him when he escaped. Such a sweet, innocent, young thing.

He thought about the events over the last few hours. Had he taken care of all the loose ends? He'd just started packing up after the conference late this afternoon when suddenly Annie charged into his room screaming at him. She made accusations that she'd been tricked. Then she started sobbing.

She claimed that she had learned their whole organization was a cover-up for a bunch of illegal activities. He couldn't believe it. He tried to find out who she'd been talking to. She wouldn't tell him.

How had she found out? Who was onto him? It was a glitch he wasn't prepared for.

She'd just kept screaming at him about being a fraud. He'd tried to quiet her. He'd even repeated his theory about the importance of stopping the government trickery. She wouldn't listen.

He recalled every second of her sudden attack.

"You're a criminal!" she'd screamed. "You're planning on destroying the only good thing this world has. I just read the files Joe and Tyler brought back from Cameron. You've twisted everything you've told us."

"Joe and Tyler? Who are they? I don't know any Joe or Tyler! What have you been listening to? What files from Cameron?" Ernie had begun to get a bad vibe, but he continued trying to calm her.

"You've got to listen to me. You've got it all wrong, Annie. Just calm down and listen to me," he'd said, trying to soothe her.

"Cameron BioTech isn't the enemy. *You* are! They're not creating a brave, new world in there, like you always claimed. You acted so high and mighty. Liar!"

Annie wouldn't shut up. "They are honestly working to improve our world. Because of the work at Cameron BioTech, we have a chance to make a world where my brother could live and walk and be normal again. They could regenerate a spine for him. And you've been either hiding or ignoring that *tiny* little fact, haven't you?

"You're the monster deceiving all of us. And what's even worse, you've been getting paid to disrupt the research at Cameron. You've been receiving tons of money. I saw it. It's all there in those files. Thousands of dollars. You've been paid! That's all you ever cared about, isn't it? The money! You're nothing more than a filthy liar, Ernie Elson! You don't care about the research at all. You lied about all of it!"

She wouldn't stop ranting. She was out of control.

She kept repeating the same accusations, "I know now that Cameron isn't creating new superheroes! Their research scientists aren't the criminals. You're the criminal! You're the criminal!" She dropped her head to her hands, wracked with uncontrolled sobbing.

Ernie recalled standing there utterly stunned. He hadn't known what to say. Where had she gotten all of this information? How could she have known?

Suddenly objects had begun to fly past his head—books, papers from all his studies, experiment results, glowing letters from others about his work in SPARTA. But when she'd wheeled around with that test tube in her hand, he knew he had to stop her. The test tube had been filled with a highly volatile explosive—one he'd been saving to use at Cameron. If she had used it, she would have blown up the lodge and everyone along with it. It would have been a waste. Her stupidity and emotional outbreak would have destroyed SPARTA along with his future.

So he'd begun talking softly to her, almost cooing, calming, pacifying, soothing. With each word, he'd stepped   closer.

"Annie," he'd appealed, "what are you talking about? Where did you get this idea? You know I would never do anything to harm you or any member of your family. You must understand that my only cares are for you. I will help your brother. I can. Together we can do these things. We just need to go about it differently. We need   to   do   what's   right."

"You're   lying!"   Annie   sobbed.

"No, sweetheart, I would never lie to you. You're the future. You're the brilliance. You're all I've ever worked for."

He stepped close enough to caress her face. She crumpled against him. Carefully removing the test tube from her hands, he pulled her closer to him while placing the test tube gently in its case on the end table next to them. It would be safe there for a while. He needed to handle her first.

"Let's sit here on the sofa and talk this out. We can make it all right for both of us. You know I've always known you were special. You're my greatest hope."

It was clear Annie desperately wanted to believe him. Ernie had given her the one thing she'd always wanted—attention and recognition. He could tell she was beginning to listen to him. He wanted her to feel he was revealing   his   real   identity.

"But why are you doing this? Is it all for the money?" She had continued crying softly then. "You'll be destroying my only hope for my brother when you blow up   Cameron   BioTech."

"Annie, I would never do that to your brother, to your family, or to your hopes for your family. I care most of all about you. Cameron can't help your brother. We can. Trust me. I know that. We'll approach it from another direction. You know I have the future mapped out for SPARTA. And there's also a future for us. We have a future, too, you know. I love you, Annie."

Annie had reached up to his face and stared intently into his eyes for truth. He knew she believed he cared for her. He had to convince her now. She'd said he was the only person who really understood her. He knew she'd loved him for a long time. She had to understand that no one else cared about her. Ernie had encouraged her to think that. Her parents seldom spoke to her anymore. They were consumed with her brother. But now they'd be proud of her. It would all work out, he promised her.

Ernie had relied on all of that. He'd played to her needs. Her tears had finally stopped. Thank heavens.

"Oh, why does this have to be?" she'd stammered. Tears clung to her dark lashes. "I love you. I've loved you for so long. You were the only one who really understood me.   I   couldn't   tell   you ..."

He'd   covered   her   mouth   with   kisses.

"I love you, Ernie." She'd returned his kisses, covering his face and neck with tears and kisses. "Do we have to hide our love? Why can't we be together? We can work together, and you can help my brother. You can make the right changes for us and for the world. We can do it together. We can be together."

Her youthful innocence won out this time. And Ernie knew what he had to do. It wouldn't last. She would interfere with everything. She would be in the way.

Responding to her emotional plea, Ernie caressed her, cooed, and whispered, "Oh, but we will be darling, Annie.   We   will   be."

He had stroked through the mass of dark curls and moved his hands down, massaging her neck while kissing her deeply. Then pressing his hands on both sides of her neck, he had quickly and efficiently twisted her neck, causing a sharp crack. It was a technique he'd learned in Nam. Quick, quiet, and efficient.

It was really too bad he'd had to do that. He'd kissed her lips gently while she expelled her last breath. He'd whispered as she slumped against him, "I did love you, Annie. You were a wonder child. I'm sorry."

But reflecting on her words, Ernie now realized there was something more important than her youthful naiveté. She'd placed his entire operation in jeopardy. He could see he'd been wrong to trust her. He realized that now. How in hell had she gotten those damn Cameron files? Nobody was supposed to be reading them without his permission. He only allowed a select few in the SPARTA group to read portions of them. He'd edited out the damaging stuff.

Annie was just too young. He should have known she wouldn't understand. Of course, he really hadn't planned to have her know all of it. No one could. So he had to get rid of her. Great kid. Great mind. It was just too   damn   bad.

That was how he'd gotten to this point. It was a tragic end to what had been a perfect weekend. His problem had been how to dispose of her. Then it was getting late. Too late. He had to get moving and clean up the mess.

He'd decided he could easily cover her absence when anyone from the group asked. He'd simply tell them she'd been called home urgently because of a problem with her brother. That was perfect. He could blame it on Annie's parents, who had gotten access to an experimental drug produced by Cameron. The kids in the group would be more incensed and anxious to put SPARTA's next plan into action. They would consider it their responsibility to help people like Annie's brother. They believed in the need to protect the weak, crippled masses from exploitation by a huge research organization like Cameron. He could use this to prove to the SPARTA group how the research was going in the wrong direction at Cameron BioTech. Then his followers would want to make it right! They would want to expose Cameron to the entire   world.   Perfect!

Yes, after a little deliberation, he was sure that he could use Annie's disappearance to his advantage. But he had to be quick. This needed to be done perfectly. Furthermore, he thought, the group might believe she'd left for home but then had been attacked by someone acting for Cameron, a spy perhaps, and had disappeared; they'd want to look for her. That was another problem.

So first of all, he had to get Annie's body out of the cabin and into her car. It had to be her car, not his. No trace, no connection to him must be found. He'd figure out how to ditch her car later and get back to his car.

It was after eleven when Ernie backed her car up to the parking spot in front of his cabin. He opened the rear door and quickly stepped back inside to wrap

74

Annie's limp body in a blanket. He picked up the bundle gently and quietly stepped out the door to place it onto the backseat. He closed the car door with a soft click.

He drove off to find the perfect spot. He knew the area. He'd spent a lot of time up here when he first returned from Nam. He remembered a side road off Highway 61 just north of here. There were about fifty cabins along that road, and they fronted right onto Lake Superior. He could head down the road a ways, find that secluded little drive he remembered, park her car in the woods, and carry her down to the lake. With any luck, no one would be at any of the nearby cabins this weekend. Annie wouldn't be discovered for perhaps a week or more. Then they'd have to identify her. It would take a while. By then, he and his group would have accomplished what they needed to do, and he would be long gone. It was perfect.

When they found her body there, authorities might think she'd been trespassing while taking a walk down to the lake and then slipped. Or better yet, the waves might just pick her up and carry the body away. There could be a number of possible explanations for what happened to her, and none of them would involve him or murder—or SPARTA.

He hoped he could count on the SPARTA group to believe his story about Cameron's interference. He'd have to make it good. The police wouldn't ever figure out what had really happened. It would be another dead-end case. He smiled and chanted, "No more school, no more books, no more students' dirty looks." He was so smart. Smarter than all of them.

He'd turned out of the driveway and headed north on Highway 61. Before long, he found the turn onto Pedagogue's Road. The dirt road was almost five miles long, he remembered. It was pitch black out with the exception of the light of a full moon and his headlights. He knew it was unlikely that he would meet any other cars at this time of night. About two-thirds of the way down the road, he turned off his lights. Slowly, the car crept to what looked like the little used drive. He pulled over and edged into the drive. Within seconds, he turned off the drive and pulled into the woods. He could carry Annie's body from here and then cut across to a flat, rocky outcropping on the shore in front of the cabin next door. The way was familiar. It was coming back to him. He'd walked down here before.

His cousin, Ray, owned this property. Wasn't that providential, he thought. Maybe God was still looking out for him. Maybe God hadn't disappeared after all.

He and Ray had never been close. But Ray had invited Ernie and his wife up here one weekend just last summer to show off the work they'd done on the property. Ernie's wife had never come to Northern Minnesota before that. Now Cousin Ray was going to provide him with a different kind of hospitality—a path to a place to leave Annie. Ernie knew that one path led from his cousin's house to the neighbor's lot next door. As he remembered it, the path ran down by the lake and then up to the neighbor's house.

Talk about the importance of gathering data, he thought. One never knew when making good observations would turn into something important and useful. And what could be better than delivering the "superior" student to the "superior" lake. He loved the play on words. It was a perfect irony, he thought. With any luck, the lake might even claim her before anyone could discover her body. It really was superior. He couldn't help chuckling quietly to himself. God! This was meant to be!

He lifted Annie carefully from the backseat. She was still wrapped up like a mummy in the blanket. He hoisted her body up onto his shoulder, closing the door quietly as he stepped back. It was a good thing she was a small girl. The walk down to the lake was going to be tricky with her body balanced on his shoulder. He carried a small flashlight to search through the thickets for the paths. The paths split into two partway across the property. One led down to the lakeshore behind his cousin's cabin, and the other path led to the neighbor's property. The latter was the path he sought out. It took ten minutes to carry Annie down the drive and then veer off to the left on a path that came out just below the neighbor's cabin. Although he could see that the neighbors were there this weekend (the car was parked in the drive), the lights were off. He assumed they must already be asleep.

He was breathing heavily now. He'd thought he was in fairly good shape, but this was almost like a boot camp march. It brought back more Nam memories than he cared to have. He needed to be especially careful these last few feet. The path dropped, and tree roots reached up through the leaves and pine needles to form jagged upheavals in the path. He slowed his pace and chose his steps carefully. After four tricky steps down across tree roots and rock outcroppings, he found himself on the boulders that formed a cratered shore. There were several flat outcroppings here.

77

He laid Annie down and unwrapped her body carefully. Then he dragged the body over to the rocks and away from the path. He looked around, surveying the area. This place should make it difficult for anyone to see Annie's body from the cabin windows. He thought it unlikely that anyone would come down here to the shore this late in the fall, even if they were still here.

The North Shore was usually ten degrees colder than inland areas. Most people closed their cabins up for the winter about this time. It was probably the last weekend for the people who owned this cabin. They wouldn't come down to the lake, especially in this spot.

It was really cold near the lakeshore now. He shivered. His breath came out in frosty streams. He wrapped his arms tightly around himself and looked around. They wouldn't be able to see the body, and now if the wind came up with good waves, the lake would take care of Annie. It was just superior, he thought again, and he smiled as he left Annie's body, grabbed the blanket, and began to make his way back.

Ernie was tired. Fatigue was suddenly closing in. He drove Annie's car back to an area near the lodge. He found a small side road with a dirt path leading into the woods. After wiping the car down and cleaning up anything that might look suspicious, he hiked back to the lodge and slipped into his room. He was glad he'd worn gloves and a cap. Of course, as cold as it was already, he'd had to wear them! But he was sure the CSI teams would swarm over Annie's car when they found it. They'd be looking for any clue, any minutiae that might lead them to find her. But he surmised even if they did find evidence of Ernie's presence, it wouldn't mean anything.

Everyone knew he'd often ridden with Annie to different events, and she'd even given him a ride to school on a couple occasions recently. There would be nothing to make him a suspect. He and Annie were close. That was all. The group knew he was her idol. He'd be properly shocked and would grieve over her death. And then he'd blame Cameron BioTech for the treachery and attacks on SPARTA.

He smiled. It was the perfect plan. Now he needed to get on with it. He had to notify his boss of a change in plans. He'd explain it all. This could work to their advantage, he'd tell him. After all, what the boss really wanted him to do was give Cameron a black eye. He would explain how this would certainly help. He'd be able to shut Cameron out of this genome race sooner than they'd expected.

Once again, his thoughts drifted to the future he would have. Perhaps now his future would be what he'd always dreamed of. *God is in heaven after all.*

"Yeah right!" he said out loud and then snorted out a laugh. God hadn't been around most of his last few years. He'd had to fight most of his life for some recognition, purpose. Now, he was finally getting somewhere.

It was the middle of the night by the time Ernie pulled into the driveway of his home in the northwest Minneapolis suburb of Blaine. He pulled his truck into the garage. Martha wouldn't bother him yet, he thought. It was early, and she'd be sleeping soundly because of the load of sleeping pills she took. He'd left Castle Danger at midnight, and it was now four in the morning. He'd made excellent time.

Later this week, he would go online with the group in the SPARTA chat room and tell them all his version of the story about Annie. Or maybe he'd only tell one or two of them and then let them spread the story. When the "line" was active, stories grew with details. It'd be even better. He'd decide which way to do it later.

It'd be a long day at school this Monday. He'd catch a couple hours of sleep and then make an especially strong pot of coffee when he got up. That would help keep him going. He couldn't afford to be absent today. If there was any suspicion cast his way, he wanted to make sure he was totally covered.

He crept into his room, locked the door, slid into bed, and drifted into a deep sleep. In the bedroom next door, Martha Elson pulled her blankets around her neck and closed her eyes.

Chapter 8

Monday mornings always came too early. Detective Swede Olson had been having his second cup of coffee when he got the first call of the day just after 7:00 a.m. He and the guys had been sitting around sharing a few jokes before they got rolling for the day. In their line of work, humor was a necessary component for maintaining sanity. Since Minnesota was the central settlement area for Scandinavians, ethnic jokes revolved around the characters of Ole and Lena and Sven. Olson had just finished telling his partners an Ole and Lena joke he'd remembered. He'd told it with all the accents of a good Scandahoovian, as the natives said.

"This one's a clean one, and an oldie but goodie. You can tell this one to anyone. Ole and Lena were standing on the roof of their home watching the floodwaters from the Minnesota River rise to the rafters. Lena noticed a pattern of movement in the water. She said, 'Look, Ole! Dere seems ta be somtin goin on in da water dere. Loookit how it's agoin back and fort in front ov da house dere. Vat do yoo tink is happenin?'

"Ole answers, 'Ah, dat's yust Sven. He sed dat he vas agoin ta mow his lawn today come hell or high vater!'"

The guys laughed even though they'd heard it before. Yeah, that was a good one. Allen had just started telling another Ole and Lena joke when the phone on Swede's desk rang.

Olson set his coffee cup aside and turned away from the group to pick up the phone. He listened intently. Charlie Frank sounded anxious.

81

"Sure, Charlie. I can come by. It'll only be a few minutes. I'll check it out for you. Just sit tight. We'll file a report."

Charlie sounded relieved. "I'd really appreciate it Swede. We go back a ways. I trust you. I can't afford a screw up on this, ya know? I can trust that you'll do the job for me."

"Well, thanks, Charlie. We still miss you around here. At least you can do security at Cameron. I know you do a good job there."

"Yeah, I guess so. I try. With my back injury, it's at least something to draw in a wage. And I have to say it's been more interesting than I thought it would be."

"Yeah. That's an understatement. Look, I'll get over there in just a little bit. I've got to set up the schedule for the guys, and then I'll be out. Okay?"

"No problem, Swede. I'll gather up the information you'll need when you get here and keep things under control until then. Thanks."

Twenty minutes later, Swede Olson was driving with his partner, Allen Jenkins, through downtown Minneapolis heading north on 35W, to the northern edge of Minneapolis. Olson began to explain to Jenkins about Charlie Frank and Charlie's job at Cameron BioTech.

"It would be hard for me to be in Charlie's shoes," Swede said. "Charlie injured his back while he was still on the force. He was helping load a gurney into an ambulance at the scene of an accident. Then he was forced into taking an early retirement because of it. I can't imagine going from active duty to being tied down in a boring security position like his. Poor guy. I have to admit, though," Swede nodded his head, absently

82

agreeing with himself, "Charlie's seen more than the normal amount action at Cameron in the last few years."

"How so?"

"The protests and demonstrations outside Cameron heated up during a convention of scientists involved in genome research a few summers ago. Don't you remember it?"

"No, I guess not. I was out east most of one summer. That must have been it." Jenkins yawned. "God, it's early, isn't it? I could have used another cup of coffee."

"I guess some crazy people felt threatened by the research at Cameron BioTech," Swede continued, ignoring his partner's disinterest. "The research labs held a national convention that brought the work at Cameron and other research labs into the spotlight. NBC, ABC, CBS, and CNN sent staff out to do interviews with some of the nation's top scientists and researchers—including some here at Cameron."

"Must have missed the news that week."

"Yeah, well, genome research at Cameron BioTech and their rivals Micron Research, Xenon Labs, and Environ Labs made the evening news all that week. The newspapers were filled with editorials and articles during the convention.

"Uh huh. So what was the big deal?"

"It was all about the ethics involved in the gene-splicing, stem cell, and genome research at Cameron BioTech. Some people were afraid that Cameron might try cloning. Even human cloning."

"No shit? You gotta be kidding! Here in Minneapolis?" Allen turned to look at Swede. Now Olson had his interest.

83

"No shit. Once the media got involved, it stirred up the scientific and religious communities, and all hell broke   loose."

Swede remembered all the problems at Cameron BioTech over the last couple years. It was all coming back.

"One day during that week, workers leaving Cameron were attacked by the protesters." Swede paused. "The riot began with a couple protesters throwing rocks and bottles at the workers. We nailed them later for inciting a riot. The riot escalated to a point where they began attacking workers and beating them on their backs and heads with picket signs."

"So how'd it end up?"

"Well, some Cameron people were able to run back into the building for cover. Others tried to get away running through the parking lot to their cars. Then a whole horde of rioters blocked and rocked one person as he tried to drive away."

"Anybody get hurt?"

"Yeah, unfortunately. Before we got there, they succeeded in turning the car over with the driver pinned inside. Our guys arrived in riot gear twenty minutes after the call came in. For some of the workers, it was too late."

"So it was bad? What happened to the guy in the car?"

"He was taken to the county hospital, HCMC, emergency room for treatment of broken bones and stitches. We managed to arrest some rioters, but quite a few managed to get away."

"Bummer. Didn't look good for the department, huh?"

Swede winced. Sometimes Allen sounded like a green, little kid.

"Yeah right." Swede decided to finish it up for Allen. "During the rest of the convention, we sent in overtime people to provide protection for everyone at Cameron. Charlie Frank was called on the carpet for not being prepared. I think Charlie earned his pay that week and then some."

"So did this Charlie Frank guy take all the blame for the riot getting out of control there? He was the security guy, right? He should've been on top of all of it."

"No, not really. Charlie did what he was supposed to. He followed protocol in getting the department there right away for support. But that wasn't the end of problems for Cameron. Charlie had to deal with bigger stuff later."

"Why? What else happened?"

"Remember that sniper shooting of that Cameron employee a year ago in September? She'd been doing a press conference about the research being done by Cameron BioTech. Cameron decided to do a press meet and greet on the front steps with a big announcement. A sniper took out their PR person before she even got started."

Allen perked up again. "Oh right. I do remember that one. She was a major player for Cameron BioTech, wasn't she?"

"That's right." Swede nodded. "Karen Thompson, the victim, was the media relations person for the company. She was also the wife of Quay Thompson, the current top dog with the BCA."

"No shit!" Allen's voice took a new tone of interest.

"Just as Mrs. Thompson started to speak that day, a sniper bullet struck her in the neck. Our investigators think it came from behind. We figured the sniper must have gotten into the building and established a position on or near a low entrance roof behind Karen Thompson. She died in front of the media cameras. No evidence of the sniper was ever found anywhere in or near the building."

"I remember that. It was big on the news for weeks. All the people who'd been in the building were cleared, weren't they? Isn't it still an open case?"

"Yep. A lot of people suspect that the shooter had to be a person working inside Cameron. Even though her husband, Quay Thompson, had connections with the BCA, they still haven't been able to determine who the shooter was, or for that matter, what may have been a motive."

"And your friend Charlie was at Cameron then, too?"

"Yep. Charlie Frank was not only on duty, he took charge and combed the building with the investigators to help search for clues. Nothing showed up."

"Interesting that he had to retire with the force and then ended up with all the stuff happening at Cameron. Not as dull as you might expect, huh?"

"Charlie did do a good job, though," Swede mused. "He was even commended by the president of Cameron BioTech as well as the BCA for his professional command of both situations. He's been given a lot of power as the head of security. Even more since then. They respect him."

"Well, he must be having a real problem now, if he's calling you in right away."

"I think Charlie's just being careful. He says he thinks they've had a breach of security at Cameron. We'll see. Looks like Charlie's doing everything possible to make sure his beat at Cameron is safe and his hide is covered."

Swede finished his story as they pulled into the parking lot in front of Cameron BioTech.

"The only thing you'll need to be aware of," Swede cautioned, "is that Charlie can get longwinded and full of himself. He likes to pat himself on the back a little bit. Just go with it. He's really an okay guy."

Jenkins nodded. "Yeah, sure. Whatever." He climbed out of the car and trailed after Swede.

As he walked up the sidewalk, Swede checked out his and Allen's reflections in the dark windows of the building's front facade. The years had taken a toll on his physical fitness. So had the traditional coffee and donuts each morning. Looking at his reflection, he decided he'd better cut back on the goodies and start working out.

That's what Jenkins did. He worked out. Youth versus experience, Swede thought. Maybe they could teach each other. Allen was a good kid. But he had a lot to learn in the police business. Personally, Swede was glad he wasn't starting all over again. The enthusiasm of innocence would disappear soon enough, he thought. But then again, maybe some of Jenkins's enthusiasm could rub off on him before the cynicism took over. He wished he could experience that feeling of excitement again.

Allen Jenkins tagged along after Swede. Swede was intent on teaching him. For now, Swede just wanted Jenkins to watch, listen, and learn. He would move up the ranks quickly if he was a good student.

Charlie Frank met Swede and Allen in the lobby. As they walked across the marble floor through the atrium to the elevators, Charlie explained the situation to Swede.

"I came on duty a bit before seven. Part of my morning routine is to check all the security monitors with our guy at the lobby security desk, Hal Jensen." Charlie motioned toward Hal as he placed the flat of his hand against the security pad next to the elevator and waited for the doors to open. "Hal said he hadn't noticed anything unusual."

They crowded into the elevator, and Charlie continued his story as he punched the button for the third floor and the elevator doors closed.

"Hal usually just spends his night watching the security monitors from each floor of the building and the cameras that are outside in the parking lot. The monitors have been beefed up since the sniper shooting of Karen Thompson," he said, looking at Swede. Swede nodded in understanding.

"Nothing looked unusual. Then after checking in with Hal, I began my usual physical sweep of the building before the workers arrive. I like to check on things myself, even though the regular night guard is supposed to have covered everything."

Swede nodded without comment. He'd begun taking notes on a small notepad he'd pulled from his pocket.

"I'd already gone through the first and second floors, ya know. It's part of my job to check all the doors and note if anyone has come in early. I always like to know who works late or comes in early. Usually the first two floors are empty at this time of day. It wasn't until I got to the third floor and tried the door at 314 that I noticed a problem."

"What was that?" Swede stopped writing and looked up at Charlie.

"The door wasn't closed tight. It looked closed, but when I grabbed the handle, it gave."

"You mean it just hadn't been latched tight?" asked Swede. He was growing impatient with Charlie now. This appeared to be pretty run of the mill. He didn't see any need for them to be here.

"Yeah. I thought maybe it was just a fluke, you know. But I didn't want to take any chances. This 314 office is the research storage room, see. All the information for the research done on the seventh floor is sent here and filed. All the heavy-duty, top-secret research is done on the seventh floor. A lot of it is filed on the computer hard drives, backed up on CDs themselves and in the Cloud. But there are also a few hard copies here."

They exited the elevator, and Charlie dismissed the guard in front of the office door.

"So what you're telling us is that you think someone could've gotten in here and gotten out some research data, right?" Swede said.

"Possibly." Charlie knew Swede was getting impatient, but he wanted to be specific. This was important.

"If a researcher wants to check back on what was done on a certain date or find out where to get more information, the request has to come through here. The assistants log all that information into the computers here."

"So did anyone come in to work early this

morning?" Allen stepped forward when he spoke.

"I asked Hal." Charlie turned to Swede and handed him a manila folder. "This is the employee list. Hal said he hadn't seen a soul. Sometimes Margie Akins is in about six. She likes to get an early start, especially if she's got something major cooking. Then she'll take a couple days off later down the line. But she's not here yet today. I checked."

Swede began tapping his pen on his notepad. He looked at the entry lock on the office door. "Didn't you say during the Thompson case that each employee has to have a handprint on file, so they can use the hand scanner to enter the building?"

"That's right."

"And handprints of people working in each area were only approved for entrance into that area?"

"Yeah, that's right. But some employees are approved for more than one area. There are always special situations based on each researcher's needs."

"So who would be using this office in this case?" Swede was scanning Charlie's employee list.

"As I said, Margie Akins was one of those people who took advantage of the optional work hours. She might work late or come in early." Charlie began shuffling his feet nervously. He looked down at the floor. "I can call Margie when we're done here. "But I really don't think there's a problem with her. No one can enter an area they aren't specifically cleared for, and she's not cleared for here."

"Have you or anyone entered the office yet?" Swede glanced into the crack of the open door. "Do you know for sure that no one is inside?"

"Well, I pushed open the door a little and just

looked around behind the door. I didn't really search the office yet. I radioed Hal to get someone up here to stand guard outside the door."

He was using a defensive tone. Charlie Frank didn't like to be told what to do in his own turf. "I just thought I'd better get you here first before we went in, so that we handled it right. I don't want to mess up anything here." He stared steadily into Swede's eyes.

"Right," said Swede. "Well, let's take a look in that office, before we do anything else. Do you have your gun? Jenkins, how about you? Don't want any surprises hiding in there." Swede was grinning.   This was for effect. They all knew it. Swede was showing off for his young partner. Charlie went along with the game.

Slipping their guns from their holsters, they entered the office. A quick survey of the main area, behind doors and under desks, revealed nothing. There were two adjoining rooms filled with wall-to-wall black, metal filing cabinets. The doors to each of these rooms had been left open with lights left on. The main area housed eight computers spaced around the room at small desks. As they holstered their guns, Charlie grunted a "Huh!"

"People usually close everything up in here and turn off lights as they leave." Charlie turned, motioning to the office furniture. "Of course, none of the filing drawers are open, no desk drawers are open, and the computers all appear to be in their sleep mode."

"What you really need to do now is to get the head of this research library in here to do a thorough check. So when does the head of this area get in?" Swede turned to face Charlie.

"Jane Reston usually comes in to work about nine thirty. Do you want me to call her now?" Charlie began to pull a cell phone off his belt.

"Yes, I think to play it safe we'd better get her in here as soon as possible. Find out if she's on the way. If someone's been playing with these computers, I'd rather have someone who knows what they're doing check them out."

"Makes sense," Allen said. "I could check the history on each of them, if you want?"

"No. I don't think that would be a good idea. Let them do it."

Swede moved away from Allen. "Would she know how everything would have been left? Or does she have a group of people in here working with her?"

"Well, usually there are four gals who come in during the week. Two of them work part-time, so they're here either on Tuesday, Thursday or else Monday, Wednesday, depending on which schedule they're supposed to follow. The other two are here five days a week. Of course, Jane Reston is the head of the research library. She's the person I was telling you about. Like I said, she comes in about nine thirty. She'd know the routine and can be sure we cover all the bases."

"Okay," said Swede, "give her a call now. We need to get something official on this, so we can write up a report." He was anxious to get this finished. Looking around, he continued, "It really doesn't look like anything's been touched. But then, I wouldn't know about the computers and who might have been messing with them. Just can't figure why someone would come in here, leave doors open and lights on if they didn't want a break-in to be discovered. Doesn't seem like much of an operation if that's what happened." It was obvious that Swede felt this was a waste of his time. He liked Charlie, but sometimes the guy was too much into overkill. This seemed like one of those moments.

"Any chance that the night custodian could have come in here to clean and maybe just accidentally left things open?"

"I can talk to him some more," Charlie said with a sigh. "I called him right before I called you. I asked him if he'd done this floor last night. He told me he usually does the top floors first and works his way down. He began last night on the sixth floor and was just getting done with the first floor when I called."

"Yeah, so what did he say about this floor?"

"He said he was sure he'd locked up everything after he finished here about 5:00 a.m. But, you never know, it could have been one of those 'off moments' for him. Everyone has those. You know how you just get so deep in thought about something and go into autopilot? Then you don't do all the things you're supposed to."

"Could be, I suppose." Swede was moving toward the elevators. "If he did turn off the lights in there and close up, that means someone was in here after 3:00 a.m. I don't know how they could have done it with all the security cameras and Hal at the front desk. There's no other way in here, is there?"

"We'll have to check all the possibilities, I suppose. You know Cameron BioTech is definitely an open target. The competition is intense. Other companies would love to get their hands on this research, and the protesters would love to shut them down."

Swede ignored Charlie's excuses and interrupted him. "By the way, did you touch anything other than the doorknob on the entry door?"

"No, I don't think so." Charlie was surprised by the question. "I just looked in, like I said, and then called Hal to get someone up here to guard the door until you came."

Suddenly, Jenkins turned and headed back toward the office door.

"What are you doing?" Swede turned to watch him.

"I'm going to retrieve that piece of paper I saw lying on the floor next to the desk in the corner of the room. It might be something."

He was moving toward the door with purpose.

Swede took three steps after him calling out, "No! Stop!"

Jenkins stopped and looked up surprised.

"Allen." Swede was talking to a child now. "You can't just go and pick up whatever you see lying around. Not until we've had the manager in here and an investigative team in to clear this area. Leave things where they are for now. We'll get a chance to check everything out in an hour or two."

"Oh, of course, sorry." Jenkins meekly backed away from the door and turned toward the elevator. Swede and Charlie exchanged glances. Swede gave a slight shrug as they walked into the elevator.

Jane Reston arrived thirty minutes later and joined Charlie, Swede, and Allen in the lobby. She was in her late thirties, carried a huge briefcase, and looked concerned.

"Hal called and said that I needed to get in here immediately." She shifted the briefcase to extend her hand to Swede. "I'm Jane Reston." As she introduced herself, she looked at Charlie with a raised eyebrow, waiting for an explanation.

"Jane, this is detective Swede Olson from the Minneapolis PD. I called him in because we may have a breach on your floor," Charlie explained. "I trust Swede and asked him to come have a look before we make any big moves on this. This is his partner, Allen Jenkins."

They nodded at one another as Jane shook hands with Allen.

Swede took over. "Ms. Reston, I will need to know when you left last Friday and if there were others still working in this office when you left." He was in his professional mode. "Then we'll need you to take a walk through the office to see if you notice anything out of the ordinary."

Jane nodded. Once again, Charlie pressed his hand to the ID pad. They crowded into the elevator. Charlie pressed the button for the third floor.

"Finally," Swede continued, "I want you to personally check each of the computers in the office. Can you tell if things might be missing or if something might have been taken from the databases of the computers? Or if they have been messed with in any way?"

Jane Reston appeared unruffled by the Swede's requests and hurried from the elevator as soon as the doors opened. It was clear that she considered this to be a no-nonsense job. She was only a petite five foot two, but she gave off an attitude that made it clear she was able to meet any challenge.

"First of all," Jane turned to Charlie, "you need to call Cindy Wylie, Betty Kraemer, Jo Adams, and Allison Brown. They are my part-time help. Hal can pull up their phone numbers."

She looked at Swede and explained. "They each have specific areas they cover. They are responsible for organizing, filing, and securing bits of information from different labs on the upper floors."

"Who else do you need?" Charlie asked.

"We'll need to call in my other two full-time helpers, Mary Richards and Michelle Wilson. Together we can quickly access the most recent log-on and entry on each computer. Using that, we should be able to tell you if someone has gone into an area they shouldn't have."

"Can you also take a quick inventory of the filing cabinets to see if any of the files are missing?" Charlie queried.

"I carry a master inventory of all files in a password-protected section on my computer." She paused, brushing a strand of hair from her eyes. "Did you want to dust for prints before we do that, or did you want us to wear gloves while we check for problems in the research library?" Jane looked at Swede with a raised eyebrow.

Swede smiled. This was going to be an easy job. Jane Reston was an efficient, no-nonsense Cameron loyalist.

"I think," Swede said, "we'd like to get our team in here to dust first, and yes, if we could get you to slip on gloves while you check the files and the computers, it would protect any possible prints left by someone else that the team may miss. That is, *if* someone else has been in here."

Jane's head jerked up swiftly. She had questions written all over her face.

"It still doesn't make sense that someone would leave such an obvious sign of a break-in," Swede explained. "I can't imagine why someone would want to let the world know they'd been in here illegally." He paused for effect. "Unless what they really wanted was to let us to know they were capable of getting in. In that case, they just left a message for Cameron BioTech."

Charlie moved closer to Jane, speaking directly to her. "We'll wait until we're finished before we call the rest of our staff." He turned to Swede, "At that point, you'll want to interview each of them. Let's get busy."

"Why are you going to interview our staff?" someone asked in a singsong voice. A young woman had poked her head into the door of the office. Charlie Frank's head jerked in the direction of the voice, and then he turned abruptly back to look at Swede. Jane stepped forward to prevent the woman from entering the room.

"We've had a problem in the research library, Sunni. This is Detective Swede Olson from the Minneapolis Police Department." She motioned to Swede, who stepped forward to shake Sunni's hand. They remained in the doorway, barring her entrance to the library.

"Detective, this is Sunni Hyun. She's one of our research partners. She works in our stem cell research division. She came highly recommended to us by her professors at Stanford. She's brought enormous expertise with her."

"Pleased to meet you, Detective Olson," Sunni said, ignoring Jane's tribute to her abilities. Sunni acknowledged Swede and then looked quizzically to Jane.

Sunni was a diminutive, young woman of Asian descent. Swede assumed she was either Korean or Japanese. He never could tell the difference between those Asians. They all looked the same to him. He gave her the once over. Sunni was wearing a white lab coat that hung to the knees of her tan trousers. He watched her as her dark eyes peered over his shoulders into the library.

"What happened?" Sunni turned to Jane for an answer.

"Well ..." Jane hesitated.

Before she could finish, Charlie interrupted. He pushed forward, out the door, to stand next to Sunni. "We think someone might have tried to send some information out of here on one of the computers last night. But it looks like they didn't succeed."

"Well, I certainly hope not!" Sunni's eyes glared at Charlie now. "We can't have any leaks happening here!" She stared for a long second at Charlie, and her chiseled features hardened as her porcelain skin flushed with what appeared to be anger.

Swede was interested in her reaction. Was there something else going on here?

"Are you concerned about losing some specific information, Ms. Hyun?" Swede said.

"Certainly. We've worked very hard on this research, Detective." She had a slight lilt to her speech, reflecting her second language. Swede immediately made the assumption she hadn't grown up in the States. She appeared evasive now, not looking directly at him. She seemed shaken by his attention.

"I don't think we have to worry," Charlie assured her. "We've got this under control for now. We'll let you

98

know as soon as we know something. There's no reason to be alarmed or to upset the staff."

"I certainly hope not!" She gave Charlie one more hard look and then turned to Swede and Jane. "Nice to meet you, Detective. Jane, I'll talk to you later." She turned and left with the same abruptness with which she'd appeared.

"Interesting young woman," commented Swede as he watched her black ponytail flip behind her.

"Well, she's a bit anal, that's for sure," Jane said. "We usually see her up here about once a day. She always wants to be sure we've filed her data correctly."

"Yeah, I think I know the type," Swede said.

"Well, let's get to it." Charlie turned and walked back into the office, effectively refocusing their attention on the job at hand. Allen followed suit.

It took three hours for the police team to dust the room for prints. They were meticulous. As they finished, Jane started checking the files. She began by matching each file with her private catalogued inventory of each file. Finally, she scrutinized the history on each of the computers for recent logons and data retrieval.

If something had been tampered with or was missing, Jane was sure she would know what it was. The research at Cameron BioTech was held in the tightest security. She took seriously her responsibility for that security. This was her office. She had also come up with an idea to keep the police occupied while they waited for her to finish her evaluations.

"I have several recently published abstracts and articles from the scientists here at Cameron that detail the research they've completed. It's pretty amazing stuff.

I thought you might like to read some of them while I finish. It might shed a light on the importance of this security."

Jane handed Swede and Allen a scrapbook of articles published in the local papers and national magazines about Cameron's most recent research.

"This might help. It might give you an idea why someone would be trying to break in here," she explained again.

Swede took the scrapbooks and handed one to Allen.

"Thanks," he said perfunctorily.

For fifteen minutes, Swede and Allen were absorbed in the articles. Finally, Swede turned to Allen. He began reading aloud an article that had been published in a recent *Star Tribune* newspaper.

"Listen to this," he said as he scanned the article. "According to this article, they've got some information that says recombinant-DNA techniques have been created that are capable of manufacturing synthetic human insulin, and a human interferon, as well as a human growth hormone, and a hepatitis-B vaccine."

He began reading directly from the article, "*Recombinant-DNA techniques, combined with the development of a technique for producing antibodies in great quantity, have made an impact on medical diagnosis and cancer research.*" He looked up at Jenkins. "Pretty amazing stuff, huh?"

Allen nodded and began reading aloud from the article he was holding. "It says here, '*Plants have been genetically adjusted to make their own pesticides. Bacteria capable of biodegrading oil have been produced for use in oil-spill cleanups. Genetic*

100

engineering also introduces the fear of adverse genetic manipulations and their consequences (e.g., antibiotic-resistant bacteria or new strains of disease).' Blah, blah, blah. This is quite a project."

"Yes, it is," Swede said in an almost, but not quite reverent tone. He looked at Jenkins, grinning slightly as he continued a voice of feigned awe. "According to the *Star Tribune*, Cameron is running precisely this kind of research. Can you imagine living in a lab day in and day out, running a bunch of experiments like these on rats, plants, and what have you?"

"I think we'd better take this break-in seriously. Do you realize the impact some of this stuff could have on all of us? No wonder they're under fire. These people are trying to discover the cures for cancer, diabetes, and hepatitis B. At the same time, they're discovering possibilities for genetic engineering of new plants and stuff like that to improve the food chain. There's no end to what they can do with this genome stuff."

"Really, kid? You know all that or did you just read it?"

"Yeah, I know it. I did learn a little bit about it in school, you know. Give the kid some credit. I know enough about it to know that this type of research can cause people to either become euphoric with hope or scared to death about the potential for evil. So this is what's going on at Cameron? Huh! No wonder they need so much security here. And no wonder they've had problems." Allen picked up another article from the scrapbook file.

"If Cameron BioTech is on the edge of engineering any of these techniques, just think of the changes we'd see in our world in the next decade, Swede.

101

And then," he added as an afterthought, "imagine the money this company could make with patents on all of it!"

Swede's features took on a slight scowl. His voice dropped to a whisper. "Kid, can you imagine the power Cameron BioTech would have if they had the control over this stuff? I remember reading an article the other day that said California passed something called Proposition 71. They want to get going on this kind of research, too. Competition must be fierce. Then the right-to-life groups started raising hell about something called embryonic stem cell research. That's just a part of it. The stem cell growth thing is major. Guess there's a lot of baggage tied into this."

Jane Reston slipped in beside Swede. "You're both right; there is a lot of *stuff* tied into this. Because of our research here at Cameron BioTech, we believe a future without fatal illnesses is not beyond anyone's hopes and dreams. We can come up with cures for cancer or even develop antibiotics to fight against new bacteria delivered by the weapons of mass destruction systems. Can you imagine what that would mean?"

She looked at Swede and then Allen and continued almost as a stern lecturer. "And yes, if we're successful with our current projects, the capability to produce millions of dollars in funding for even further research would be astronomical. Success here would mean a snowball effect for future research. The success of this research could make the company holding the keys the next closest thing to a world power." Jane eyed both of them seriously. "That's why we're so careful about our security."

"Yes, ma'am," Allen said respectfully. "So, I can also understand why the protest groups are so hot to trot, ma'am. Look at the last paragraph of this editorial." He looked down at the newspaper clipping again, reading aloud, "*On the other hand, if Cameron BioTech hired the wrong scientists and headed in another direction, they could also be looking for ways to control the world with threats of using antibiotic-resistant bacteria or a cloned superhuman with worst possible human traits. It might be possible to even create a soldier/killer clone. Things could get ugly if there's no real control placed on a corporation like Cameron.*" He paused and looked up. "Does the government have any say about what you're doing here?"

Jane didn't answer.

"Don't know." Swede smiled.

Swede shifted and laid the scrapbook on the desk, heaving a sigh. "But right now, that's not our problem. Right now, we've got to find out if Cameron really had a break-in, and if they did, we need to know what was taken. Cameron might be morally on the up and up, but if the wrong group got hold of some of this information, they could use it to create a monster just like you described."

"I agree government control is not your concern right now, Officer." Jane Reston was obviously irritated. "You just need to find out who or if anyone was in here. We'll take care of our business; you take care of yours."

It was obvious she didn't care for the direction their conversation had taken.

"Yes, ma'am. Right now, we've got to find out if they really had a break-in," Swede repeated. "And if they did, we need to know what was taken. Just the facts, ma'am." He nodded and grinned at his attempt to sound just like Detective Joe Friday.

Charlie walked in just in time to deflect any further retort from Jane Reston.

"I hope they get finished in there soon," Charlie said as he nodded toward the offices. He was pointedly ignoring Jane. "The longer it takes, the farther away a criminal can get with stolen research!"

Jane Reston turned and walked back to the filing cabinets.

Chapter 9

Quay stopped at the Getaway Lodge to check out and pick up his clothes and fishing gear. It was late Monday afternoon. Sam had checked into the lodge the night after they'd covered the crime scene and had a late dinner with Quay's brother, John.

Now Sam waited outside in her car. Her car was not quite the vehicle Thompson's was, she mused. She'd just pulled in next to Thompson's dark metallic gray pickup. He'd picked it up from the dealer before just leaving for the North Shore. With gray leather seats, all the bells and whistles, including four-wheel drive and an extended cab, the vehicle had elicited more excitement in Quay than she'd seen in a long time. It was big enough to pull his boat and get him into the backcountry during hunting season, he'd said. And he claimed it didn't cost him an arm and a leg for gas. That was important these days, he'd added.

Quay said his good-byes to his brother, John, outside the motel. John agreed to take Quay's boat to his place and store it until he could get back up north and pick it up. After a quick discussion about procedural details with the case, Quay threw his duffle bag of clothes, fishing rods, and tackle box in back and led the way south on Highway 61, with Sam following in her car.

They made good time caravanning into Duluth and then onto 35W to the Twin Cities. Just four hours later, they were at the BCA headquarters getting ready to dig into Sam's computer files on SPARTA. With his usual cup of coffee in hand and a fresh stick of bubblegum in his mouth, Quay leaned forward as Sam pulled up the information.

"I've accumulated a lot of material on SPARTA, but most of it is over a year old," she explained as they waited for the information to load. "I'll need to get online now to see what I can find out about their most recent activities. Maybe there's some activity in their chat room that will give us some information about the murdered girl on the North Shore. It might be something that we wouldn't have noticed before."

Quay watched as Sam logged into the chat room. The online room was active with at least seven different participants. Sam had established an identity with the online group. Her login name was Hotchick1. Quay laughed at that.

The group was in an active discussion today about the "acropolis" meeting that had been held recently. No one was giving the location, but it was clear their rhetoric was building. Identified as only CI, Cameron BioTech was at the center of the discussion.

"This might be interesting," Sam said as she settled into her chair. Right now she wanted to just follow the conversation rather than become an active participant. They read the chat together with Sam interpreting the chat room lingo. They read together silently.

—*Suzy Q*— How can our government let a company like this continue to operate? It's criminal!

—*ArmNHammer*— LOL. You don't really think the American government is clued in on what's going on there? IMHO The whole thing is a cover up.

Sam interpreted for Quay, "LOL is *laughing out loud*. IMHO means *in my humble opinion*."

—ArmNHammer— The company isn't going to let others know the whole picture. They don't want to have another company steal their work and make a breakthrough ahead of them. They'll only let out what they want others to think.

—SugarBaby— E is right. Gotta get in and stir it up. Gotta publish their real research, so public can know.

—Batman— FYI, we know that. BTW I was really impressed with E's speech at the acropolis. He hit on every point. He's right ya know. We need to get our army moving.

—ArmNHammer— We are going to make the world sit up and listen! GMTA! most people don't really get what an Einstein he is!

Quay interrupted Sam's reading. "What's GMTA?"

"It's *great minds think alike.*" She continued reading, with Quay looking over her shoulder.

—SugarBaby— Me2. Too bad Smartypants wasn't there at the keynote. Where was she? Anybody heard from her?

—ArmNHammer— IDK. Got a good hacker in the room? EG—I have some ideas I'd like to try out.

Sam explained that EG was *evil grin.*

—Spideyman— WebWire is rounding up some material. He'll be in later.

—ArmNHammer— Are we meeting with E again this month? I haven't heard anything from Smartypants since before the big arena meeting at the acropolis.

107

Where is she? We need her to pull her weight in order for this to come together.

—*SugarBaby*— IDK. Last she told me she was meeting with E and then taking some time to put it all together. E told me we were going to meet in our place on 10/10. That will be the planning night for our big event. Smartypants will be there with all the background stuff. GR. CYA. BB

—*Batman*— M2. CYA soon.

Sam clicked out of the website.

"Well," Quay observed, "it looks like they're getting ready for something, whatever the big event is. We'll need to keep an eye on them. Did you catch the comment about 'Smartypants' not being there?

"Sure did! I wonder if that's our girl. From what I've gathered in their chat room in the past, this group's always got plans for Cameron BioTech."

"That could be a problem, right?"

"That's a definite concern for the local BCA and the FBI as well. They've been under observation for quite a while."

"Yeah I remember them." Quay's voice dropped, and he turned away toward the door.

"The FBI said the leader of SPARTA," continued Sam, ignoring Quay's reaction, "is a high school science teacher, who appears quite innocuous on the surface, but the general tone of the chat room information and other info on the net is that they're about as radical as you can get. They aren't afraid of a fight, and they're talking about weapons. We really need to get someone inside there, but they're hard to break into—very closed, guarded, and naturally suspicious of anyone who might not be in league with them."

Quay had turned around and was staring at the blank screen.

"But what really amazes me," he said, "is that they're willing to 'chat' online like this, when a more private conversation could be held through something like texting or Facebook inbox messaging. Why are they so open about this?"

"The chat room provides them the opportunity to lure in others, where texting doesn't. Did you notice that they didn't make any comment about my being there?"

"Yeah, why?"

"Their roles sound glamorous enough and important enough to make other bored teens and college kids want to get in on the action. A conversation using texting or inbox messages would be more secretive, and they probably do use that for some more private conversations, but here it's an open invitation for others to join. They want to increase their numbers."

"In that case, isn't there someone we have who would be a willing participant? We must have someone who we could get to infiltrate and fit their profile."

"We're working on it, Quay."

"Let's see if we can join their next chat and then push for a meeting. We might be able to arrange it. We need their identities. The group evolves constantly. That's got to be the way in the door there." He blew a huge bubble and popped it. He was anxious to make things happen.

Sam looked at him and grinned, then turned serious. Her voice lowered.

"You know we thought about doing that two years ago after the sniper killed Karen, but the chief nixed it.

109

He thought it would be a waste of time, because he didn't think there was enough to indicate their involvement." She paused. "I think we've got enough this time to take another look at the group. I'll talk to Boogie, our resident computer jock, in the morning. Elson just might fit the description of our perp! We need to talk to him. Should I talk to the boss too, or do you want to do it?"

"This is one of those times I think you should talk to him." Quay was running his hand through his hair. Then he fished in his pocket to produce a new piece of bubblegum. "He'll just think I'm trying to dig up more unrelated stuff on Karen's murder. If it comes from you, it'll sound more like a serious investigation into this little girl's murder."

"Okay. Why don't you call John and see if he's come up with an ID on the girl yet. That will give us another lead. I'll talk to the boss."

"Okay, I'll get on it. Then why don't you call it a day?"

Sam hesitated and then agreed. "Fine, I'll see you right away in the morning. Then we can begin fresh. You get some sleep too, Quay. You're going to need to be clearheaded tomorrow."

"Yeah, I will," mumbled Quay as he headed out the door and turned toward his cubicle. A slight feeling of satisfaction was creeping in. This one could be the solid lead he'd always been hoping for. Karen's murderer could be tied to this little girl. He could finally solve it, if they'd let him stay on this one.

Hope springs eternal, he thought grimly. *Funny, they say men "replace" when they lose a spouse*, he mused. He blew a huge bubble, sucked it in, and popped it. Unfortunately, he hadn't even considered it. As far as he was concerned, there was no replacement for Karen. Not yet. He had to find her killer first, and then maybe she could finally be put to rest. Then and only then would he be able to find peace.

Chapter 10

Ernie Elson's brief respite from fear of discovery ended late Tuesday afternoon after school when he pulled into his driveway in his northern suburb and found a dark gray pickup parked in his driveway. A man and a woman got out and approached him as he got out of his truck.

"Hello. We're looking for Ernie Elson. Would you be Ernie?" The man was smiling, looked friendly enough. He was taller than Ernie, wearing a light tan Columbia jacket over a blue denim shirt with button-down collar. His shirt was open at the neck. *Another one of those yuppies*, Ernie thought as he eyed the navy Dockers pants.

"Yeah, I'm Ernie," he answered. "Who are you?" He realized he sounded gruff, but he really was tired and didn't need to be bothered with these types. They were probably delivering a *Watchtower* magazine or something of that sort.

"I'm Detective Quay Thompson, and this is Sam Atwood," Quay said, indicating the woman standing next to him. The woman looked to be in her early thirties. She pulled the collar up on her olive green jacket, which bore an LL Bean logo, and extended her hand to Ernie. Ernie could see a tan turtleneck underneath her jacket. Her matching slacks were cuffed over brown boots.

She's a yuppie, too, Ernie thought as he finished giving her the once over. He noticed she wasn't wearing any jewelry except small gold hoops in her ears. No rings, either. Her auburn hair was pulled loosely back and held at the sides with a comb of some sort. Pretty good looker, Ernie thought. He began to get more interested.

"We're with the BCA."

Ernie's interest died as suddenly as it had risen. He thought he could feel himself pale. His skin suddenly felt tight.

"We're here for some information about a group called SPARTA, and it's our understanding that you're the head of that group. Could we step inside? We won't take much of your time."

Ernie felt like he'd been doused with ice water. "Well, my wife doesn't handle strangers too well," he answered quickly, motioning to the house. "She's not well, and she gets pretty nervous with people around. If it's not going to take too long, could we just talk here?" He shuffled from one leg to the other.

"Okay, sure," Quay answered, glancing at Sam.

"Early Monday morning," Quay began, "a body was discovered on the North Shore of Lake Superior. She was a young African American girl. Her body was found just north of Lutsen down near the shoreline of one of the properties there. It appears that she'd been placed there after she died."

Ernie shifted uneasily.

"I don't understand what I could possibly do to help you with that," Ernie said.

"There's a possibility she was murdered. The part that you might be able to help us with, Mr. Elson, was her SPARTA connection. She had a necklace in her hand with the SPARTA logo etched on the back of a gold medusa medallion. We haven't been able to identify her as yet. We think she may be a member of the SPARTA group that you lead. We were wondering if you could help us out. Would you mind looking at a photo of the body?"

"SPARTA, huh. You guys are always trying to find something on us. Okay. No problem." Ernie gave a small sigh of relief. This wouldn't be any problem. He could handle them. It appeared they didn't know anything. They were just looking for her identity.

"We aren't an illegal group. We aren't like that, you know. I'd be glad to help you out if I can," he said and smiled confidently. "But you know our members are spread all over the country and even in international parts of the world, so I doubt if I'd really be able to ID one member. It's a growing organization, you know. We are a grass roots group whose goal is to try to stop the big conglomerates from misguided genome research. Our country is headed in a dangerous direction."

"Yes, Mr. Elson," interrupted Sam, "but we really need to know who this girl is. Any help you could give would be appreciated."

"Sure, I'll do what I can. Let's see the picture."

Ernie's hands trembled slightly as he took the picture Quay held out. He stared at the lifeless face of Annie Bell. *Too bad*, he thought again. He shook his head.

"Yes, unfortunately, I know this girl. Her name is Annie Bell." Attempting to show surprise and concern, he stared at Annie's picture briefly.

"She used to be one of my students." He was twisting the photo around in his hands. "A superior student, too!" He smiled to himself. "What happened? She was at a SPARTA conference with us this weekend up north." He offered the information, assuming they must have done their homework and knew about the convention. He continued, "But I heard she left early. I didn't see her after the last session. I do know she was worried about her brother," he added. "She has a brother with health problems, you know. Her family devotes a lot

114

of time to him. She talked a lot about him this weekend. I guess I just thought she left early because of a family problem back home."

Ernie thought it was always better to tell part of the truth. They would find out that much anyway. He could give them Annie's name and a little about her family but let them scout out the rest.

He was surprised that Annie had been discovered this quickly. The necklace was a stroke of bad luck. Now he'd have to do some quick covering. He'd also have to notify his boss. That wouldn't be a good thing.

He hadn't gotten around to telling the boss about Annie's death yet. The discovery of her body so soon could really be a problem. Damn, this wasn't going to go as smoothly as he'd hoped. But he thought maybe he could still control the situation. He had covered his tracks. There wasn't anything to lead the police to think he had killed her.

"Do you know where Annie lives, Mr. Elson?" Quay asked. "We'd like to visit with her family."

"Yeah, I'll see if I can get her address for you. Boy, this is some shock! Annie was such a great kid. Who would do this?" Ernie decided to build his act up a little more. "What do you suppose happened to her after she left the conference?" He looked boldly at Quay.

"Well, Mr. Elson, that's what we are trying to find out. Did you see her leave the conference?"

"Not personally, no. I just mean we ended about seven Sunday night. I didn't see Annie after the last group meeting ... in fact, now that I think about it, I'm not even sure she was at that meeting."

"Did this girl hang out with any one in particular?" asked Sam.

115

"Not that I ever noticed. Everyone sort of hangs together. There's always lots of conversation and discussion about group strategies. She's in on most of that."

"What exactly is the focus of the group, Mr. Elson?" Sam asked.

"Well, as I said, SPARTA is a group you probably already know about. I founded SPARTA. As a person with a science background, I've had many concerns about the direction genome research is taking." He had an open door, and he was going to use it.

"Our goal is to stay informed about research accomplished by various companies. When we see a possible misuse of information or a misdirection with the discoveries made, we make it a point to publicize what the company is doing. If we can redirect or in some way slow down misguided research that could harm our country, we begin active protests. It's always quite legal." He took a breath. Quay interrupted.

"How far do your active protests go? Have they ever gotten violent?"

"Oh no. Definitely not! That would be going against our own beliefs. We are definitely pacifists— against violence, I mean. We use nonviolent demonstrations to make our statements. Gandhi couldn't be more proud of how we operate!" He chuckled.

Ernie was still holding the picture of Annie's body lying on the rocks by the Superior shore. He repeatedly rotated it in his hands as he talked. He shifted from foot to foot while occasionally glancing at the picture. It was difficult to look at her, but he seemed to be drawn to her picture. It made him nervous. He swallowed his chuckle, calmed his nerves, and looked up at Quay with steady eyes.

"How old was Annie?" Quay asked.

"She couldn't have been more than eighteen or nineteen. I usually only see her—saw her—at the SPARTA meetings now. I had her in class in high school when she was a junior. She was a brilliant science student!" Ernie pushed a wayward strand of graying hair behind one of his ears. His fingers were trembling.

"I'm sure," answered Quay. "Would it be all right if we checked back with you again after we visit with her family?"

"Yeah, I'll be here, but call first so we don't upset my wife, okay?"

"And perhaps you could also provide us with more information about the other members of SPARTA?"

"Well, I'm not sure about that. Privacy information act and all that, you know. I can't just give out information about members without their permission. Besides, I don't know why that would be necessary."

"It may be necessary if we begin to believe that one of your SPARTA members had a hand in her murder," answered Sam.

"Oh, I would never believe that! No way could that happen!" Ernie spluttered. "As I said, we are dedicated to only peaceful demonstrations. It is totally against our position to be involved in anything violent. No. No way!"

"Well, we'll have to see. In the meantime, can you get Annie's address for us now? We really need to talk to her family, and you could help speed things along."

"Sure, I've got SPARTA membership papers in my truck. I'll get it for you."

Ernie walked over to his vehicle, leaned in, and pretended to rifle through a stack of papers in the front seat. He knew Annie's parents' address and phone number by heart. He had talked to her often enough when she still lived at home. Grabbing a pen from the dash, he scribbled on a piece of scrap paper and walked back to Sam and Quay.

"Here you go," he said, handing the slip of paper to Quay.

"Thanks." Quay took the paper, folded it, and stuck it in his pocket. He looked at Elson and gave him a quick smile.

"We'll be in touch with you again later tomorrow if that's all right. That should give you enough time to talk with your SPARTA members and get permission for us to interview them. Thanks again for you help, Mr. Elson. I'd like to leave my and Sam's card with you in case you think of something else. Please give either one of us a call!" Quay handed their cards to Elson.

They shook hands with Elson and walked back to Quay's truck. Elson watched them as they backed out.

"Well, that was certainly interesting," said Sam, once they were in the car. "That guy is some sort of wacko. I haven't seen hair that long and stringy since the seventies. I can't believe he's a teacher. Who'd want their kid in his class?"

"Yeah," Quay answered as he reached into his pocket for his bubblegum. "Did you notice how edgy he was? He kept turning the picture in his hands and fiddling with it. He didn't even have to take a good look

118

at her. He wasn't surprised she was dead. I'm guessing he knows a lot more. We'll give him a little time to think about things, and then we'll pay him another visit to shake him up a little more. He'll slip up eventually, and we'll get more out of him." He blew a huge bubble and popped it with a grin. He was feeling good about this.

"Sounds like a plan." Sam chuckled.

As Quay drove down the county road, he processed his instincts about Ernie Elson. He guessed there was a reason that Elson lived out in the middle of nowhere. Only in Minnesota could you find isolated places of wilderness like this so close to the city. Elson was tucked away in his own little hideaway. Quay definitely wanted to get more background on Ernie Elson.

"Let's go back over what we already know first," Quay suggested. "I know the department checked into SPARTA a couple years ago, but I've got a feeling the department has more buried there. Before we head back to the office, let's look up that address Elson gave us for Annie Bell and meet with her family. We can at least give them the news. They can ID the body when John releases it. Let's call John and tell him we think we've got an ID."

Chapter 11

Ernie watched the pickup back out of his driveway before he turned and slowly walked up to the door of his home. As he opened the screen door, his wife jerked open the interior door, facing him with a scowl.

"Who was that?" Martha asked anxiously. "What did they want? I saw them out there with you. Why were they talking to you? Are you in trouble, Ernie? Were they asking about me?" Her voice rose in pitch with each question until she was nearly screeching and out of breath.

"Relax! Relax, Martha," Ernie tried to reassure and calm her. "It's okay. It wasn't about you. They were just asking some questions about a former student of mine. It doesn't affect you or me. Just forget about it."

"What former student? Is that girl in trouble? Did that girl who was always hanging around here get you in trouble? You're always off messing around with that SPARTA stuff. She dragged you into something, didn't she? It was about that girl, wasn't it? Who were they? Tell me!"

"Relax!" Ernie's voice rose as he began to lose patience. The last thing he needed right now was to deal with Martha. He had to calm her down. "It's not a problem. I can handle it."

"Well are you going to tell me who they were, Ernie?"

"His name was Thompson." Ernie sighed with resignation. She'd never quit. "He's with the detective division or something like that with the BCA. He's trying to get some information on Annie Bell."

"Annie ... Annie ..." She rolled the name over, thinking aloud. "Annie!

Annie Bell! She's the one. Ernie, what have you done?"

"Nothing, I told you!" he snapped. He took a deep breath and tried to calm himself as he continued. "It's just coincidental that I knew her," he said in a soothing voice. "Her death has nothing to do with me."

"Death? Death! What on earth? Ernie! You'd better not be involved in this. Death? Oh my God." Her voice was rising again to a high-pitched screech. She began pacing, wringing her hands as she walked. "Now you've done it! I always knew you'd gone off the deep end. You're in over your head. Now what will I do? Who will take care of me now? Oh, Ernie." She began to sob. Martha was building up to a full-fledged meltdown. He had to slow her down and do it quickly.

"Would you relax, Martha? I told you it has nothing to do with me. She's just a girl I knew, a student I had in class. Nothing more. She also knew a lot more people than just me. Who knows what happened to her? It wasn't anything to do with me. You've got to believe me, Martha. Now go take your afternoon meds, and you'll feel better."

"Ernie, don't talk like that to me. I know you, Ernie. I know you! This is just the start of more trouble!" She turned away abruptly and walked to the cupboard above the stove. Opening the door, she selected two medicine bottles from her collection stored there and emptied her required pills into her shaking hands.

Ernie took advantage of the respite in his wife's harangue to exit the kitchen and scurry upstairs to his den. He closed the door and pushed the lock on the doorknob. He'd had enough confrontations with her to know how this would end. She'd take her pills, scream up the stairs at him for a few minutes longer, and then go to her room. He wouldn't see her again until morning. She'd be all right. He just couldn't deal with her now, too.

He didn't want to be disturbed. He had important work to do. He had to compose his message to his boss. He decided he'd write it out first so that he'd have the perfect wording in the message. There couldn't be any room for error. This was literally a matter of life and death. It could mean his death if he didn't handle it right. Martha was right. He was in over his head.

His boss, The Manager, as Ernie called him, would want to know the particulars about Annie. But Ernie knew he could take care of it. This wasn't going to be a problem. Ernie was sure of that. He just had to make sure The Manager believed that, too.

Ernie waited until eight that night before he quietly slipped out the back door. His truck was still parked near the end of the driveway. He walked quietly down to the truck, hoping that Martha wouldn't wake and hear it when he started up the engine. He was fairly sure she had taken her meds and gone to bed. Or at the very least, she was in bed watching the television. That was her usual evening routine anyway. She'd left him alone after her outburst. That was a relief.

The two of them barely spoke to each other anymore. His role as a husband was simply that of a caretaker. He was there to be sure she took her meds for her paranoia. She couldn't work anymore. She claimed she was agoraphobic. It was true she was afraid to leave the house. She also panicked anytime she had to be around people. That was okay by him. She was less trouble if she stayed in the house. He never knew when she'd go off on someone.

He climbed in his truck, clicked the door shut, started the pickup, and backed out of the drive slowly. He headed toward the Blaine City Library. They were open until nine. He knew he had time to get there and e-mail his message to The Manager. He'd have to wait until tomorrow to get the reply.

Ernie always sent his messages to the e-mail address of Manager@hotmail.com. The guy was good. He wouldn't be easily found. Ernie decided to just go with it. Take the money and run, so to speak.

He'd received his first contact a year ago through the SPARTA web page. After that, they'd set up this e-mail system of communicating, but he'd still never met his mysterious Manager. After mailing a message using the public library Internet, Ernie wouldn't usually receive a response for at least twenty-four hours. Often the return message would come to his yahoo e-mail address from The Manager account at Hotmail. The information and directions he got from The Manager never gave away any hints about his identity. The messages just told him when to pick up the next set of directions. To get the complete set of directions, he had to go to a drop location in the parking lot of a nearby strip mall. A large manila envelope would be taped to the back of a dumpster behind the building.

Ernie's instructions were never handwritten; nor were they ever sent online. They were always printed out using a computer printer. They were never signed. After the assignment was complete, his money was delivered using the same methods. The e-mail accounts were both under false identities. Nothing could be traced. Everything was done with absolute anonymity. No clues to any identity were ever established. That was the way The Manager wanted it.

Ernie had expressed an interest in this guy's name, but The Manager had made it clear he was better off not knowing. Ernie was smart enough to know that if any of this went down, he was standing alone. He'd decided he was going to do some research after today. This was becoming too big an operation, and now it was also too dangerous.

He'd send his standard e-mail. This time when The Manager's reply came back, he was going to try to track it back. There must be a way to do it. He'd ask Mike, the tech guy at school, if he knew about tracking e-mail identities. He could tell Mike he'd been getting some harassment e-mail that appeared to be coming from a student. He'd explain that he wanted to track down the culprit.

His e-mail to the Manager was simple and to the point.

> *We've had some trouble. A group member found some Cameron info at meeting site and threatened to expose us. Had to make decision quickly. Had to remove her. I took care of details, but the police are nosing around the group. Police found group logo on necklace she'd hidden on her. Came to me with questions about former student and our group. Nothing more to indicate any suspicion here. Confident there will be no further connections made. No other data to tie her to me or group. Shouldn't be any other problems. Thought you should*

124

know. Watch the press for further info. We can play it up as a company attack on a protestor. You decide and direct how to proceed from here. Will pick up response tomorrow no earlier than 1100 hours. — EE—

Ernie sent the message and left the library. He drove back to his house feeling even more confident. All would work out just fine. At nine thirty, he crept quietly into the house and up the stairs to his secure room, carefully locking the door behind him. He would spend a long, restless night wondering what The Manager was going to do. This would all work out, he assured himself, but the escape he'd been planning for himself may have to happen sooner than he'd expected.

Chapter 12

After meeting Ernie, Quay and Sam drove to St. Paul to make a quick stop at the BCA Headquarters. Quay was going to make a call to John while Sam tracked down the office tech guy, Boogie, to see if he'd come up with any news.

Boogie was an expert with computer forensics. He could trace almost anything. His computer talents had helped the BCA solve several crimes that involved use of computers. All sorts of crimes were committed daily through the use of the Internet, and one of Boogie's jobs was to ferret out Internet criminals. He was good at tracing white-collar crimes as well as the hard-core crimes like sex crimes, porn, and fraud.

On the way in, Quay and Sam had discussed the possibility that Ernie Elson may have used e-mail as a method of contacting his SPARTA members and anyone else connected to the group. If they could track his e-mails and conversations with the members of the group, it just might lead them to information or even a solution to Annie's murder. That's where Boogie came in.

Boogie's office was a window cubicle tucked away in a corner of second floor of the BCA headquarters. He was in charge of a small cadre of techie jocks. His support team worked from a maze of cubicles arranged outside his office. Together they formed a nearly invincible data recovery group, with Boogie as the company's uber cyber king. A window office was wasted on Boogie. He pulled his blinds to reduce the glare on several computer monitors. Books and papers were strewn all over the office on every available surface. Boogie's filing system consisted of papers stacked in corners, on the bookcase, and on the only chair in his cubicle besides the one at his desk. According to Boogie, it was ordered chaos. He claimed he always knew where everything was.

Boogie was a lanky, six foot two, forty-three-year-old who lived for his cyber world. His humor was quirky and quick. So was his mind. He came to work in baggy jeans. His standard uniform was usually completed with a T-shirt bearing something like an Apple logo with "Bad to the Core" stamped across the front. Boogie didn't care to look like anyone connected to the BCA. He was also not into the latest fashion trend; he wore jeans with holes as he crawled around behind his desk to change hookups on his computers or as he sat on his knees searching through his books and papers for more information.

Like most techie geeks, he was a confirmed PC lover. But Macs worked, too. It depended on what his needs were. His long, dark hair was tied back into a ponytail and was starting to gray around the temples. Although his hair was turning silver, his outlook on life remained golden. He was a teen at heart.

Boogie had a system, and it really pissed him off whenever someone suggested he clean up his office. So Sam made it a point to swing by every so often just to give him a little advice on organization. Boogie knew Sam well enough to put up with her needling, and he enjoyed bantering with her.

Today, as usual, Boogie was buried behind one of the three computers lined up on his desktop. He used two desktop computers with side-by-side screens and a laptop. It looked like he had pulled up information on all three computers, and he appeared to be working on each of them simultaneously.

"Hey, Boogie," said Sam as she peeked around the door of Boogie's office, "got time to talk?"

"Oh, sure, I've always got time for a sexy lady like you, Sam." He barely looked up at her. He was reading a page on his screen. "You'd never believe some of the stuff I've been coming across today. Did you know there's a group of teens online who are now in a competition to see who can make someone else pass out the most times using the Vulcan Hold used by Dr. Spock on *Star Trek*? These kids have just discovered that they can do a pinch on the nerve on the neck until you pass out. Remember that old party game?"

"Good grief. I guess we should thank Leonard Nimoy for that one, huh?"

"No ... more like Rod Serling. These kids are in a *Twilight Zone*, and I know, don't say it—that dates me!" He chuckled. "So anyway, what brings you to my corner of the world so soon?"

"Well, I was just wondering if you were going to clean up this mess anytime soon."

"Aw give me a break, Sam. I'll clean it up when Apple merges with Gates's empire."

"Well, the least you could do is give your window office to some other soul who would really appreciate it. Someone like me, perhaps?"

"Like you'd need it. You never work anyway. You're always out running around having fun on company time."

"Touché." Sam laughed.

"So what's really on your mind?"

"Boogie, remember that group called SPARTA that we followed for a while?" She took a stack off the chair in front of his desk, carefully placed them on the

128

floor, and sat down, leaning forward with her elbows on Boogie's desk.

"Sure, that group was the one we checked into when Quay's wife was done in by that sniper. And it's the one we could never nab." He turned on his swivel chair to face her.

"Yeah, that's right. Well, they're rearing their ugly heads. Quay and I just began working a homicide that we think might have connections to that group. A girl's body was found up on the North Shore just past Lutsen on Monday. Quay's brother, John, asked Quay to take a look at the scene, and Quay called me to join him when they discovered a SPARTA necklace in the girl's hand. We've traced her back here to the cities, and we think we may have an identity on her.

"We talked to a guy named Ernie Elson, who is the head of SPARTA. He lives just north of the cities. He identified the girl when we showed him her picture. He got pretty agitated. He denies any knowledge of what happened to her, but the SPARTA group was meeting up near Lutsen this last weekend." She was spilling out the information to Boogie in a race of words. Boogie was nodding.

"I just followed some conversation in the SPARTA chat room, but I need more. Quay and I would like you to dig into the people in that chat room and see if you can find out more about them—names, backgrounds, etc.—anything you can find out. Also, we'd like to know more about their leader, Ernie Elson. Can you come up with an e-mail address for him, or a website, and check out anything you can find about him on the Internet? We think we may have something to nail this SPARTA group with this time."

Boogie nodded and then asked, "Got an okay from the chief?"

"I'm heading in his direction right now. You just get started, and I'll have the okay for you before you get into that chat room!" Sam started walking out the door.

"Hey, Sam?" called Boogie. "If I do an extra good job, will you take me on in a game of Guardian?"

Guardian was a computer game that Boogie had developed in his spare time. He claimed he was a certified gamer extraordinaire. His career at BCA was just a byproduct of the genius he used in his "hobby" of writing game programs. Boogie often made jokes about being a geek, but he was hardly a geek, thought Sam. His intelligence was off the boards.

"Sure, Boogie. I'd enjoy whomping your butt. Just let me know when you've got the time."

Boogie grinned, flipping a Vulcan V, and calling, "Live long and prosper," as she walked away.

While Sam was following up with Boogie, Quay was placing another call to his brother, John.

"Hey, John. I'm just checking in. Sam and I have been doing some follow-up on your Jane Doe up there. I think we've got a lead."

"Well, that's good news. We just got the autopsy results. It's a definite homicide. Somebody just wrapped his hands around her neck and snapped it. I say 'his hands' because it had to be a man, considering the strength needed to accomplish a death like that. There weren't any other marks on her body. She didn't appear to have even put up a struggle. Nothing under the fingernails, no other scratches or bruises. It was just quick and efficient. Almost looks like he had experience or training on exactly how to do it. There was nothing more at the site where the body was dumped. If there were tire tracks, they'd have been covered with all the traffic. We're looking for any abandoned vehicles in the area. We're also checking with the local inns and resorts. Someone may have seen her. What have you got on her?"

"We believe her name is Annie Bell. That SPARTA necklace was a big help. We interviewed the leader of the SPARTA group. He lives down here. Guy's name is Ernie Elson. He ID'd the picture we showed him of the girl's body. He even admitted she had been up there at SPARTA conference last weekend. The group met at the Flying Eagle Lodge in Castle Danger. You might want to check that one out. Claims he doesn't know anything about what happened to her though. Says she left the conference early. Sam and I are going to visit with her parents in the morning. I just wanted to check with you first. Can we send the girl's parents up there tomorrow to ID the body? Once her identity is confirmed, we can get moving on this."

"Sure, send them up. The body is ready," answered John. "Do you think your guy is the man?"

"Hard to say at this point. He's quirky. We're digging a little more into the SPARTA group. Once we get the ID, we can interview the SPARTA members. I'll talk to you more about it tomorrow when we come up."

"Okay. I'll go check on the conference at the lodge at Castle Danger. We'll talk later. Good luck."

Quay hung up and thought about Annie Bell's parents. He wondered if they had any idea that Annie was even missing. She hadn't been living at home, according to the records he'd just dug up on her. Her current address was a townhome near the U of M. He didn't know if she had roommates. He hoped he'd find out more from Annie's parents. This was one time that he was really glad he had Sam for a partner. It was going to be a difficult call. Sam would know how to handle something like this better than he would.

Chapter 13

Quay and Sam made their visit to Annie Bell's parents early the next morning. Quay called the parents first to ask if they could stop by. Quay had prepared the Bells, stating the reason for their visit was the possible disappearance of their daughter. They were greeted at the door by a red-eyed Mrs. Bell. Mr. Bell, a small, graying African American man dressed in jeans and a sweatshirt, appeared next to his wife at the door and placed his arm around her shoulder. He led her back to the living room while inviting Quay and Sam to follow.

"This is just a formality, Mr. and Mrs. Bell. Annie has been found. We believe Annie was murdered late Sunday night."

Mrs. Bell crumpled into her husband's arms, sobbing softly.

"She was identified by using a picture. A former teacher was able to identify her for us," Quay continued. "We couldn't be sorrier to bring this news. We're going to be looking for answers for you."

"Was that teacher who identified our daughter a man by the name of Elson?" asked Annie's father. His voice cracked as he obviously tried to contain an edge of anger.

"Yes, it was. Do you know Mr. Elson?" Sam looked at Mr. Bell and glanced at Quay.

"Hell, yes!" he exploded. "He was a major source of trouble in our household. We had so many nights of arguing with Annie about her visits to his home and the amount of time she spent with that man. It just didn't seem right."

"And on top of that," inserted Mrs. Bell, drying her eyes, "he was always filling her head full of ideas about how research science was being twisted by the government." She began sobbing again.

"I'll just bet he knew where she was this weekend, didn't he?" stormed Mr. Bell.

"Well," Quay stalled, "we'll be sure to look into that. We really appreciate any help you can give us. We're going to find Annie's murderer, you can be sure of that."

Sam and Quay spent several more minutes with the Bells as they shared everything they could about Annie's current living situation and her patterns of activity. They shared about Annie's invalid brother and her studies at college. It seemed to calm them to talk about Annie and their family. As Sam and Quay prepared to leave, they assured the Bells again that they would keep them informed of anything they discovered.

They walked back to Quay's truck in silence. It had been an emotionally draining visit.

Sam put away her notebook. "I guess we'll be paying Ernie Elson another visit?"

Things definitely looked bad for Ernie Elson. Quay pulled his cell phone from his pocket and hit the speed dial for his brother. He told John about their meeting with the Bells. It was clear to both Sam and Quay that Annie's parents had no idea she'd been involved as deeply as she was with SPARTA.

"According to her parents, Annie Bell was a top student, a good girl, a wonderful daughter. They gave us a lot of information about Annie and her studies at the college.

"However, it was fairly obvious as we talked with them that they had had very little time for their daughter," Quay continued. "She caused no trouble, and they were busy caring for her paraplegic brother."

Sam could barely hear John's deep voice on the other end of the line.

"No, I don't think so." Quay looked at Sam for approval and answered John, saying, "Their guilt is pretty understandable." Sam nodded.

"Anyway, we provided them with directions and your phone number in Lutsen. They're going to make the trip later this morning. I think they were leaving right after we left. I don't think there's any doubt that the body found on Lake Superior's shore was that of their little girl, Annie. We're going to be heading up your way, too, a little later." He paused and listened, then looked at Sam, who nodded. "Yeah, we'll see you there."

Quay said good-bye and hung up. Turning to Sam, he said, "Now it's time to begin digging. Let's see what we can find."

When Ernie turned on his classroom computer Wednesday morning, he was surprised to find a response to his e-mail in the Yahoo account waiting for him. He hadn't expected The Manager to respond this quickly. Then as he read the message, his stomach began to clench into a knot. The message had no greeting.

> *This was not part of the agreement. You were to keep a low profile with your group until I told you otherwise. We need to meet today. Our contract is finished. The final installment will be paid. There will be no further contact. Be at the drop sight at 8:30 p.m. Don't be late.*

Ernie didn't like the idea of this required meeting with The Manager. If The Manager wanted to actually meet with him to make the final payment, that meant he was willing to reveal his identity. That could only mean one thing—the Manager wasn't worried about Ernie's being able to identify him. Ernie was not going to be paid; he was going to be killed. It was time to move. Now.

He left his room and walked quickly down to the main office. As he entered, he did his best to look suitably sad and at the same time upset.

"Ellen," he addressed the head secretary in a low voice, "I'm glad you're here right now. Do you have a minute? I know this is a busy time for you in the morning before school, but I have an emergency. Can I talk to you in private?"

"Of course, Ernie." Ellen trusted Ernie. She was truly concerned.

"Come in and close the door," she said.

"Ellen, I've told you in confidence about Martha and her problems. I know I can talk to you and it won't get around. Sometimes, I just have to unload on someone." Ellen nodded sympathetically.

"Well, it's gotten to the point where I just can't leave her alone. I'm afraid she'll do something to herself. Last night she had a really bad spell. I thought we could work through it, but this morning she was even worse. She was screaming and hallucinating. I had to lock her in her room so I could leave her safely for a little while. I hated to leave, but I had to get my lesson plans in order. I'd like to call a sub and go home to take care of her. Can you cover for me?"

"Oh, Ernie, I'm so sorry," Ellen said. "You've had such a rough time. I'll call the sub for you. Do you have a special sub you want?"

"No, just someone that you know we can rely on. I think I'm going to have to be gone for several days to get this taken care of. I think I'm going to have to commit her, Ellen." Ernie hung his head and let his eyes begin to fill with tears.

"I'll take care of it, Ernie. I'll just tell our principal that you have some personal problems to take care of. He'll support you, don't you worry. You just get things settled and come back as soon as you feel you're able."

"Thank you. That means a lot to me, Ellen." Ernie gave her a quick hug and shuffled out the door, wiping his eyes as he left.

"Just take care of yourself, Ernie," Ellen called after him.

As soon as Ernie left the office, he hurried to his room. He passed several other teachers without acknowledging them. He kept his head down and tried to look appropriately absorbed.

He left brief notes for a sub, gathered up as much of his personal material as he could carry without looking too conspicuous, grabbed his jacket, and pushed through the groups of students who were just entering the front doors of the building.

His pickup was in the middle row of the parking lot. He'd have to go back to his house to pick up his laptop and some other bank papers he had hidden away. Maybe he could sneak in before Martha was awake. It was only seven fifteen. If he could be out of the house by eight and on the road, he could head onto 35W and on toward Canada. He could conceivably be out of the

137

country by nightfall. That was all he needed to do. Get out of the country.

Ernie's haste prevented him from noticing the gray sedan that crawled out of the parking lot behind him. He drove north toward his rural home. The last four miles were gravel road. As he turned onto the county road, the gray sedan began to close in behind him.

Ernie was driving on autopilot, lost in his plans for his new life in Canada. It wasn't until he'd driven a mile down the gravel road that he noticed the sedan edging up behind him. His alarm grew when he realized it was closing in on him too fast. He slowed slightly, hoping that the car would just pass him. Clouds of dust and gravel spun up behind the sedan. That guy was really crowding him.

A chain-link fence paralleled the gravel road. Boulders, cement culverts, and mounds of sand and gravel lined at least an acre of fence. Several yellow, full-size road graders were parked beyond the building materials behind the fence. This was a storage facility for the county road crews.

Suddenly the sedan swerved out and pulled alongside. Ernie looked over at the speeding vehicle as it sped up to pass him. The driver was wearing a hood. Ernie's skin tightened. This was no ordinary driver in a hurry to pass. Ernie's heart raced. He was in trouble.

He wasn't sure what to do. If he'd been one of his students, he would have thought the guy wanted to drag race. The car maintained the same speed as Ernie, running parallel with him while crowding closer.

Finally it dawned on him that the sedan was going to run him off the road. He knew if he hit the ditch at this speed, he'd fly through that chain-link fence and into the cement culverts and gravel piles there.

At that moment, Ernie Elson was sure he going to die. He had nowhere to go. In panic, he stomped on the gas pedal to accelerate and pull ahead.

The sedan kept pace. Suddenly, his right front wheel caught in the loose gravel on the shoulder. In his panic, Ernie overreacted and pulled the steering wheel into a hard left. Gravel peppered the sides and undercarriage of his truck. Dust covered the windshield. The back end of the pickup began to fishtail toward the ditch. Ernie tried to compensate by flipping the wheel back to the right and hitting the brakes at the same time. He was desperate to get the pickup back on the road.

Terror took over. His foot slid off the brake pedal accidentally and pounded onto the accelerator.

Everything was out of control. His truck became a metal projectile. Dust gathered in great brown clouds as gravel continued to ping the sides of the pickup. His wheels spun, unable find traction in the soft soil of the ditch. Finally the pickup righted and flew forward directly into the ditch. Ernie's head hit the ceiling as he bounced over a culvert and took off airborne at fifty miles an hour. He was aimed directly toward the chain-link fence.

Strands of Ernie's long, graying hair flew wildly into his grimacing face and terror-filled eyes. He gripped the steering wheel in a white-knuckle grasp and instinctively stiffened his arms to brace against the coming impact. Both feet pressed against the brake pedal now, pushing it all the way to the floor. The motor roared in his ears as the front bumper began its impact with the fence. The boulders and culverts loomed ahead of him. Ernie screamed, but his voice couldn't be heard over the screeching metallic grind of the car against the wall of chain-link fencing. The piercing whine of the motor and Ernie's shriek coupled in a frenzied symphony as the pickup sliced through chain link. A sudden thunderous clap joined the symphony, created by the motor's roar and Ernie's scream. The pickup finally slammed into the boulders, bringing the vehicle to a sudden stop. As the steering wheel made impact with Ernie's chest, Ernie's scream silenced.

The front end of the pickup had collapsed like a paper accordion. The impact pushed the engine nearly into the seat of the truck, finally coming to a rest close to Ernie. As the engine slid into the passenger compartment, Ernie's head flew forward into the windshield. A spider web of minute cracks spread from a bowl-size crater that formed from Ernie's skull. In the next instant, Ernie's head whipped back. Ernie hadn't taken the time to put on his seatbelt. There were no airbags in his old pickup. Simultaneously, the pickup's doors on both sides flew open.

Ernie's twisted body tumbled partially out the open door as blood oozed from various cuts. His head drooped at an artificial angle. His right hand still clutched the steering wheel. The motor continued to whine briefly. Then an unnatural silence settled over the truck. Dust slowly drifted over the vehicle and settled downward, forming a ghostly gray-white coating on the crumpled vehicle.

Chapter 14

Tracking data took time. It was Wednesday morning before Jane Reston finalized her analysis of the various logins and retrieved data from all the computers in the library research office at Cameron. She met Charlie Frank, Swede Olson, and Allen Jenkins in her office and announced her findings.

"After intense tracking though computer files and e-mails, our group at Cameron has to admit that there has been a security breach and a break-in over the previous weekend. However, our researchers have said they believe the data taken wasn't significant enough to place any of the current work at Cameron in jeopardy. Most of the data has already been made public knowledge through recent interviews and published essays," Jane explained to Swede and Allen. "However, the security breech is still of major concern."

She looked directly at Charlie. "If Cameron computers could have been entered that simply without detection, our entire research facility could be in jeopardy."

"Only one computer appears to have been compromised. It shows that data we had thought to be secure has actually been accessed on that computer. There has also been an e-mail sent from that station to an address at hotmail.com. The name attached to the address was simply 'Manager.' The history had been wiped, but we were able to recover that much."

"Do you know anything about the e-mail?" asked Swede.

"I'm not sure what was e-mailed to that account," Jane explained. "I can call in the person who normally works on this computer. If she sent out an e-mail to that address from this computer, it would have been highly irregular and certainly unethical."

"Hotmail.com is a free e-mail site. Anyone could have used it," Allen speculated.

"Exactly." Jane turned to Charlie. "For the sake of security, no one is allowed to access outside e-mail accounts from these computers. Everyone signs an agreement."

It was obvious that Jane Reston was upset. Her workers were supposed to be completely reliable. She'd discovered a flaw in her formerly perfect system.

"Well, Ms. Reston," Swede said, chewing on a toothpick, "let's see if we can get that person in here for a few questions."

"I'll call Betty Kraemer right away. She's one of our part-time people. Let's see what she has to say before we make any decisions."

"Okay," agreed Charlie. He appeared relieved that Jane was taking charge. "I'll make sure the room is blocked to anyone else. I'll notify Hal at the front desk to begin backgrounds on the other workers on this floor." He was already walking out the door as he finished the last words.

Charlie Frank was barely holding together. He seemed angry and frustrated. Cameron's own internal investigation had been unable to determine the person or persons involved. They had also been unable to determine how the break-in had succeeded. There were no indications that anyone had entered the building through open doors or even secure entrances. Security cameras showed nothing unusual. This was now the second time Cameron had been hit with security breeches on Charlie's watch.

Swede guessed correctly that Charlie was experiencing no small amount of pressure from Cameron execs. He told Swede that his boss had informed him that it was vital that they learn how much had been leaked, to whom, and how. He had assured his boss that they'd find out who and how. Charlie told his boss that he had given Swede the computer entry logs for every day of the previous month. He and Swede had poured over the logs looking for names of persons who shouldn't have had access to the computers.

Since the head of Cameron's research labs was demanding action, Swede decided they should contact the BCA. He assured Charlie they'd get more help and would get it faster if the BCA was involved.

"I suppose you're right. It's time to bring in the big guns," Charlie admitted. "I really didn't want to do that."

"It'll be okay. They can help. I'll get on it right away." Swede made the initial call to his superior at the Minneapolis Police Department. It wasn't long before the request was forwarded to Boogie, the computer forensics expert at BCA.

In turn, Boogie called Jane Reston to set up an appointment for her to come into the BCA headquarters. Jane didn't waste any time arriving to meet with Boogie.

"Cameron stands to lose millions if the vital data from their research is leaked to anyone or pirated by another company doing similar research," Jane explained to Boogie. "This was a minor leak, but its import is life-threatening for this company."

Jane was maintaining a business-like composure, but it was obvious to Boogie that she felt a vested interest

143

in Cameron, and that was behind the edge to her tone.

"This genome research is a race to discover, validate, and direct future medical breakthroughs," she continued. Boogie just nodded.

"Absolute secrecy is necessary to secure Cameron's entrance into the world of cancer cures, the elimination of diabetes and various other diseases, as well as the possible regeneration of nerves and cells. This is a broad field that opens the door to infinite discoveries in the medical community."

Boogie continued nodding. He picked up a pencil and began doodling on a scrap of paper near his computer.

"Other companies are also in the chase," continued Jane. "It is quite possible that this could be a case of corporate espionage." Jane's voice was rising now. She was trying to impress the need for priority investigation from the BCA. Boogie looked up and simply raised an eyebrow. She settled back into her chair and continued.

"If Cameron loses the data that gives them the lead in this research, they also lose financial support to continue future research. Cameron needs to be in the lead of this research so they can generate ongoing financial backing for research." Jane finished with an exasperated sigh.

She waited. Boogie nodded again. He laid down his pencil. He understood what Jane was saying. But it just wouldn't pay to get all whacked out about it. She might be right. This could be a matter of corporate espionage, or it could be just a bunch of hackers from a small, obnoxious protest group. He tried to be diplomatic.

144

"Well, Ms. Reston, I guess the best thing we can do is try to discover the source of your break-in." He could see her relief at his agreement to take action. "I believe, from what I've been told, that I can track the path of the data sent from your computers in the research library. However, there's no way I'll be able to determine what was done with the information once it was received. At that point, we'll need to organize a detail of BCA personnel who can track down the person who received the data. I need to assure you that this isn't going to be accomplished in a matter of hours or possibly even days."

"I understand." Jane smiled at Boogie for the first time. "I'm glad someone is finally agreeing to do something. But we need to have answers as quickly as humanly possible. We can't have this happen again." She adopted a professional, administrative tone. "At least for starters, we need to know how someone was able to penetrate the security system at Cameron."

"I think I can do that for you," Boogie assured her. "Give me a few hours in your research lab. Can you get me the clearance?"

"I can get that for you today." She stood and gathered her things. "Let me get back to the office. I'll call you as soon as I have the approval. We'll have a pass waiting at the front desk for you by early this afternoon."

Boogie showed her out of the office and returned to his desk where he picked up his phone to give Quay Thompson a heads up. After hanging up, he grabbed his pencil to resume his doodling. He needed to process.

In another part of the Cities, Ernie Elson's Manager was not doodling. Ernie Elson's death would

145

clearly look like an accident, but worry had taken over the Manager's thoughts. At first, there had been an enormous sense of relief that Ernie Elson was taken care of. There was no chance now that he could talk and implicate anyone. But then worry and the reality of the situation began to creep in.

SPARTA could no longer be used as a reason for the problems and break-ins at Cameron. SPARTA would surely die without Ernie Elson. Any necessary bad press and disruption of research at Cameron in the future would have to be developed in some new and creative way. That was definitely a problem. And then there was that need to keep the people with the money happy.

But, on the other hand, the upside was that maybe Quay Thompson would be heading this way with questions. The big guy from BCA. *Well now*, he thought, chuckling to himself, *it might be coming together after all. There could possibly be a bright side to all of this.* A brilliant idea kindled. The Manager began hatching a plan that would allow him to take care of Quay Thompson once and for all. The final countdown could begin. It would bring about the end of Quay Thompson's career, and best of all, Thompson wouldn't even know it until it was too late!

Chapter 15

While Boogie followed the e-mail trail of a Cameron user simply named Manager, Quay and Sam began another trip up 35W north to visit John up at his North Shore office near Lutsen. Annie Bell's parents had completed their formal identification of the body late that morning. That opened the door for the BCA investigation into SPARTA. Quay and Sam would make their first stop at John's office. Now the tedious, methodical questioning of witnesses and pursuit of the killer would begin.

When they arrived at John's office, Quay and Sam found John had already started an investigation portfolio. The starting point of their investigation would be the Flying Eagle Motel in Castle Danger where the SPARTA convention had been held.

"I've already talked to the lodge manager," John reported. "He gave us the names of each person registered at the lodge over the weekend. We have people who attended the convention as well as two other families who stayed there that weekend. The manager said all the SPARTA reservations were made by Ernie Elson. Elson made reservations and provided the name of at least one person for each of the rooms occupied. Three of the people who were registered listed the same address as Ernie's home address on their reservation info. It looks like they gave their true names, though."

"Well, it's a good start," said Quay. He was anxious to get going.

"This is clearly a paranoid group of people," John added. "They're wary about anything that might come out about their membership in SPARTA. To me, that could indicate that the group might be involved in some kind of illegal operations."

"So let's get moving. I think we've got enough." Quay looked from John to Sam for agreement.

"Okay, little brother." John slapped Quay on the shoulder. "It's your case. Go ahead and run with it. Just remember, you might find out more than you want to," he cautioned.

Quay nodded. "I can handle it, John. I've got to find out what happened before I can move on with my life."

Quay pulled out his cell phone and dialed a long-distance number.

"Yeah, this is Thompson. Get me a subpoena for the computer at Ernie Elson's home as well as the one at his office at his school. Get all of his files in both places and any address books he kept. Somewhere, Elson had to have a roster of SPARTA members. Get someone out to Elson's home immediately to pick up what they can. I'm going to want any loose papers. Go through his files, desk, business papers, phone bills, whatever. Then will you also pull a record of all the calls from his home as well as his cell phone? Let me know as soon as you know something, okay? Thanks, pal. I appreciate it." He disconnected and turned to John.

"Okay, what's next?"

John flipped through the file.

"Our crew completed a sweep of Ernie Elson's cabin and also the cabin used by Annie Bell. The manager noted that their cabins were next to each other. Annie Bell and Ernie Elson were not sharing the same cabin. He said the group was pretty docile and hadn't been the partying type of group." John scanned through more notes.

148

"They requested a large meeting room and refreshments. The refreshments consisted of colas and fresh fruits and breads, no alcohol. They met until about ten the first night—that would be Saturday night."

Sam pulled a small notebook from her purse as John continued. Quay watched her and grinned.

"What's this? Double trouble?"

"Just making notes on John's info, being thorough. That's all." She pretended to glare at him and then lowered her head to hide a sly smile.

"They met again early on Sunday morning," John continued. "Most of them had checked out and left by eight that Sunday night. The manager wasn't sure when Ernie Elson left. Everything had been paid for up front. Elson checked in with the manager Sunday afternoon to be sure all the charges were complete."

Sam finished her notes and looked up at John. "Is there anything else beyond what you've got on the convention?"

"Well, in addition to that, we found Annie Bell's car."

Quay raised his eyebrows.

"That's a pretty good addition," Sam commented. "Where was it?"

"It had been driven onto a remote side road just north of the lodge. Evidently, the killer thought it wouldn't be discovered for a while. I'm guessing that he walked the rest of the way back to the lodge. We're checking for fingerprints on the vehicle as well as footprints away from the car."

Quay started figuring the logistics. "If it wasn't more than a mile, and if he returned late at night or early in the morning, chances are no one would have seen him come in on foot."

"Makes sense," John agreed. "We'll follow up on that just to be sure."

"Anything else?" asked Quay.

"Nope. That just about sums up what we have."

"Okay. So now that we have that out of the way, can we eat?" Sam was holding her hand over her stomach.

"Woman! You are always hungry!" Quay sounded exasperated but smiled.

"Okay, let's head up to Grand Marais," John suggested. "There's a neat, little restaurant right on the breakwater there. I'll drive."

The Wild Goose Café was located just off the breakwater with a clear view of Lake Superior. The log-paneled interior displayed a patchwork of wildlife and scenic paintings by local artists. Quay and his brother moved to a booth at the windows in the back of the café where they could view the water and the entry at the same time. They sat facing the door—a practice common among police officers. Not able to do the same, Sam took the seat opposite them. They each turned and took in the panoramic view of the lake in silence. Today, the lake was roiling with waves crashing against the breakwater, shooting foamy, white sprays of water skyward. The early afternoon sun shimmered silver through the spray, forming small rainbow-colored prisms here and there. The rocky breakwater named Artist's Point by the locals ran several hundred feet out into the lake paralleling the shore. The reef served as a wide trail for nature lovers and artists that wanted to get closer to the lake. Quay observed as the artists arranged their easels at various points along the reef. He pointed at sweeping gulls that nearly brushed the easel of one artist.

"Look at that. It's such a perfect picture. I don't think anyone will actually ever be able to capture it on canvas."

The repetitive thundering of the waves against the reef could be heard in the café. The sound calmed and hypnotized Quay. Lake Superior always had the same mesmerizing effect on him. He could watch the waves breaking for hours. He suspected it had the same affect on John and Sam, too.

Somehow this moment brought some clarity to his direction. He thought about why he'd originally agreed to come up here this week. The North Shore. The great escape. The perfect natural retreat. He and Karen had always had special weekends here next to the Great Lake. But one thing had led to another, and then it was gone in a flash of a moment. He'd needed to come back, he realized. He was hoping for closure. This case was beginning to look like it might just provide that.

The waitress arrived and took their identical orders for coffee and the special fresh catch of the day—walleye.

Now, as the three of them sat in the booth, Quay sat back and let the lake infuse him with peace. His mind cleared. The details associated with Annie Bell's murder began to assemble into a clear composite. He began to formulate a new hypothesis.

"What if," Quay mused aloud and then paused, running his hand through a mass of unruly blond hair as he put his thoughts together. "What if Ernie Elson is just a pawn in the SPARTA network? What if he's really just creating a distraction with his protesting? A distraction he's been ordered to create. You know SPARTA claims to be against the genome research at Cameron BioTech. Elson makes it a point to be extremely vocal about his beliefs. And his group has accelerated their activity while at the same time always claiming they're just peaceful protestors trying to stop what they call dangerous research."

"Yeah, and?" John didn't see where Quay was going with this.

"And, largely due to SPARTA's activities, Cameron has been bombarded with bad press: a barrage of violent protestors in addition to SPARTA, Elson's news making comments, and Karen's murder." Quay continued working his way through what they already knew.

"But that's just what happens—bad press," Quay continued, looking at John and Sam. "Maybe that's the point. They're supposed to stir up things against Cameron BioTech just enough. And perhaps destroy Cameron's image in the process so that they begin to lose money and lose donations. Then another company comes along and sweeps up the disillusioned donors. It seems like things happen, and then all of it's swallowed up and leads to nowhere. But perhaps other things are happening. Things that make a difference are really happening behind the scenes at Cameron BioTech.

"Maybe our Mr. Elson has learned more about Cameron BioTech and the industry than he should," continued Quay. "Maybe he has a different agenda now than the one he was originally presenting."

Sam excitedly picked up the direction of her partner's line of thinking. "We know Annie Bell followed

Ernie around like a little puppy, according to her parents. She adored him in high school, they said. But she wasn't Ernie's student anymore. Maybe she wasn't as naïve anymore as she'd been in high school either. Would she have expressed some kind of dissension with Elson? Maybe she even accidently discovered some things about Elson that she shouldn't have. Maybe she became disillusioned with SPARTA and with her dear Mr. Elson. Maybe Ernie had to stop her from revealing those things she'd discovered."

"And, so?" John asked, trying to follow their line of thinking.

"And so, there's something else going on at Cameron," Quay continued. "I learned from Boogie just before we left the office today that there was a break-in at Cameron BioTech over the weekend. It sounds like they believe someone got into their computers and stole some of their research data. In fact, whoever did it was able to send several research files out of their lab. So the SPARTA group has always claimed their only aim is just to disrupt Cameron BioTech's work—but maybe that's not all they're doing. Maybe there's something more going on. Maybe there's a hidden agenda known only to our Ernie Elson. SPARTA met up here over the weekend. Those files e-mailed out of Cameron could have been sent directly, or indirectly, to a SPARTA source at the conference."

"Yeah, I get it. So where are you going with this?" John asked.

"If those files were delivered to Elson while they were at the conference, and if Annie Bell accidentally happened upon them, she might have gone after Elson. She could have been angry, disillusioned. Maybe he'd

153

always stressed to Annie and the rest of the SPARTANS that they weren't doing anything illegal. But now, there it was. She caught him. Something illegal. Maybe Miss Do-Gooder Annie Bell threatened to expose him and his pet organization, SPARTA.

"According to her parents, it sounded like Annie had always been pretty naïve. Elson was her idol. Maybe his crown suddenly became tarnished in her eyes. According to her parents, she wouldn't have gone for anything that was illegal. Annie was always on the straight and narrow."

"Okay, I guess I can see that," John said. "But why did Ernie Elson need to get rid of Annie Bell? Seems like he could have handled her without killing her. She was still naïve enough to follow after him. Murder is a pretty major reaction."

"And do you think he might be the one who directed the break-in at Cameron? If so, why did he need to do that?" asked Sam. "If that's what happened, we need to prove how the break-in was related to Annie Bell's murder and the conference. Why would Elson have been involved in all of that? What would have been in it for him?"

Quay stared out at the lake, still focusing on the breaking action and erupting spray of the waves. John and Sam followed his gaze, each processing the possibilities in silence. It began to make sense.

"Could it be," mused Quay as he continued watching the waves and sipped his coffee, "that whoever slipped the files out of Cameron this weekend was also running Elson? He could have been a pawn for someone or something bigger. Maybe our little professor unwittingly caused unwelcome attention to the Cameron situation. The kind his partners didn't want."

His theory, now crystalizing, came out in a rush. "And, just maybe, our real problem isn't with SPARTA at all. This whole SPARTA group could be just a façade for the real game being played out with Cameron BioTech's genome research.

"Maybe someone, possibly even someone inside Cameron, wants Cameron to have problems. That someone might be even funding some of the people, a.k.a. SPARTA, causing the uproar against Cameron." Silence grew among the three as they processed what Quay was putting together.

Quay's mental marathon raced on at full speed. This couldn't have been just a group of random incidents. He was beginning to see a whole larger picture. If his hypothesis was true, this was huge. Much bigger than any of them had ever imagined.

Sam and John looked at Quay, listening to what he was saying and watching his excitement grow. They'd nodded as he outlined the entire scenario. This made sense. It put everything into perspective.

"Okay, so if that's really the way it is," added Sam, "we have a clear direction. We need to follow up at Cameron. We need to know what Annie Bell might have discovered. We also need to know what Elson knows and doesn't know. And we need to find out who's been running Elson."

John joined in. "If he had any inkling about suspicions we may have about his connections to Annie Bell's death after you questioned him, he may just have talked to someone else. He may have needed to explain why you were there. He needed to protect his own assets, so to speak."

"That also might be enough for that someone he talks to to decide to eliminate Elson," speculated Quay. "Elson may know too much incriminating information about the whole deal."

Sam jumped in. "Annie's death hasn't hit the news yet. SPARTA people may not know. We'll have to work fast."

Quay shifted in the booth and looked back at Sam and John. "I think we need to err on the side of caution. We've got the search warrants going. I don't want any more suspicious minds at work before we uncover what's going on.

"First, let's see if we can interview some of the members of SPARTA. I want to find out if they know who their money source is. Who's been funding their activities? We may be able to find something on Elson's computers, but I doubt it. He would have been pretty careful."

"You're right. There has to be a money trail there somewhere. Let's see if we can look into his bank accounts too." John pulled his notebook from his pocket and started a list.

"All right, let's get going on it." Quay took a last sip of coffee as he stood. He dug into his pockets for tip money. There wasn't time to waste. John and Sam caught up with him as he walked out. Quay turned back to them, walking backward through the parking lot.

"John, is there any chance that you can help us work this one down in the Cities?"

John was already nodding. "I was hoping you'd ask."

"It looks like we could use your eyes and expertise on this one, and it really is your case and district. I'm

156

guessing that this one will have several districts involved."

"I'll talk to my deputy when we get back to the office," John said. "I'm pretty sure we can work together. I'll have to check in with Sharon and the kids. Then I'll put together some things and meet you at your place later tonight so we can map out our plan. Sam, can you join us at Quay's?"

"Sure, I'll just have to check my date book," Sam said sarcastically as she flipped open her notebook. "Let's see ... I think I can squeeze more work hours in my day. Nope, nothing going tonight. And besides, I get paid so much overtime!"

"Yeah, don't we all?" Quay laughed. "Come on, Sam. Let's get those long legs of yours working. I've got better things to do than admire scenery all day."

Sam laughed as he opened the pink wad of gum. He casually tossed the bubblegum into the air and successfully caught it in his mouth. He grinned at Sam as she shook her head.

"Aren't you just amazed at all the talent I have?" He laughed at himself. He was definitely feeling better. And he had to admit the bubblegum finally seemed to be squelching his desire for the tobacco. Maybe this bubblegum bit might be working after all. Actually, he thought, a lot of things might be working after all.

Sam and John looked at one another smiling as they recognized the change in Quay's demeanor. He seemed to be moving with a real sense of purpose for the first time in a long time.

He almost seemed to be truly happy, Sam thought. Quay was usually so serious. As she watched this new Quay walk out to the parking lot flipping his keys in from hand to hand, she realized that she'd never really thought much about how good looking Quay really was. When he was like this, though, he was just downright studly. A long-forgotten little spark ignited. Nope, she decided. She purposefully squelched it. She wasn't ever going there again. She could just be happy that it was refreshing to see this change in her partner.

John noticed the change, too. Quay exhibited a new, upbeat confidence. John assumed the reason was that Quay had decided this case was related to Karen's death. Quay's talent was his ability to compile random strands of data and piece it all together. John had always enjoyed watching his brother work up a case before—before Karen. Quay always used to say that new cases were like putting together jigsaw puzzles. As each piece fell into place, Quay became more confident and more driven. He said, "When the pieces fall into place, they create a cop's Mona Lisa."

Quay stopped next to his truck, waiting for John and Sam to catch up.

"You know, I think I could compile a complete joke book with the jokes from these stupid bubblegum wrappers." Quay was holding the tiny wrapper close to his eyes as he squinted at the small print. "I should have been saving them from the start. Just didn't feel too funny at the time. But now I'm beginning to feel there might be a funny bone in me after all." He looked up at John with a silly grin on his face.

"Yeah, right," laughed John. "I think I know just where your funny bone is!"

Sam burst out laughing as Quay shot John one of his big-brother glares.

"Oh you're real good, little brother! The emphasis for you is on little!" Quay couldn't contain his smug grin as John gave him a punch on the arm. It felt good to laugh.

As Quay climbed into his pickup, Sam remembered that over the last couple years, Quay had reminded her of Joe Btfsplk from the old comic strips. He always seemed to have a dark cloud hanging over his head. They really made a fine pair, she thought. She'd had the broken engagement and then a marriage that fell apart after a miscarriage. She wasn't even close to being in the market for romance. She'd been burned twice and wasn't anxious to try again. No rainbows over her head either, she thought cynically.

Maybe that was why she and Quay were so comfortable with each other now. They'd both had their share of misery, and neither of them had any great expectations anymore. They both understood where they'd been and where they were now. So they could just forget about the social life and dig into the job. It was easier that way for both of them. No expectations.

Chapter 16

An hour later, Sam and Quay sped toward the Twin Cities. Quay was particularly eager to get started. It felt like he had a personal, vested interest in this case.

The scenic Highway 61 from the North Shore to Duluth gave Sam cause to interrupt Quay's rambling about the case.

"Just look at that. Sam remarked as they flew past the brilliant array of fall colors. Isn't it just incredible?" Quay nodded absently in agreement.

Then suddenly realizing that Samantha was not talking about the case, he answered, "That's just one of the reasons I love it up here."

"I totally understand. What's not to like?"

"Only the winters, but even with the cold, the views are still spectacular. Can't beat them."

It was true. The North Shore scenery was incredible at any time, but it was especially spectacular in the fall. As they sped south toward Duluth, the evergreens, birches, maples, and oaks flew by in a kaleidoscope of reds, oranges, browns, and greens. The leaves were just coming into peak color. The sparkling diamonds on the sapphire blue lake to the west provided a brilliant frame for the flaming colors.

While Quay drove down the winding lakeshore Highway 61, he and Sam halted their discussion of the case several times. Quay eagerly pointed out each particularly picturesque point. He slipped in a CD, and they listened to the tunes of Kenny Chesney accompanying the autumnal panorama of Lake Superior.

"A little traveling music," he said. Sam smiled and laid her head back against the seat.

Quay flew on through Duluth and south on 35W to the Twin Cities, eager to get to headquarters. It was late afternoon by the time they finally arrived. Sam decided to check in with Boogie first. She hoped Boogie might have been able to uncover more information in his search through the e-mails at Cameron.

Quay headed off to meet with his secretary, who was trying to come up with the list of SPARTA members. He hoped that someone in the group might have information.

Quay's secretary had done her job well, as usual. He could always count on Bonnie. She'd pulled together a list of all the current SPARTA members. The warrants would be ready if he needed them.

As Quay looked through the list, he picked out two names that he thought would be of help. They had both been informants for him in the past. This was an unusually fortunate turn of events. Now all he had to do was track each of them down and get some answers. He decided to work this one without the warrants. He thanked Bonnie and headed out in search of Sam.

Sam was ready with information, too. She joined Quay in his office.

"I talked with Boogie. The computer from Elson's home revealed nothing more than usual household data, as you expected. However, Boogie's working on Elson's school computer right now. The guys were able to pick up two computers, the one in Elson's classroom and the one in his science department office. One of them is bound to reveal some information.

"By the way," she continued, "Elson's out on a 'sick' leave. He told the secretary at his school that his wife was ill. His wife was the only one home when they

161

picked up the home computer. She was pretty distraught. The guys couldn't get anything from her that made sense. She couldn't or wouldn't give any information about Elson either. What do you have?" She looked at the papers Quay was holding.

"Well, we'll have to deal with Elson later. Sam, I've can't believe what a break I've got! *We've* got," he amended. "I've got a lead here with the names of a couple guys from the SPARTA group. These guys used to be snitches of mine. Do you want to tag along? I'm going to try to track these two creeps down. I think I might be able to shake something out of them."

"Sure!" Sam jumped to her feet and grabbed her jacket. "Just let me check in with Boogie once more before I leave. I think he might have something more on Elson's work computers. At any rate, I want him to call as soon as he gets something."

Sam grabbed a cup of coffee on the way out and jumped in Quay's truck just as he began rolling out of his parking space.

Quay's energy and tension was evident. He began talking to Sam before she could shut the door. "Isn't it interesting how things can just overlap sometimes? These two guys were snitches for me on a drug bust a few years back. I haven't seen either one of them for quite a while."

"Who are they, Quay? Would I know them?" asked Sam.

"No, I worked with them before you started with the department. They're both just a couple of tweaks. Knowing them, I think we'll be able to pick up enough from them to find out about any possible funding Elson might have had elsewhere."

"Where are we going?"

"Well, we'll start with what I was able to dig up for current stats on both of them. According to our last records, they were both living near the Uptown area in Minneapolis."

Quay wove in and around cars on the freeway. His destination and possible answers were only twenty miles away.

It was nearly six when they turned onto Interstate 94 off 35W. They slowed as they neared the Hennepin Avenue exit. Quay turned south into the Uptown area and pulled up in front of a small Thai restaurant.

A neon sign advertising spicy, Thai cuisine flashed in a double window. Quay and Sam could see a few couples seated at oilcloth-covered tables. A group of noisy college kids was just entering. Just a couple yards to the left of the restaurant door was a red, unmarked door that led to apartments over the restaurant. Quay stepped in and motioned for Sam to follow him. The walls of the dimly lit stairwell had seen several coats of paint over the years. Here and there, chips pulled away, revealing burnished golds, army greens, and light taupes of years past. At the top of the stairs, five doors opened onto the narrow hallway. Quay stopped in front of a door marked with a tarnished number three. Sam flattened against the wall on the opposite side of the door as Quay knocked.

They could hear someone moving inside the apartment. Muffled sounds were coming from a television, but no one answered the door. Quay knocked again and then decided to call out.

"Hello in there. James Weston? Jesse Weston? It's Quay Thompson. I need to talk to you."

Again there was a sound of movement, but now it became a dull, urgent thumping and thrashing.

Quay jiggled the doorknob. The knob turned easily in his hand, and he slowly cracked the door open about six inches. At that moment, two silenced revolver bursts slapped through the doorframe directly above Quay's head.

Quay ducked and lurched back. Sam immediately fell to a crouch on the floor.

"Jesus Christ! Will you hold it for Christ's sake! All we want to do is talk!" Quay called out.

Another shot clipped through the doorframe.

"I guess they don't want to talk to us," Quay said loud enough for them to hear as he grinned and motioned to Sam. She drew her gun from her shoulder holster and nodded an assent of readiness. Quay pulled his Glock 9mm, lowered his right shoulder, and sharply shoved his full weight against the door. The door responded with a sharp crack as it flew back into the wall. Quay charged through the opening, dropped to the floor, and folded into a somersault roll. Sam followed at a crouch, shouting, "Hold it right there!" She aimed her gun directly at the opposite window.

Two figures were silhouetted against the window. Quay spotted one of the men leaning with one foot out the window, the other leg pulled up ready to complete the escape. Sam focused on the man who was still inside. This one was apparently trying to steady his brother with one hand while aiming a small pistol directly at Quay with the other.

"Drop the gun, you idiot," demanded Quay. "You don't want to do this. We're just here for a quiet talk. That's all."

The tall, lanky fellow with the gun responded with a tone of disdain.

"You don't know what you're talking about, Thompson. There's no such thing as just a quiet talk with you,"

"Just drop your gun, and we'll see," said Sam. "We can work something out. At least give us a chance."

"I see you at least brought along someone easier on the eyes. Who's she?"

"This is my partner, Sam," Quay answered.

"Sam? Sam's her name? And she's your partner? You're really sinking low, Thompson."

Despite his derisive attitude, he slowly released his gun, laying it gently onto the floor. He nodded at his brother and tugged on his belt. His brother climbed reluctantly through the window back into the apartment.

The two of them stood near the window, each doing his best to present a belligerent glare at Quay.

"Okay," Quay began as he moved into the room. "Let's do some talking." He carefully edged closer and kicked the weapon in Sam's direction.

"What's going on with you guys?" Quay asked. "What are you two so jittery about? Have you got something to hide? By the way, Samantha Atwood, this is James Weston." Quay turned to Sam as he pointed to the tall, lanky fellow who had been holding the gun. Quay holstered his Glock. Sam nodded a solemn greeting as she retrieved James's gun.

"This other fellow is his little brother, Jesse. They used to be somewhat reliable."

"We don't have anything to hide," whined the one called James. He rocked back onto his heels while shoving his hands in his pockets.

"Keep your hands out where I can see them, James." Sam motioned toward a chair with her gun. "You need to have a seat."

"We just don't want to get involved." James reluctantly pulled his hands into view and let his arms dangle awkwardly at his sides. "There's something big going down. People are getting killed. We didn't do anything."

"So tell us about it," Quay said as he pulled out a chrome chair with a torn, red vinyl seat. "Why don't you join us at the table, fellas," he said, pointing to the chair. His tone indicated it clearly was not a request.

There were three other chairs in similar condition crowded into the tiny dinette area of the apartment. The table was littered with several days' worth of newspapers, partially filled coffee cups, and empty beer bottles. Quay nodded to Sam, pointing at the mess on the table when he noticed that several articles in the newspapers had been circled. Sam edged over to the table to begin a closer inspection.

"There's nothing to tell," whined Jesse, still not willing to move toward the chair.

"Sit down, Jesse!" Quay demanded, losing patience.

"We weren't doing nothing, man," protested James. "What's the problem, man? You got nothing on us."

"Well I can honestly say you're right there," Quay answered, settling back in the chair. "Except that you just shot at two officers of the law. You see, you made it seem like you had something to tell when you took those shots at us and tried to scramble out that window."

"You scared us, man! That's all," responded James. "We're just a little edgy, nothing more."

"So tell us what you're so edgy about," interrupted Sam. "I see you've had some interest in the recent write-ups in the *Star Tribune* about the SPARTA murder." She pushed the newspapers toward them. "Want to talk about that?"

"All we know is what we read," answered Jesse, nervously shuffling his feet. "We went to a couple of those SPARTA meetings, and we were interested in what happened to that girl. We know Elson. He runs SPARTA. We wondered what happened. That's all."

"Ah, shit! Would you just shut up?" James yelled at his brother. "We don't have to tell them anything."

"I'm not telling him anything!" Jesse glared at his brother. "You want to talk to the man, go ahead. We don't have anything to hide."

Quay sighed, settled back in the chair, and stretched his legs up onto the table. Sam leaned forward, resting her elbows on the table and settling her chin in her hands.

"We're willing to take as much time as you need," Sam said.

"James," Quay reached into his shirt pocket, "I can probably help you out here. I'm guessing you know enough about Ernie Elson and SPARTA to run the operation yourself." He pulled out a piece of bubblegum and began to slowly unwrap it. "Want to tell us what's new with the SPARTA gang? I'll help you today if the information's good. Or," he paused, popping the gum in his mouth and shoving the wrapper back in his pocket, "we could just go downtown and lock you up for firing on officers of the law. How about that?"

Jesse and James exchanged looks. Quay saw a slight nod from Jesse and the unspoken agreement.

"Look, man," James began, "you were always fair with us. We just don't want any trouble."

Quay shrugged. "Not a problem if you just give us some info." He leaned forward, settling the chair on the floor with a thump. Jesse made an involuntary jump. "I need to know if either of you attended a SPARTA conference at Flying Eagle Lodge up by the North Shore recently."

"Yeah, we were there." James looked nervously at Jesse for support. Getting the nod again, he continued. "SPARTA seemed like it was a good idea, ya know? Dude, the group really wants to help people get rid of corporate interference in our lives. They know things that some of these big corporations are doing. The rich guys are trying to take over our lives. They're really going to ruin our future, ya know, dude? And they're doing a lot of undercover stuff, too. I don't think our government even knows everything. It's bad, dude."

"So," probed Sam, "tell us about it, dude." She used the moniker with a smile, establishing an appearance of understanding as she lightly touched his hand. "Let's start with how well you two know the leaders of this group. Did you know Elson personally?"

"Sure," Jesse jumped in, eager to demonstrate his knowledge now that it looked like they were off the hook. "We met him a couple months ago. First we talked with some of the group in one of those online chat rooms. Ya know? Then they invited us to a couple meetings. We met this Elson guy in person at the first meeting. He seemed like a cool dude. Really smart, too."

"If things were looking so good with SPARTA, what they were doing? What spooked you?" asked Quay.

"Well," James picked up the story, looking at Jesse again for assurance, "when we went up to the conference up north, there were about forty or so people there." Jesse was nodding in agreement. "Everybody up there was gung-ho about protesting at research labs like Cameron and stuff. They wanted to get the media involved. There was a lot of talk about genome research and stuff that Cameron was doing secretly."

"How did Elson know what Cameron was doing secretly?" asked Quay.

"That's what made us change our minds," Jesse said. "He got up at the last session of the conference and made this big speech about Cameron research. And it was really interesting, but what really scared us was this girl named Annie Bell who sat next to us."

Quay perked up. "What about her?"

"Well," Jesse hesitated, looking at James for approval. James nodded, and Jesse continued.

"Annie was reading through a bunch of papers in one of those file things, ya know, while Elson was speaking. All of a sudden, she started talking under her breath about how Elson was a liar, and she said that he'd actually stolen some secret research data from Cameron. Then she said something about money. She said she'd just gotten the 'real research plans' related to the stuff at Cameron."

"Did she say who was involved and where she got the papers?" Sam asked.

"Nope. She just said the whole deal wasn't right and that Elson had to be stopped. She was pretty mad, man. She said she had found proof that Elson was involved with stealing some information, and according to what she saw, he was twisting and perverting the research. Dude, she really got up a head of steam. She was actually getting scary."

"What'd she do with the papers?" interrupted Quay.

"We don't know," answered Jesse. James was nodding his head in agreement. "She took the stuff she was looking at and walked out before Elson's last speech was over. She stormed out, actually."

"Did Elson see any of this?"

"Uh, no, I don't think so," answered James.

Jesse said, "Everyone was standing and applauding Elson—except us, of course. We were too scared at that point. We didn't know what to do. We just tried to be inconspicuous and duck out. It just looked like a whole lot of trouble was brewing if that Annie girl could do anything about it. We left right away before anyone else."

"Yup! We sure did!" James was confident now. "Went right back to our cabin, packed up, and left."

"Then today we heard on the news that a body had been found farther up along the shore from where we'd been meeting. That was really bad," added Jesse. "We were afraid it meant trouble for us because we'd been at the conference. Ya know what I'm saying, dude? We just knew the cops would be all over us." He paused. "And then you showed up."

"So what else can you tell us? Tell us everything you saw, noticed, who was there—we need all of it." Quay's voice had become husky and demanding.

170

They spent the next forty-five minutes grilling James and Jesse while at the same time reassuring them that they'd be protected. By the time they were done, it was dark out, and Quay and Sam had filled in a few of the blanks. Quay believed they had enough preliminary information to establish a sound BCA case.

When they were finished, Quay and Sam set up protection through the BCA for the boys until the investigation was finished and the case was ready for trial.

"We're going to need your testimony to establish motive," Quay explained to the brothers as they got up to leave.

Sam continued, "This is far more than Elson being the possible murderer of Annie Bell. It looks there are much bigger issues here. Annie Bell was just caught in the web. She was an innocent."

Sam and Quay escorted James and Jesse Weston out of the building. They were met at the curb by a waiting unmarked BCA car. The brothers would be driven out of the Cities to a safe house. Their affidavits would be taken. Now it was up to Quay's group to do the rest of the legwork.

Chapter 17

It had already been a long day by the time Quay and Sam arrived back at BCA headquarters. They had begun the day at the North Shore and ended in the Uptown section of Minneapolis with a few stops along the way.

While Quay and Sam were meeting up with the Weston brothers, John had driven down from Lutsen and was waiting in Quay's office when they arrived. Quay quickly brought John up to date on the information they'd gleaned from James and Jesse.

"Looks like you may have nabbed the girl's killer already," John said as he drained the last of his cup of third cup of coffee. "Now what?"

"Well, even if we think we've figured out who murdered Annie Bell, that's not the end of the story, John. I think there are bigger things going on. We still have to find out who was funding Ernie Elson."

"Funding him? What are you talking about? Do you have proof on your theory?"

"It looks like Ernie may have just been a peon like we thought. Someone was giving Ernie Elson orders. Someone wanted Elson to do some dirty work at Cameron. He screwed up when he killed Annie. He'll be in trouble now. If we give Elson enough rope, he may just hang himself and lead us to the big fish in the process. We've just got to put all this together before we can make any arrests."

"How do you know all this? Did James and Jesse give you some good info?" asked John.

"Yeah, I think at least a little hint," said Quay. "They overheard Annie Bell talking about some discoveries she'd made about Elson's connections with Cameron BioTech. It sounds like there may be someone inside Cameron stirring things up. It's not really clear what the motive is at this point.

"First, I think we need to check in with Boogie to see what he's got from his e-mail search on Elson. Then tomorrow we need to pay a visit to Cameron BioTech. Somehow, it's all tied together with that break-in at Cameron over the weekend. It happened while Elson was meeting with the group up north.

"Whatever she found, Annie Bell was very upset about it. I'm thinking that's what got her killed. Elson's got connections here with Cameron. Connections he doesn't want anyone to know about. Maybe his funding was coming from someone at Cameron. We'll need to talk to him again."

"But what I can't figure out," said Sam, "is why someone in Cameron would be paying Elson to cause trouble for their own research labs. What's with that?" Slumping into Quay's office chair, Sam pushed her legs out and stretched back to pull her hair off her neck. She was tired, and this case was becoming overwhelmingly complex.

"Well, let's just find out what's with that," Quay said as he unwrapped his fourth pink piece of Double Bubble Gum for the day and popped it in his mouth. He grinned and inhaled like he'd just taken a refreshing puff on a cigarette.

Sam and John watched him and shook their heads in unison.

"Man, you are really strange, you know that?" commented John.

"Yeah," Sam joined in, grinning. "And what's worse is I have to work with him!"

Quay just smiled, blew a huge bubble, popped it, and stood up. "Let's see if Boogie's still here."

Sam groaned as she pulled herself out of the chair.

"Can't we just go home now?"

"Pretty soon."

John repressed a chuckle as Quay led the way out the door toward the second floor.

It was late, but Boogie was still there buried behind two computers. He was clicking away on one while reading data scrolling on the other. The third computer in his office was lit and seemed to be processing something else all by itself.

"Hey, Boogie," John called out as they entered. "Don't you have a life, either?"

"Got anything for us, Boogie?" Sam asked as she brought up the rear of the procession into Boogie's office.

"Oh, hi, guys. You're still here, too, huh? I think I may be onto something here. It's taken a while, but I'm closing in."

"What's that?" asked Quay as he leaned over the top of the computers, scanning Boogie's screens.

"I've been able to trace those e-mails sent to Elson. I began following a string of addresses from the e-mails he got from someone calling himself The Manager. We got that off his school computer. It looks like The Manager guy wanted to remain anonymous, even to Elson. I don't think Elson knows who he is. The e-mails indicate Elson was instructed how and when to protest in front of Cameron Research Labs several times over the last couple years. It even goes back as far as the time Karen was shot, Quay."

Quay's head shot up, and his gray eyes bore into Boogie. "What are you saying? Do you think Elson was in on that? What else have you got?"

"I'm not really sure other than Elson was instructed to get SPARTA involved with the protests and to create a disruption at Cameron BioTech several times. According to one recent e-mail, he was also supposed to get someone to break into the computer lab library at Cameron. This Manager person told Elson he'd have no trouble getting in. The Manager told him how to do it. He set up a drop point with the directions. Clever, huh? Then the perp was supposed to e-mail certain information out of Cameron to Elson. They weren't supposed to bring out any actual hardcopies."

"Then what? I don't get it. What was Elson going to do with the stuff?" asked John.

"That's what you guys will have to figure out. It's not clear what they actually took out of the lab library at Cameron." He paused. "Oh yeah, you guys don't know this yet."

Boogie filled them in about the meeting he'd had with Jane Reston discussing a break-in at Cameron and the problems Cameron had had over the weekend.

Quay, Sam, and John listened intently without interrupting. This fit in neatly with what Jesse and John had said.

"I haven't gotten into the enclosure on the e-mail they sent out. I also haven't been able to catch the identity of this Manager guy. But I'm close. It looks like he used a public Internet hookup somewhere and then got on with a fake ID. If I can come up with a location for the public hookup, you'll probably have to do the legwork from there. The location might be a help to nailing down

175

his or her identity. But we'll need to get some possibles from Cameron so you can show pictures around."

Quay flashed back to something Karen had said about the protest e-mails she'd received. The protestors always used public computers at libraries to send their little sermons and threats, she'd said. And they were always anonymous. Quay was sure that's exactly what she'd said. Things were definitely looking up.

"They may have used a library. Okay, Boogie. Good job!" he said, clapping him on the back enthusiastically.

Boogie grinned in appreciation. "Glad I could be of some help, guy."

"Go home, Boogie! Call it a day!" Sam said as she, too, patted him and walked out.

Quay could hardly contain his excitement. He hadn't even listened to Sam.

"Great work," Quay repeated, "and keep at it, fella. Give us a call the minute you track down anything else. We'll head over to Cameron and talk to the security chief and also the cops from MPD. They were the ones who first went over to check things out."

Quay's energy level had definitely revived. He was so revved up that he'd forgotten about the time. He wanted answers now, not later. He'd waited long enough. He could feel this. He was finally getting close to answers.

He pulled on his jacket while giving more instructions to Boogie. "Let's get going," he said as he glanced at Sam and John and then strode out the door and down the stairs.

"Quay, do you know what time it is?" John reminded Quay as he and Sam followed him out the door. "The chances of getting any information tonight are slim to none. Let's call it a day and start fresh in the morning."

Quay's pace slowed slightly. He stared ahead and said nothing.

"Come on, Quay," Sam said. "You know he's right. I know how much you want a solution to this, but—"

Before she could finish, Quay turned to look at both of them and snapped, "You don't have any idea how much I want this to be done. Neither one of you knows."

"I think we do," Sam said quietly as she edged closer to Quay and grabbed his arm.

"This isn't just another case now." Quay was almost growling. His voice had become deeper, heavier. "This one is now personal."

He turned to his brother. "John, you understand, don't you? You've got to. SPARTA has the answers I need. I've waited a year for answers. That's a year too long! I'm not going to stop until I have someone put away for this." He paused. "This girl's murder and Karen's murder. It's finally going to happen. I can feel it."

"Quay," Sam said, "we'll do it. We will follow every lead until we get the answers for you. But you have to rest. You don't want to make mistakes. This has to be picture perfect. You know that. You want to make it stick. *We* want to make it stick. Let's just call it a day. We can start early tomorrow. We'll be with you all the way. You know we want to help."

Quay nodded. "All right." He let out a huge sigh as if he'd been holding it for the entire last year. "Sam, we'll meet tomorrow at the headquarters at seven. From there, we're heading straight to Cameron." He climbed into his pickup and slumped behind the wheel.

177

Sam reached forward to put a hand on his shoulder. "Let us stop with you for a bite to eat first. You could use some food and some company for a while tonight, I think!"

John said, "She's right, Quay. Let's head over to that little bar we used to go to on the corner of Hennepin Avenue and Fourth Street. Paddy's? We can grab a bite to eat and have a drink there. Then we can call it a night."

They left the parking lot in a parade of three vehicles turning in the direction of downtown.

It's still going to be a long night, Quay thought.

Chapter 18

Quay was tense and sullen when they settled into the booth at the back of the bar. He stared down at the beer bottle he was squeezing, silently picking at the label. Boogie's information had just reignited every memory and every ounce of anger he'd ever felt. The emotion was so intense it exhausted him.

Why hadn't they been able to nail SPARTA a year ago? What had been SPARTA's purpose? What was going on at Cameron BioTech? Was it someone who had a problem with Cameron or was it someone who had a problem with Karen? Had Karen discovered something and not known it? Had someone been intent on killing Karen after all? What did Elson know? What was his role in all of this? Or was it possible that this was all about Cameron—and Karen had just been an innocent bystander who'd gotten in the way? Why?

Questions and scenarios were swarming around in his mind. He wanted to pound through walls. He wanted to storm Cameron. Most of all, he wanted answers. Rationally, he knew he couldn't bring back Karen. But he could find answers. He could connect the dots and get the bastards behind her death. He could let her rest in peace. He had to admit to himself that was what he wanted more than anything now.

The trio waited for their burgers in silence while Quay sipped on his beer and collected himself. He hunched down in the booth and was leaning over his beer bottle, still picking at the label. John settled in next to Quay and pulled off his jacket. Sam sat across the table and stared at the two of them. She leaned her arms on the table and bent forward toward them. She sighed and then finally broke their musings with a quiet voice.

"Quay, you need to let us into that head of yours. What are you thinking? If you share your ideas, I think we can work together on this thing. It doesn't have to be yours alone."

He shook his head. "I don't know. I'm so damn angry. I can't begin to tell you." His voice was just as ragged as the look in his eyes. "When Boogie said that it looked like someone in Cameron had set Karen up, I wanted to smash things. How did we miss this two years ago? Who dropped the ball? From what Boogie's suggesting, we could have prevented it! We knew the SPARTA group was pinpointing Cameron. The BCA did nothing. Was there information staring us in the face that we ignored?" He shook his head again. "There must have been something."

His face had become tight, his gray eyes filled with a stony intensity neither Sam nor John recognized. Quay was a handsome man, but now his face had taken on a hard, cruel edge. It didn't become him. He radiated anger. The easygoing bubblegum guy was gone.

"Quay," began John cautiously, "we'll get this figured out. We'll work with you. But, man, we've got to do it right this time. Like Sam said before, we don't want to screw this up. Don't let your emotions, and most of all your anger, lead you headlong into disaster." He took a drink of his beer and waited.

Sam added softly, "Quay, we both care about you. You have to know that. There's no way we'll let you down on this one. We're behind you all the way. We'll make sure you get the answers."

Quay looked up at her and then at his brother. Slowly his eyes softened. He took a drink and set the

180

bottle down carefully. He stared at it as if trying to bore a hole through the bottle.

"I know you will. I know," he finally mumbled. He took a deep breath and added, "I know you're right. I'll be all right. Thanks for being here. Both of you."

He looked at Sam.

"You've been a great partner, Sam. You've been the best thing for me this last year and a half. You've never pushed into my private life, but you've been a quiet support. You've always been here. Thanks."

Sam lowered her head, hiding the tears that began welling in her eyes. This was the first time Quay had actually acknowledged any satisfaction in their work together or—perhaps more importantly—their friendship.

When she'd first been assigned to Quay, he'd been so cold, aloof, and intense that she hadn't known whether she'd be able to continue to work with him. He seemed to resent her and closed her out each time they took on a new case. She had tried to just be the kind of partner he could count on. She knew that trying to be anything more would be an insult to him. She also knew she had to prove her worth to him. Gradually, Quay warmed up and finally had confided little bits about his life to her. But he'd never talked about Karen.

She'd learned about Karen, though. Others in the department had told her, warned her: "Step gingerly around that one, Sam. He's a volcano ready to explode." And so she had. She hadn't let him push her around too much on the job. She'd asserted her competence, but she had never invaded his privacy.

He had shown more confidence in her abilities as their partnership grew. In the last few months, he had asked for her input more frequently. To have him say this to her now was more than she could have hoped, she thought.

Slowly, she realized she'd come to care for Quay. Now he was more than a partner and perhaps more than a friend. For the first time, she admitted to herself that she might be falling for this fragile giant. Given their combined history and her past, the thought frightened her.

Sam swiped her eyes with the back of her hand and studied Quay as he looked away. He was thinking back to the lake again. *What a complex man*, she thought. John watched her gaze and nodded.

They ate quickly and agreed to meet at BCA headquarters by eight the next morning instead of seven. They needed a little break. Sam took off for her place while John followed Quay back to his home. He'd be bunking with his brother until they got some of this case settled.

When Sam walked into headquarters the next morning, she expected to find Quay in his office. Instead she found him up in Boogie's office. Quay had gone there as soon as he'd gotten in. Luckily Boogie had gotten in early, too. He hoped Boogie had new information for them.

Quay walked behind the desk to get a look at Boogie's computer screens. He was standing with his hands in his pockets looking over Boogie's shoulders. When Sam walked in, Boogie appeared to be annoyed.

"Thompson, man. I left work right after you last night. I just got in," Boogie was saying. "I'm not superman, ya know. I'll get it done as fast as I can for you. You know that."

"Sure, Boogie. I understand. This is just especially important to me. Call me on my cell as soon as you have anything else. I mean *anything*!" He turned to leave and saw Sam standing silently at the door. Boogie looked up and nodded a hello at her. Quay turned and walked slowly toward Sam. He grabbed her elbow, turned her around, and steered her out.

"Good morning, Boogie," Sam called over her shoulder as Quay led her away.

"Hey, Sam." Boogie smiled and waved. "Nice talking to ya. Have a good one!"

When they got back to Quay's office, John was sitting at Quay's desk waiting. "Grab a cup of coffee and let's go," Quay ordered. He was already pulling on his jacket and pulling keys out of his pocket.

While John was picking up coffee for Sam and himself, Sam sat down beside Quay's desk. She reached over to the dish he kept on his desktop and grabbed a couple square, pink packets from it, placing them in her pocket. Quay was making a quick call to Detective Swede Olson at the MPD. He was asking Olson to meet them at Cameron.

According to Boogie's information, Swede Olson had done the first investigation of the break-in at Cameron BioTech this fall. Quay and Swede had worked a couple other investigations together. He trusted Swede. He wanted his input on exactly what he'd seen and done on the previous investigation. He believed he was a thorough and honest cop. That said enough about him.

183

Quay tucked his gun away in the console between his front seats. John opened the glove compartment and wedged his gun under the vehicle identification papers. Sam climbed in back. She'd left her gun in the trunk of her car. She didn't think she'd be needing it for this interview. Quay pulled out and headed north up 35W toward Cameron BioTech. Since it was the morning rush hour, they were caught in the thick of the morning traffic. It would take them about fifteen minutes longer than normal.

Quay was silent during the drive. It was obvious to Sam and John that Quay was completely absorbed with this mission, and they were both worried about the tension they saw building in him.

The toll this trip was taking on Quay was evident. Quay's complexion was slightly gray, and his expression was haggard today. His hair, not combed as impeccably as usual, displayed blond strands belligerently curled in different directions around his face and ears, giving him an unkempt Robert Redford look. He had thrown on an old pair of faded jeans and added a navy crewneck sweater that bore a Ducks Unlimited logo on the right front. A gray T-shirt peeked above the neck of the sweater. His hiking boots seemed out of place here, but he'd obviously worn them for comfort. It was clear he didn't care about his appearance today, anyway.

He had pulled on his wrinkled Columbia jacket at the last minute after retrieving it from a loosely crumpled ball of clothes in the backseat of his truck.

Funny, Quay had thought to himself this morning while getting dressed, he sure would never be any competition for that Lucas Davenport who was the main man at the BCA. That Davenport guy could actually pose for a *GQ* magazine. "Just not my style," Quay mumbled aloud now, thinking about it again. Sam and John looked at him in confusion, not understanding what he was talking about.

Sam and John, on the other hand, had both dressed up a bit today, both making an attempt to be on their professional best for their meeting at Cameron. John had worn a navy sports jacket over a pair of Khaki pants. But he hadn't relinquished the plaid shirt with the button-down collar underneath the sports jacket. Nor had he worn a tie. He'd thrown a sweatshirt in the truck when he and Quay had come in this morning. It was cool, and he figured he'd be able to ditch the sports jacket as soon as they were done.

Relinquishing her usual blue jeans, Sam had pulled on khakis and topped them with a tan Sherpa jacket over a navy blue turtleneck. She thought the plaid, navy and tan flannel lining of the jacket made her look like she'd worked on coordinating a fashion statement. Not that she could ever lay claim to that kind of fashion thing.

Like Quay, Sam claimed a mantra to comfort. Her low heels had been the one concession to style. It seemed like a good idea. Her added height gave her body a slim model's look, and besides, she liked being on eye level with the guys when she went on one of these calls. Sam had tucked her auburn hair behind her ears and let it fall loosely over her shoulders today, so that she presented a more feminine form. With these two outdoorsmen, she'd thought to herself, she sometimes needed to accentuate her feminine points. Being uniquely feminine could come in handy sometimes. Regardless of their diverse

185

appearance, the trio would present a confident, unified, although semiprofessional front when they entered the doors at Cameron BioTech.

When they found a parking spot, John and Sam jumped out, following Quay who led at a brisk pace. Sam was first to notice Quay's second of hesitation, his halting steps. It was just the briefest moment. Then he paused and stared at the building. She and John looked at each other, realizing at the same time what this visit meant for Quay. They stopped, waiting for Quay to take a moment for reflection.

He began talking quietly. "This is the first time I've been back to Cameron since Karen's death." He remembered that day as a sharp, black and white, slow-motion video. He didn't even remember what he did after seeing her slump at the podium. How he'd gotten to her. He remembered holding her. He remembered the investigative crew had politely told him to leave even though he'd flashed his badge and demanded to stay. A fellow officer had calmly told him that he knew who he was and that at that moment he just needed to move away. Let them do their work, he'd said. He had to leave Karen to them. There was nothing more he could do. They'd told him they would handle it. He was supposed to go home and wait.

They'd told him that, but he hadn't been able to leave. He'd walked over to a nearby tree and lost everything in his stomach. Then he'd sat on the curb of the parking lot wondering how he was going to survive. And when they were done, he'd had to make arrangements to pick up her car and her belongings. There weren't words to describe the pain. It had been excruciating.

Now he was here again just a little over a year later. The first time back. The memories returned in floods of Technicolor. He swallowed hard, reached in his jacket pocket, pulled out a piece of bubblegum, deliberately opened the wrapper, and placed the square of gum in his mouth. He took a deep breath of the crisp autumn air and exhaled.

"Okay, let's do this." Sam and John moved in alongside him, and the three of them walked together toward the building.

Chapter 19

Detective Swede Olson greeted them in the lobby. When Quay had called to ask for help, Swede sounded pleased to be able to help him. He'd left his office at the police station as soon as he got the call. He knew and admired Thompson's diligence on any job. He pulled on a drab brown suit from a downtown men's discount store for the meeting, but he still looked fashionable compared to Thompson.

They shook hands all around as Quay made the introductions.

"As I told you on the phone, we've got a case developing that may tie into the break-in here. We need to know all the details you have, what you discovered when you got here the day after that last break-in," Quay began. "Who did you talk to? What were you told? What evidence were you able to collect?"

Swede noted the urgency in Thompson's voice and began.

"Sure. I'll tell you what I can. First, let's call the head security guy to join us. He's the one I worked with. I didn't give him a heads up about our coming today, but I think he's probably in."

Swede walked over to the security desk at the side of the lobby. He spoke with the man stationed at the desk, and the guard picked up a phone and placed a call.

Returning to the group, he explained, "The head of security will be right down. His name is Charlie Frank. He's a former MPD cop. Got injured a while back on the job and took an early retirement. Ended up here as security chief at Cameron."

"Oh, I know exactly who he is," interrupted Quay. The tone of his voice indicated that he wasn't impressed. "He and I had a few run-ins when we both worked MPD. I wasn't his favorite guy. This isn't going to be easy."

"Sorry, I didn't know that," answered Swede. "I've known Charlie a long time. He's always seemed like a steady kind of guy."

"Maybe he was at one time. And maybe he is now. But he sure didn't take it too well when I was promoted over him for the sergeant position. After that, he got into several questionable scrapes. I had to respond to a couple Internal Affairs interrogations about him."

"Oh, really?" Swede became even more interested. He stepped closer to Quay.

"He held a grudge, blaming me," Quay continued, "and from then on, it seemed like he tried to meddle in or obstruct every investigation I ran. When I picked up the job with the BCA, he let me know that he was glad I was leaving the department. He told me I didn't belong there, either. Called me an elitist and a few other choice terms. He was really pissed."

"You're kidding! I never would've believed it. I never heard anything about this. I thought he was glad to leave the PD."

"Yeah, he didn't mince words about his feelings for me. I guess he just thought he was the better cop and had been ignored."

Sam listened, shaking her head. "So what's his real problem, Quay? Do you think he was good enough? Or did he just think he was?"

"He was a little lazy. Screwed up a couple investigations by not doing the paperwork. Then there were questions about his being on the take. Something related to operations at a local bar. That's why he got passed over. But really he just wouldn't accept responsibility. He was the kind of guy who had a quick temper and was always quick to blame anybody else for his mistakes. In my opinion, it caught up with him."

The elevator doors opened, and Charlie Frank walked out, scanning the lobby and then spying the small group huddled off to the side. He smiled and waved at Swede Olson.

He appearance had changed since Quay had seen him last. He was balding now and had gained enough weight to produce a considerable paunch, which he'd tried to pull in by over-tightening his belt. Frankly, Quay thought, Charlie Frank looked like the stereotypical cop who'd had one too many Krispy Kreme donuts. His brown security uniform shirt was stretched taut across his chest and belly, and he looked as though it might pop the buttons at any moment. His bald pate gleamed under the lobby lighting, and remaining strands of graying hair were slicked back on the sides. Charlie Frank walked with a slight swagger toward the group, but when he spotted Quay, a scowl flitted briefly across his face.

He recovered quickly and managed to smile again as he reached out to shake Swede's hand.

"Hello, Swede. Good to see you here. I see you brought company. What's the occasion?"

Swede turned to Quay, John, and Sam, quickly introducing them.

Charlie glanced at Quay, then turned and directed his response to Sam and John. "Well, I know Thompson, but I don't think I've had the honor of meeting you two. Good to meet you." He extended his hand to them, ignoring Quay.

Sam and John both extended their hands and murmured hellos to Charlie.

Charlie turned back to Swede for an explanation.

"Well, Charlie, Thompson here called and asked me to meet him here. Your woman from the data room has been talking to the tech fellow at the BCA about the break-in you had here."

"Yeah? And?" Charlie couldn't hide his contempt as he looked toward Quay.

"Well," Quay picked up the line, stepping forward, "we've got some questions about the break-in and the e-mails that were sent from the Cameron computers. We have reason to believe they may be connected to something else we're investigating."

"Let's go upstairs to my office where we can talk in private." Charlie turned abruptly and began walking toward the elevators. Quay, Sam, and John looked at one another, shrugged, and followed.

Swede hesitated a moment then said, "You know what? I think I'll wait here for you awhile. I think Charlie can fill you in."

Quay turned and nodded. His look indicated that he understood that Swede realized his presence might cause more friction and bravado from Charlie while he was being interrogated by Quay. "Just don't leave yet, Swede. We'll still want to talk to you. This'll only take a few minutes, I'm sure."

"No problem. Got to do my detective thing, ya know. I just think it'll be too much extra paperwork," he joked as he walked toward the security desk in the lobby.

As they entered the elevator, Quay began explaining to Charlie the reason for their request.

191

"We've come across some information that may tie a murder into your recent events at Cameron."

"You've got to be kidding, Thompson. All we had was a break-in. Not a murder. You out drumming up business now?"

Sensing the tension between Quay and Charlie, John took over. He turned to Charlie as the elevator doors closed.

"Charlie, we think the break-in may have been more than—"

Charlie interrupted. "I don't understand. Is there something more here that we didn't find? I thought we had settled it when we figured out that there had been an e-mail sent from here, but that it didn't seem to have done any harm. We never had any proof of who sent it. Have you guys come up with something?" Charlie appeared to be becoming agitated, maybe even defensive.

"Well, that's what we're working on," explained Quay. "We have reason to believe that at least one, if not two murders were committed, relating to work being done here at Cameron. One may have been as a result of that e-mail. It has something to do with a group called SPARTA. You may remember them from some of the protests against Cameron BioTech."

When the elevator doors opened on the third floor, they stepped out, and Charlie led them to the right to his office at the end of the hall. The building was quiet today. Each of the office doors along the empty hallway was closed.

"Sure, I remember SPARTA," Charlie responded. "But that outfit turned out to be pretty harmless. What do you think you have now?" Charlie began nervously shuffling, moving from one foot to the other as he stopped outside the door to his office and fumbled in his pocket for keys. To Sam, it seemed to be unusual behavior. Why would Charlie seem so nervous about the mention of SPARTA?

Quay's cell phone suddenly erupted with an impatient ring. Quay reached into his jacket pocket to retrieve the phone and stepped several feet back down the hall to take the call. He nodded to Sam and John to stay with Charlie.

Sam and John stopped to wait with Charlie outside his office door.

"He said two murders. What's he talking about?" Charlie looked to John for the answer.

"Well, we believe a young girl connected with SPARTA, by the name of Annie Bell, may have been murdered by someone as a result of information she discovered about SPARTA's involvement with Cameron BioTech."

"Bullshit! I don't see how that could possibly be part of this break-in deal, and who was the other murder he was talking about?" Charlie attitude was defiant.

"I think Quay believes there may also be some tie-in to his wife's murder a year ago," Sam said softly.

"Oh, right! I knew it!" He bristled. "He'd try anything to cause trouble here. He'll look for any little clue to put it on Cameron and me as the head security guy." Charlie turned to point at Quay. "You know that guy has always had it in for me. He's done his best to ruin me."

Quay turned his back to them and listened intently to his caller. It was Boogie.

"Hey, Thompson, I think we've got something here. You know we decided the anonymous e-mails to

193

Elson were coming from a free account at a public location. Well, we were able to trace the incoming e-mail to Ernie Elson from a Minneapolis Public Library down by Lake Calhoun. Fortunately, the library is next to a Wells Fargo bank on a dead-end street. Also, lucky for us, the bank has security cameras on the roof that cover the street. We just met with the security at the bank and started looking at the films of cars passing through near the times the e-mails were sent. The same car was present each time. We were able to zoom in to get a good look at the plate. We just got the info from the databank."

"Good work, Boogie. What did you come up with?"

"Well, I think we got a bingo. The owner of the car is your security guy at Cameron."

"No kidding! You know our location?" Quay was speaking in a subdued voice and kept his back to the group down the hall. He didn't want to give away too much in case Charlie was listening to his conversation.

"Yup! That's why I thought you should know ASAP. You be careful out there, man. Charlie Frank may be your Manager who was running Ernie Elson."

"Will do, Boogie. Good work. Thanks for the heads up. You deserve a day off!"

"I'm going to take that recommendation to the top, man. Talk to you soon."

Quay clicked off and walked back over to join Sam and John in their discussion with Charlie. Charlie had become even more agitated, and his anger was clearly directed at Quay. The trio was still standing just outside Charlie's office door when Quay walked over to them.

"Well you oughta know, Cameron's my beat, guys." Charlie tried to resume a normal attitude but stared at Quay. "I would know if there was something going on here. I always figured it was outside. It has to be. There just hasn't been anything here to indicate it was an inside job!"

"As a matter of fact," Quay interrupted, "I just got word from our tech man at headquarters that he's traced some of the e-mails. Some e-mails regarding Cameron were sent to a fellow by the name of Ernie Elson. He's the head of the SPARTA group. We were able to follow the e-mail trails and also read them. The e-mails came from a public library down by Lake Calhoun."

Sam and John turned to look at Quay.

"What'd they find out?" Sam interrupted before Quay could finish.

"Well, it's very interesting." Quay looked intently at Charlie. "Seems that our man Charlie, here, was at the library each time an e-mail was sent to Elson. How do you explain that, Charlie?"

"What are you talking about?" Charlie's voice seemed to raise an octave. "You can't think I'd be involved in this. Here you go again, Thompson, looking to get me. Can't I even go to a public library? Why would I be doing something like that? What motive would I have?"

"That's what we'd like to know, Charlie," answered Quay as he moved to block the path to the elevator and Charlie's possible escape. Sam and John edged closer to Charlie.

"I've actually got a lot of questions." He decided he was going to do a little fishing and push Charlie a little harder. "I'd like to know why you were ordering Ernie

Elson to create disruptions at Cameron. And how did you get the money to pay him for his protesting and break-ins? He had to have been paid. That's where SPARTA got their money. The money trail had to come from somewhere. Want to clue us in, Charlie?"

Charlie glared at Quay. "Ernie Elson?" Charlie feigned ignorance, but it was clear he was rattled. "How the hell could I know him? You said he's connected with SPARTA. I wouldn't have anything to do with some crazy terrorist group."

Then he launched his preemptive attack.

"You always thought you were such a smart guy, didn't you, Thompson?" he sneered. "You always had to be in the spotlight, the big top dog. Climbing up the ladder is all you ever cared about. Always making a big name for yourself, aren't you? You're doing it again, just like before, aren't you? You don't care who you climb over. You had to push me right out of the system, didn't you? You knew I was better than you, so you just had to see to it that I was out of the way. Now you're still after me. With no good reason."

"What are you talking about, Charlie?" Quay sighed. "You and I used to work in the same unit in Minneapolis. But I never did anything to cause you trouble. It seemed more like you caused your own trouble."

Quay remembered Charlie's constant run-ins with the Internal Affairs guys. Charlie's name had come up frequently for alleged abuse and battering during the arrests he made. His name had also been connected with some cops who were on the take from a couple local bad guys. There was also the bar serving to minors. Charlie had known and ignored it, for a fee. Charlie had always been on the fringe of the accusations, but he'd managed to slip away from actual conviction. When Charlie Frank had injured his back on the job, it was a convenient way for the department to release him. He probably could have stayed on in a desk job, but the department didn't want him. Quay had been interrogated by IA when they were investigating Charlie. Quay had told them what he believed, but there wasn't any actual proof. After that, there wasn't much good blood between them. And now this.

"You were the cause of my trouble!" Charlie's voice was getting louder. "You always were a hot dog. Now you want to be a hot dog again and try to drag me into this murder investigation you've got going. Well you're not going to do it!"

Sam moved closer to Charlie, hoping to subdue him if necessary. Then with one sudden motion, Charlie grabbed Sam around the neck, dragging her roughly in front of him. At the same time, he yanked his gun out of his shoulder holster with his left hand brushing her breast as he reached across her. Sam jerked defensively. She tried to grab at Charlie, but he'd been too quick. His gun was pushed against the base of her head.

"Hey! Charlie! No!" Quay and John both yelled in surprise. Quay began to reach for his gun and then remembered he'd left it in his truck. They stood for seconds in a frozen tableau. It was up to Charlie to make a decision. For a big man, he could probably still make the moves, Quay thought.

Charlie smirked slightly as he pushed the gun harder against Sam's head. Slipping to the side of the hall, he yanked Sam out of Quay and John's reach. Sam said nothing but continued struggling against Charlie's control. In the struggle, she twisted her ankle, grimaced in pain, swore aloud, and stumbled forward as one of her heels broke. Charlie tightened his grip and yanked her back and up so that she was forced to stand on tiptoes and lean against him until she regained her footing. Quay and John tried to reach out to catch her, but Charlie quickly pulled her further out of their reach.

Ominous silence filled the hallway. Quay and John stared at Charlie. Their eyes shifted to Sam in unspoken communication. *It'll be all right*. Strands of auburn hair fell loosely over Sam's grimacing face as she gasped to catch her breath. She renewed struggling and pushing against Charlie's hold, hoping to find a weak resistance point, but Charlie pulled his arm more tightly around her neck, closing off her air. She began gasping slightly.

"You're not going to do it to me again, Thompson," Charlie began softly in a smug tone as he struggled with Sam. "I'm going to do it to you this time. Maybe it wasn't enough to lose your wife. I thought that would be enough to shut you down. How about your partner, too? Want to lose another woman? Want to take a chance?"

Quay felt like he'd been sucker punched. What was Charlie Frank talking about? What did he mean that losing his wife wasn't enough? He stood in paralyzed shock as Charlie dragged a struggling Sam down the hall. Charlie was moving toward what appeared to be the door to a back stairwell. Sam was grunting, gasping, and cursing at Charlie, fighting against each step.

"You idiot! You damn idiot! What are you doing? You dumb sonofabitch! Let me go! Now!" Sam's gasped in a raspy voice. Her voice was actually rising with each curse as she tried to pull more air into her lungs.

"Now, that's no way for a lady to talk." Charlie chuckled. He pressed the gun barrel hard into her temple until she was still as he used his other arm to pin her arms tightly against him.

John was the first to snap into action. John lunged toward Charlie. Quay stared at Charlie and Sam, frozen in disbelief. This man had truly gone crazy.

John and Quay realized pulling a gun now would only incense Charlie more. As John moved forward, Quay spoke clearly and calmly to Charlie.

"You don't really want to do this. You can make a different choice, Charlie. You know this isn't necessary. You know you can't get out of here that way. Let's just talk about this before you do something you'll regret. You haven't got anything to worry about yet, man. We can work something out. Just talk with us."

"I'm not talking to you," Charlie roared. "You can go fuck yourselves. I'm walking out of here with your sweet little partner, Thompson. You just wait and see. If you want her alive, you'd better stay right where you are for at least ten minutes. I might release her later after I get out of here, or I might just have to get rid of her—permanently. It's up to you whether she lives or dies."

His eyes were blazing with a mad passion. Then he paused, and a malevolent smile spread across his face. His eyes crinkled a bit at the joke he was making. "You get to make the choice again, Thompson." His tone was mocking now. "You should like that. You always did like making decisions."

He shoved the gun barrel harder against Sam's temple while pulling her more tightly to his chest. Sam flinched at the pressure of the gun barrel but picked up on Quay's attempt to divert him and joined in.

"Charlie." Sam tried to keep her gasping voice calm and soft. She tried to angle her head away from the gun barrel to look at Charlie. "Listen to them. You don't want to do this. Just let me go now. We can work out something to help you out."

Sam was truly frightened. She'd been caught totally off guard. She knew that she was in terrible trouble. Sam could see that Quay was still processing what was happening with Charlie. He was clearly numbed at the magnitude of the hatred Charlie had toward him. Sensing Quay's confusion, Sam eyed John who caught the look and took charge continuing the dialogue.

"Charlie, just think for a minute," John began. He looked again at Sam. Sam's eyes were pleading. John nodded slightly at her silent signals.

John began to concentrate on possible maneuvers Sam could use to escape. He was hoping he could signal Sam. But right now, nothing seemed possible. Charlie was an experienced cop. He knew all the moves, too. Hopefully he could distract Charlie long enough to give her an edge.

"Charlie," John continued as he took a tentative step toward the two of them, "give yourself a chance. You're closing out any opportunities for yourself here. At least let her go. Then you can go."

Charlie had backed all the way to the exit door at the stairwell. Making an awkward adjustment with the gun and Sam, he swiftly reached across Sam and placed his right hand over the smooth, black security panel next to the stair door and then resumed his defensive stance.

The framed panel was a high-level security clearance device. It identified users by their handprints. As soon as Charlie placed his hand on the panel, the automatic door began to swing open to the stairway. Realizing Charlie's plan, John and Quay sprang forward.

"You can both go to hell. See ya, suckers," called Charlie as he pulled Sam in front of him for cover while he quickly backed through the open door and slammed it closed. Wheeling around, Quay and his brother watched through the door's glass panel as Charlie made a clumsy grab at Sam's arm and dragged her struggling against him down the stairs.

Quay and John lunged and reached the stairwell door just as the door clicked and locked. Quay's fingers slipped off the edge of the door as the sound echoed through the hall. Instinctively, he tried to push it open. There was no doorknob, no lock to grab, no window to break. This was a secure door. It could not be opened by anyone but those who had authorization. Charlie had timed it perfectly. He was now in a secure stairway, heading somewhere out of the building. He knew this building better than anyone. He could go anywhere.

Quay pulled his cell phone from his pocket to call in support as he and John turned to race to the elevators. They both had the same thought. Get to the main lobby to have the building secured. Maybe they could beat Charlie, and they could lock him in.

Hal at the front desk answered Quay's call.

"Hello, Cameron BioTech Security. This is Hal."

"Hal!" Quay was yelling now. "Hal! You've got to lock up the building. Understand? Lock down! Now! Charlie Frank's just taken a hostage. He's trying to leave the building."

201

Hal seemed perplexed. "Charlie Frank? What are you talking about? Are you sure, man?"

"Yes, dammit, I'm sure. Now get on it. And while you're at it, have Swede there call in the MPD to block roads out of here. Now!"

"Right, I'm on it," Hal said and hung up.

The elevator seemed to crawl down to the main floor. When they reached the lobby, John veered off and ran to the security desk while Quay sped through the front doors and onto the plaza. John began shouting to Swede Olson and Hal at the front desk as soon as the elevator doors opened. "Get help! Get the roads blocked! *Now!*" The brothers were both on their phones.

Quay stopped on the plaza. The sun was bright. His eyes had to adjust. He squinted and scanned the parking lot. There were too many cars. He saw five vehicles pulling out. He made note in his mind of the color and make of each one. They were too far away to get the plates. He pulled out his cell phone and punched in speed dial for the dispatcher at the BCA.

"This is Thompson, and it's an emergency. Get the make, model, and tag number of a vehicle belonging to Charlie Frank." He paused and listened. "Yeah, I do mean the guy who heads up Cameron's security. He just took a hostage—my partner, Sam. And get any addresses connected with him. And I want it yesterday!"

Adrenaline flushed through his system. His confusion about Charlie's statements had worn off. He pushed it all to the back of his mind. He'd figure it all out later. His professionalism and experience took charge. He had to be detached and clearheaded if he was going to save Sam. This wasn't the time to go for a detailed evaluation.

This time, he swore to himself there was no way he was going to let Charlie Frank get away with his bad cop routine. He wasn't going to let him take Sam away from him.

John urged Quay into action when he came flying through the doors and out onto the plaza. He didn't slow as he passed Quay. He called over his shoulder on the run.

"Come on, Quay. He got out the back! They weren't able to secure the building soon enough. The security cameras show him taking Sam to a black Chevy Avalanche pickup out behind the building. Hal says it's got a big engine, Quay. He'll call us with the year and tag number." He was puffing as they climbed into Quay's vehicle.

Charlie's rage combined with panic to erupt into a volcanic flow of irrational thinking by the time he had pulled Sam out the back door. Sam continued to struggle against him, alternately digging her heels into the ground and kicking his shins. She was not going to go willingly with this crazy guy, by God. He tightened his arm across her chest and shoved the gun up under her breast.

"Listen, lady, if you want to live until we get to the truck, you'd better start cooperating. Otherwise, I'm gonna drop you right here. I don't need the extra baggage anyway, understand?"

"Why not just let me go then? That is, if you don't need me," Sam taunted. She was limping awkwardly, her one good heel clicking on the pavement as he pulled her along with him. She hoped she could get him talking. Maybe that would be the way out.

"I don't need you. I want you! You're the one who's really going to make Quay Thompson suffer. He deserves to suffer. Just like I did. I could see he's got a thing for you. Didn't take him too long to get over his little wifey, did it?"

"She was murdered more than a year ago. You're crazy! Besides, what are you talking about? Quay and I are just partners."

"Yeah, right. I thought maybe he'd slow down when I took his wife out. I thought—"

"You what?" Sam couldn't hide her astonishment. "*You* took his wife out? You killed her? What are you talking about? What'd she do to you?" Bile rose in her throat. The heat of anger overwhelmed her. She surprised herself with her bravado. She kicked her heel hard into the shin of Charlie's leg, slammed herself back into him, and pushed Charlie back against a nearby car.

But Charlie pushed back. He pulled her around and almost fell as they struggled. Then he regained balance. He was in control once again. Grabbing a handful of her hair in one hand, he pocketed his gun and seized her arm with the other. He dragged her roughly past three more cars parked up against the back of the building. After yanking open the driver's door of a black Chevrolet Avalanche pickup, he threw her violently onto the seat.

"Get down on the floor over there, bitch," he said as he continued to shove her onto the passenger floor.

"Curl up under the dash, dammit!" Charlie jumped into the driver's seat after Sam. He drew his gun again and pushed the muzzle against her back. Sam scrambled across the seat, twisted her body around, and sank to the floor on the passenger side. Her feet stretched up on the seat until she shifted enough to pull her feet together onto the floor. This wasn't a tiny pickup, but it was tight under the dash. The area she was now cramped into wasn't overly roomy, but she figured it was probably better than what she'd find in most pickups. She closed out Charlie's continued ravings. Surveying the truck's interior, she mused that this vehicle must have cost Charlie Frank a bundle. Now she dared to glare up at him.

"What'd Thompson's wife do to me? You asked. You really want to know? Nothing!" He revved the engine, threw the pickup into gear, and squealed away from the building. Speeding out of the parking lot, taking a left turn onto the exit road on two wheels, he began swerving in and out of city traffic. As traffic slowed, he veered to pass on the right. Angry horns blared and tires screeched as Sam tried to find a grip to steady herself.

Taking the pursuit into the parking lot and scanning the lot for Charlie's truck, Quay backed out of the narrow parking space and raced up the row to the end of the parking lot, then hesitated.

"Which way?" he asked and looked at John. John was on his cell phone. He was waiting on the Cameron people to come up with the info on Charlie.

"They have everyone's info on file at Cameron. The guy at the desk was in panic mode. It'll take him a minute or two. We can start to head out in the direction we think Charlie was going, though. This way is probably my best guess. Maybe we can catch him." John pointed to the right, giving Quay directions as he listened on the phone.

"I put a call into the headquarters, too," said Quay. "They're sending in cars, and they'll call back with addresses and car info, too. We'll need to direct them where to head. What do you think?"

Quay floored the accelerator and flew toward the nearest exit. He was glad they had come in his truck. He knew his way around the Cities and was most comfortable handling his own truck. He had selected the biggest engine he could get when he bought it. At the time, he'd needed the extra power to tow his boat. In addition to the extra horsepower, he had the added advantage of sitting high enough to see over the tops of several vehicles ahead of them. He just hoped he had the speed to catch up to Charlie.

"Has the guy at Cameron come through with an address on Charlie yet? Do we even know what he's driving? Where's he headed? We need to make a decision soon."

John turned to Quay as he listened intently on his cellphone for a second. "The guy at Cameron said he was probably headed west. He's driving a black Chevy Avalanche. He thinks he must be heading toward the frontage road and onto the freeway. Is that to the right?"

"Yeah. My best guess is that from there he'll head out to the 35W freeway and go north. He probably thinks there'll be less chance he'll get caught up in traffic going that direction. It's early yet. Let's try that direction. With the bulletin out to the locals and state patrol, we'll have a spotter soon."

As soon as his call went to dispatch at the headquarters, all units would be pulled. This was one of their own who had been kidnapped. There wouldn't be any lingering around the coffee pot with this one. Sam was well liked.

Quay almost pitied Charlie. Poor, dumbass Charlie didn't stand a chance. He just hoped that Sam did. Charlie appeared to be crazy enough that he just might kill her. Especially if he thought he was going to be caught. He was a desperate man. The last thing Quay wanted was a standoff with negotiators using Sam as the bait. Charlie was experienced. Despite the fact that he was completely irrational, he knew all the negotiation strategies.

Quay raced furiously, dodging in and around moving vehicles, blasting his horn angrily at anything and anyone who got in his way. John fumbled around under the seat.

"Where's your bubble, Quay? Don't you have one?" he yelled, referring to the portable, flashing, blue strobe light for the roof.

"Ah, shit. I threw it under the backseat the last time I had the truck detailed. Can you crawl back and find it?"

John released his seatbelt and pushed his lanky frame across the center console. He stretched to reach back and under the seat until finally his fingers touched the smooth plastic of the flasher light. He tugged it toward him, latching on the globe. He twisted back into the passenger seat, snapped his seatbelt, reached out the window, and attached the bubble light onto the roof.

Once the light was in place, vehicles began to pull over in response to the light flashing behind them. If they still didn't notice the light, they heard Quay's incessant honking. Finally, Quay had a free lane to maneuver. His engine roared as he pushed the speedometer up.

Suburban houses sped by in a blur. Black and whites responding to the call now blocked traffic at the side street intersections as Quay's dark gray truck streaked past. John waved a salute of thanks to the brothers in blue as they passed.

Quay began to feel a belt of tightness clenching at his chest. He focused on the road ahead, straining to see Charlie's black Avalanche moving through the traffic.

"Damn, damn, sonofabitch! Why didn't I see it coming?" Quay vented his anger as he pounded on the steering wheel. His misguided judgment frustrated him.

"We'll get him, Quay," John assured him. "Sam will be okay. She knows how to take care of herself." But it was clear the brothers shared their fear. This wasn't going to be easy for any of them.

Chapter 20

Charlie continued boasting to Sam as he drove. Sam listened in silence.

"Thompson needs his comeuppance. He needs to suffer a little. Actually he needs to suffer a lot. He needs to know what I went through. I lost my life. He just lost his wife! I don't feel sorry for that sonofabitch in the least."

When Charlie had forced Sam to crawl down onto the floor of the passenger side, she'd managed with no small effort to turn herself around and was now curled up facing Charlie. Her knees wedged against the seat, with her feet squeezed between the middle hump and the bottom of the seat. She jutted her head out from her uncomfortable niche and tilted her face up at an awkward angle toward the driver's seat and Charlie. Her left ankle began tingling and throbbing, and she knew it would become numb before long. She wished more than ever that she hadn't chosen to wear her heels today. One heel was poking into her opposite ankle. So much for demonstrating her powerful femininity, she thought. She could barely move. She wiggled her toes, trying to push out of her shoes to give her feet and legs some comfort. Maybe it would help with what already felt like slowly swelling ankles, too.

She cocked her head to the side and looked up to get a clear view of Charlie. She knew she needed to have eye contact with him. He had to see her as a person, not just a cowering, simpering female he'd captured to get revenge on Quay. She had to somehow involve him in a conversation with her. He appeared to want to defend himself. He wanted to vent, to brag. So she decided she'd give him his forum. It might be enough to distract him. Maybe she could take his mind off his driving and escape. Maybe the conversation would create a false sense of security for him.

Sam had to admit to herself that she was scared, really scared. But she knew she couldn't expose any fear. If she did, Charlie would see her as weak and easy to manipulate. She also reasoned that by now, John and Quay would have gotten out of that building and would be racing after them. She knew Quay. He wasn't about to allow Charlie Frank to get away. Her job right now was to stay alive. Quay would have said it was her prime directive. Her experience also told her that keeping Charlie distracted might help. Distracting Charlie would be her job while Quay and John did theirs.

Chapter 21

Ernie Elson considered himself to be one lucky man. Contrary to what his anonymous attacker believed and definitely desired, Ernie had not died when he'd been forced off the road and crashed. Sometime after the crash, Elson had squeezed open his eyes and looked into the concerned face of a woman. He had no idea how long he had been out. He recognized the woman's face. She was a neighbor lady. She told Ernie that she was driving home when she saw the wreckage and realized someone was still inside. She realized it was her neighbor's vehicle. Clearly distraught by her discovery, she pulled "poor Mr. Elson," as she kept calling him, out of the wreckage. He'd had to assure her repeatedly that he was all right and there was no need to call anyone. She had finally agreed to just drive him to a nearby doctor's office after he'd refused to go to the emergency room. Too far to go, he'd insisted. Luckily for him, he thought, she'd bought it. She had even insisted on waiting for him and giving him a ride home.

The doctor told him he had a couple broken ribs and a concussion. He also stitched up a good-size cut on his forehead. One ankle was sprained. But fortunately that was all. He knew it was incredible that he had so few injuries—what's more, even survived. Other than the few bruises and sore muscles he'd been nursing, he was all right. He was alive. That was all that mattered. Still he hurt like hell. It was difficult to move with any speed.

The doctor told him he was very lucky. His wife had nearly fainted when he'd walked in later that day. She'd gone overboard playing nursemaid to him while at the same time nagging and cursing him for his stupidity. She'd called to have the car towed to a local body shop. All the loose ends were wrapped up. And his attacker obviously didn't know that Ernie was still alive or he'd be at his door right now.

Evidently no one bothered to notice that there was no news about his death or his accident for that matter. If he had been following up, he probably would have come back for Ernie again to finish the job. Maybe he was busy or too distracted. It'd only been a couple days. Ernie decided that was his advantage.

Ernie Elson was smiling now. He believed it was more than luck that had kept him alive. It was fate! He had been saved from death to be the one who revealed the true evil lurking at Cameron BioTech. He knew now that evil wasn't only lurking in the research being done by Cameron. The evil also lurked in the form of its employees. And he was confident he knew which ones they were.

Ernie was sure his life had been spared for one reason only. He was meant to make a difference in the world. He was positive he had a mission. This was a new mission. A mission more important than any he'd ever had in Nam.

He knew The Manager. He'd seen him. He'd seen that face when the man had driven by to take one last look at Ernie in the wrecked truck. Ernie had been barely conscious, but he'd seen that face through his bloody haze just before passing out. Ernie had memorized the face. He realized he knew the man from Cameron BioTech. He was sure of it. And now that he'd discovered who his Manager was, he knew he could do it. He could shut down the research labs. He could discredit Cameron BioTech. Their operations would come to a satisfying ending, all thanks to him.

He didn't go back to work that day or the next. He called in sick. He was sure that no one would question his absence. He'd provided a solid cover with his stories about his wife. That was just one more reason he was sure this was meant to be his mission. He'd been inadvertently prepared for it.

The first thing he did the next day was to begin his own detective work. He got online and managed to pull down a list of names of employees from the Cameron website. Fortunately for him, and unfortunately for his attacker, most of the employees also had pictures next to their names. He recognized Charlie Frank as the head security man at Cameron. That was the man. The man's picture was next to his name right on the main site. That face was etched in his memory.

How interesting, he thought. That very man had been opening the doors to thieves at Cameron BioTech while pretending to be a person who provided security for the company. Well, well, well. There was much more here than met the eye, Ernie realized. The bile of revenge rose in Ernie's throat. He would make a difference, and it wouldn't just be something he did for SPARTA. He would make a difference that would affect the world.

Ernie Elson began to plan how he could bring Charlie Frank down. He was an evil man. He must be stopped. And then there was all the evil happening daily behind the doors of Cameron BioTech. Two kinds of evil must be dealt with here. He needed a plan that would bring Cameron BioTech down at the same time as the cunning Charlie Frank, his Manager. The very thought of holding such power at this moment made him smile. He'd show them what a lowly teacher could do! And his brainchild SPARTA would gain fame to boot. This was going to be a "twofer," he thought with a contented smile.

Ernie had just pulled into the Cameron parking lot to make a surprise visit to Charlie Frank when Charlie Frank flew by. He recognized him as the driver in the familiar black Chevy Avalanche pickup. Then, in what seemed like seconds, another sleek, dark gray pickup flew by, following and obviously chasing Frank. He'd seen two men in the second pickup, and from the looks on their faces, he thought they were pretty angry. And he was positive they were cops. He'd gotten just a glimpse, but he recognized one of the men as the one who'd visited his house to ask questions about Annie.

Ernie smiled to think that Charlie might have gotten himself in a jam. How fortunate. Maybe Ernie could help with Charlie Frank's problems. *By adding to them*, he thought happily. He could already guess where Charlie was heading. Ernie Elson had done his homework on Charlie Frank. Ernie wouldn't need to join the chase. He knew of a way he could beat them all. If Charlie Frank was heading north to his cabin, and he was fairly certain that he was, Ernie was going to make sure there was a surprise waiting for him. Ernie turned his car around, exited the parking lot, and headed toward the small Crystal Airport in the northern suburbs.

Ernie had been careful with his money. He had managed to put away quite a reserve as a result of his SPARTA activities as well as his work for the Manager. He'd used part of it to purchase a small property in the north woods near Lake Superior. Then he'd invested in a small plane, which he stored in a rented hangar at the Crystal Airport. He'd never shared his successes and private joys with anyone, not even his wife. Now everything was all coming together.

Chapter 22

Sam had curled as well as she could under the dash and now rested her head against the edge of the front passenger seat. God, how she hoped Quay was okay. She was sure all of this would have stirred up all the old anxieties for Quay. She worried that he would be having flashbacks to Karen's death.

He'd finally begun to pull away from that. Recently, she'd also begun to sense that Quay was beginning to have different feelings toward her. Feelings that weren't just limited to her as a partner. They understood each other. They had bonded.

Sam now realized she had to stay alive for more than just herself. She had to come out of this in one piece for Quay. He didn't need to add another woman's death to his suitcase of guilt just when he was beginning to emerge into real life again. He would blame himself all over again. One more death would mean a kind of death for him, too.

Sam wanted a good life for Quay. He truly was a good man. He didn't deserve this. Right now, she was also beginning to believe that maybe she cared for him and wanted some kind of a life with Quay—if not together, at least as partners. That settled it. She would do everything in her power to stop this madman.

As Charlie Frank sped on to the 35W freeway ramp heading north, Sam's mind became a wild eddy of scenarios. She lifted herself up a bit to see over the seat and peer through the back passenger window. She tried to see billboards and signs on the southbound side of the freeway as they flew past. She knew where she was. She guessed where Charlie was heading. Then she began developing her survival plan.

Sam surveyed the interior of the vehicle. She'd seen a black, canvas duffle bag perched on the backseat. So, perhaps Charlie had already been planning on a trip of some sort before this day began. He was packed for travel. Hopefully, he was going to be in the open so Quay would be able to give chase. That meant they had to stay on I35W going north.

She and Quay had surmised that Annie Bell's murder scene at the North Shore was chosen because the killer had connections there and perhaps had knowledge of the area. Maybe Charlie had connections to the Bell girl's murder, too, since everything seemed to be linked to Cameron BioTech. Charlie might even be returning to the scene of the crime. She didn't know anything for sure, but she did know that right now it appeared that Charlie was getting away and taking her along for the ride.

Where was Quay? She prayed a fervent, silent prayer that he and John were following and knew where she was being taken. She wished there was some way she could signal Quay and John.

While Sam silently processed her situation and plotted her next move, Charlie intently plotted his escape. He'd hoped that if he hopped onto north I35, he would be able to get a decent lead. He might even be able to lose anyone pursuing him. He knew Thompson and his brother would be pulling out all the stops. They'd call out the cavalry. He knew the routine.

Thompson had to be so pissed. He laughed to himself. Served Thompson right. Charlie was just beginning to serve up payback. Thompson wouldn't even have the beginning of an idea of what had happened.

217

Right now he was well ahead of the pack. Further up the road, he had a spot where he would pull off the freeway onto a side country road. He knew this part of the state better than anywhere else. This was his home territory. Thompson was in so much trouble and so out of luck—again. He laughed again.

When he reached Sandstone, he planned to pull off the freeway and take a county highway up to Duluth. From there, he could circle west around Duluth and take another county road through the backcountry up toward his cabin. He'd pull back onto Highway 61 when he got close. Thompson and company wouldn't be expecting him to take the back roads. They wouldn't be able to track him there. He would fly like an eagle! Such satisfaction. Such purity of planning. It was such providence that he had mapped out this route and packed it all up this week. Getting rid of Elson closed that door. This run ahead of Thompson was just a little hitch. He could still get away. He had the means and the cash. And the brains. He laughed out loud. He'd done it all.

He was so elated he couldn't help bragging to Sam.

"You know what's happening, missy? I've outmaneuvered your buddy Quay Thompson and his group. It's all about what I know and the rest of them don't."

Sam noticed his eyes had taken on a wild, edgy look. This guy was purely crazy. She shivered. He had begun sweating profusely; the combination of what she believed was his adrenaline rush and the exertion of kidnapping her had created a shower of sweat that was now pouring in winding rivulets down the sides of his forehead. Sam watched as sweat stains bled slowly across his tan security shirt where his paunch bunched into rolls and pushed against the steering wheel. He'd laid his gun next to him on the seat. She watched as he pulled a cloth handkerchief out of his back pocket to swipe at his brow.

The he continued with his monologue. "What do I know that they don't, you're thinking. What I have, my dear, is a neat little hideaway north of Duluth. I told some of my friends that I have a place up past Duluth, but they don't know exactly where. I never told them! And Northwoods Country is a big area. They'll never find me. They'll never find you! And we'll be long gone by the time they figure it out." He laughed again and threw the handkerchief down on the seat where it covered his pistol.

Sam squirmed to get into a better position. Now she bent toward the seat so her back wedged tightly against the bottom of the dash and her knees tucked snuggly up to her chin. Thank heavens the passenger seat had been pushed back for more legroom. She still had to arch her neck and lift her head at an awkward angle to look at Charlie. Her bare heels were wedged against the console, which lay between the leather bucket seats. She thought she must look like a crunched up comma. She tried to readjust herself to give her legs more room by pushing her back more toward the door. Her ankle hurt, and she reached around to rub it. She pulled off her knee-high socks and concentrated on her throbbing ankle. Maybe she could play on his sympathy, get him to drop his guard. Then she could get the gun!

"Charlie," she whined, "I can't ride like this way all the way to Duluth! Don't you think I could sit on the seat next to you?" She squirmed to reposition herself and display her discomfort.

"Nice try, little chicky, but not a chance." He glanced toward her. "You're just going to have to stay put for a while. I might let you up later—that is, if you're really good." He made what sounded like a snorting laugh.

Charlie's nervousness was escalating despite his bravado. She'd noticed how the stain of his sweat continued to etch across his shirt. She would have to make a move soon.

Sam eyed the pistol on the seat. The barrel was just peeking out from under the handkerchief Charlie had thrown there.

Charlie glanced at her and followed her eyes as she looked at the pistol. He reached out and snatched it up, handkerchief and all, in a move that would have impressed a snake flicking its tongue.

"No way," he growled. "You're not going to stop me. Nobody is—not even your boyfriend, Quay." He swiftly tucked the pistol into the side storage pocket in the driver's side door.

Sam made a decision. She used Charlie's distraction with the gun to slide her hand out of sight and into her pants pocket. Her cell phone was on. All she had to do was get it on, push the mute button, and dial the preset number she had for Quay. Then she would leave the line open. If she could slide it up close to the console, Charlie wouldn't be able to see it, and the console would hide it. It would be tricky, but it was worth a shot. Quay would be able hear any conversation and could use her cell to track them.

Charlie continued his rant. "The trick is how to get to and around Duluth. With any luck, we could get there in a couple hours. Then, from there, it'll only be a little over an hour to the cabin, if I can maintain the speed." He was talking to himself, ignoring her. He turned on the police scanner he'd installed on the dash and began listening to the chatter. Sam was glad for the noise. It would cover any beeps from her phone.

The police scanner was mostly static. They were out of range. Charlie fiddled with it, trying to pull in departments as they passed each city. Several units had called in, trying to get the description of Charlie's pickup. They were rounding up support, he noted. The hunt was on. It also sounded like the Thompson boys were on the freeway somewhere behind them.

"Do you hear that?" needled Sam. "They're already out after you. They know where you're going. You don't stand a chance. Give it up, Charlie. You're going to lose again."

"Shut up!" Charlie glared at Sam. "You just shut your face. I'm listening. What I know and they don't is that I'll be past Duluth and almost to my place by the time they even begin to figure out where I'm heading. You just shut the fuck up when I tell you to. I've got the horses with my truck. I can take all of them. I'll outrun even their fastest vehicle. I'll be through before they even begin!" He stomped down on the accelerator, and the pickup lurched forward at renewed speed.

The scanner continued with frenetic chatter among police departments and their patrols. They were reaching out for the state patrol now.

Charlie's pickup was edging toward the 100 mph mark now. He pounded his horn madly while flashing his lights as he approached cars in the lanes ahead of him.

"Charlie," Sam said. "It's warm in here, don't ya think? Why don't you turn on some air? You're sweating a bunch."

"I told you to shut the fuck up!" Charlie screamed. He reached across the seat and smacked her with an open hand across her cheek. An angry welt rose on her cheek; blood began to trickle toward her chin from a small cut caused by his ring. The sudden motion caused Charlie to swerve onto the shoulder. He adjusted and pulled back into the lane but had to swerve to the side again when cars refused to move out of his way. Several times, his rear wheels spun into loose gravel on the shoulder of the road. The pickup fishtailed wildly, but his four-wheel drive kicked in, and Charlie quickly brought it under control.

"I knew this'd be a rough chase, but I also know that I've got the edge. I was a cop. I know the tactics. I know the standard strategies, but I'm thinking outside the box. I will pull this off. It'll be tricky; timing is everything. But I have the plan. It's an excellent plan. A perfect plan. And those guys don't have any idea what my plan is. They can't catch me if they stick with the standard police procedure. That alone gives me an extra edge. I'm a lot smarter than you think, little girl."

Sam retreated further under the dash, closing up her comma shape, wedging herself tightly against the underside of the dash in an effort to protect and steady herself. She listened to the scanner chatter. She understood she had no idea what this guy was going to do. He was a ticking time bomb.

Through it all, the horn blaring, the lights flashing, the rear tires swerving off the road, Charlie smiled. A broad, toothy grin covered his face. My God, Sam realized, he was enjoying this!

Charlie was enjoying this. In fact he was having the time of his life. He had been involved in his share of car chases in his day. So this was a piece of cake. He was actually having fun. No problem. No problem at all.

Beneath him, huddling on the floor under the dash, Sam's terror was mounting.

Chapter 23

By the time Quay and John entered the ramp to I35W, Charlie was twenty-five miles north, flying past Forest Lake. Charlie had a good lead. But with any luck, Charlie didn't know what Quay had in mind. Quay had begun to put together his own plan.

Quay was waiting to hear from the choppers. They needed those choppers here now, this minute, to keep track of Charlie. They couldn't lose Charlie now. Quay's cell phone rang. After the initial chatter with the various departments, Quay and John had agreed to stay off the regular two-way as much as possible. The scanner was open to the public—and possibly to Charlie if he was using a scanner. And he probably was. Charlie would have planned for an escape.

After a few calls, the various departments and patrols had agreed to put on an act for Charlie's benefit. Quay hoped Charlie would be lulled into a false sense of security by what he was hearing on the scanner. Any false leads they could throw at Charlie would help them.

His cell phone jarred him back. He grabbed for his jacket pocket while holding the wheel with his left hand.

He tapped it open and answered abruptly, "Yeah? Thompson here."

The line was silent—except he could hear a background noise of some sort. Quay listened intently and then heard the sound of a police scanner. A muffled voice overrode the scanner. It was Sam. She was talking to Charlie! She had gotten her cell line open somehow. *Good thinking, Sam!*

Quay listened as Charlie began ranting about a place past Duluth.

Quay covered the mouthpiece and turned to John.

"John, it's Sam! She's got a line open on her cell! Charlie doesn't know. He's talking about some place up past Duluth."

Relief began to sweep through Quay. Sam was all right. And she was thinking. She was helping.

"We need to keep my line open, too. Use your cell to call in and see if HQ can get a fix on her phone. And find out about helicopters. Is the highway patrol working on getting their choppers in the air?"

John called BCA headquarters and waited for what seemed to be an excruciatingly long time. Finally an answer came through.

"Quay, they're working on the phone. Boogie thinks he can track her as long as the line is open," John said. "We should hear about the choppers in a couple minutes."

Seconds later, John took a call from the security officer, Hal, at Cameron. He grabbed a piece of paper lying on the seat and began writing furiously.

"Thanks, Hal. You're a good man," he said as he signed off.

Turning to Quay, he explained, "Hal pulled up the information on Charlie's vehicle. It's a 2008 Avalanche. He's got the license number. And he says Charlie's supposedly got pretty good power in that truck. He's been bragging to the guys that he got it trucked out with a special V8 engine. He'd crowed about how he souped it up to have the speed of a Corvette. The problem is, with speed like that, he's taking a chance of going airborne with the weight of the light truck bed. We'd better not push him too much."

"There's a lot more. Hal says Charlie's probably headed north of Duluth – just like what you heard from Sam's cell phone. Hal says the word around Cameron is that Charlie has a cabin up off Highway 61 by Temperance River. He was somewhat secretive about it. Nobody knows much about it, except that he did let it slip a couple times when he was yakking it up with the boys in security at Cameron. Couldn't resist bragging about it, I guess. It sounds like it's more than a cabin, from what he was telling the guys. He also bragged that he's got a stash of money, but he wouldn't say where it came from.

"According to Hal, the guys were always needling him about his expense account. They couldn't figure out where he was getting all the money he flashed around. The Bureau is following up. They'll get Charlie's W-2 records from Cameron, his bank records, and a record of the income from his disability pension payments from the police force. The guys are also working on locating real estate listings under his name. They can track that down through real estate tax payments. Boogie talked with Hal and asked him to tell us as soon as he has the location for us. We should have it within the next few minutes."

Quay heaved a deep sigh of relief. He began to ease back on the accelerator.

"Well, at least we've got a glimmer of good news. It sounds like he's most likely heading to that place of his north of Duluth. Let's just take it easy. Those damn choppers are coming, aren't they?"

"Yup! They should be up soon and heading onto I35 north according to our boss at the Bureau. We'll be up there ahead of Charlie Frank. We're not going to let harm come to one of our own. We'll get Sam back, Quay."

"The combination of the state choppers and keying in on Sam's phone GPS should help locate him. Then we can just let him go on his way. We'll be able to sneak in ahead of him. He'll have a false sense of security."

"Sounds good to me," John agreed.

Heaving another sigh, Quay changed the subject. "You know our new state patrol choppers have got the same capability as army choppers. I was just thinking about that. Charlie's got that brand-new Avalanche. If it's tricked out like he claimed it is, my best guess is that he's got a GPS tracking system." Quay looked at John and grinned with satisfaction. "Poor Charlie's favorite vehicle is going to do him in."

"Oh, right," John answered as he put it together. "The chopper guys will be able to lock onto the vehicle's GPS. Charlie can travel wherever he wants while his own GPS continues to track him without him even knowing it. Once it's locked on, he can't get away. So we won't need to track Sam's phone."

"Right," answered Quay. "We won't have to worry about her losing signal. As soon as we know they've locked onto Charlie Frank's pickup, I'll be able to close down the phone line with Sam. Then she won't have to worry about discovery. Who knows what that idiot would do if he discovered she was signaling us. I hope she'll figure that out when the line goes dead."

"If we can pull all this off, it will make nabbing him a lot easier." John let out a sigh of relief.

"I'm really glad we won't have to get involved in a high-speed chase with Charlie. I love the speed and adrenaline rush, man, but it puts too many innocent lives in danger, and frankly, I'm getting too old for that stuff."

"I'm with you," John agreed. "Okay, why don't I check in again? They should have some news by now. I'm guessing the chopper guys will have thermal imaging capability, too. That will come in handy, too."

"Yeah, but you know that, contrary to Hollywood's fiction, we won't be able to use it while they're in the pickup. Thermal imaging can't see heat of objects through insulated materials, or metal. It probably will be useful later, though, if he's out in the open at that cabin or in the woods."

John's phone rang. He answered and listened, said a quick thanks as he rang off, and turned to Quay. "Two state highway patrol helicopters have just lifted off from the downtown St. Paul airport, so it'll take them just a couple minutes to catch up to our location. Then they can move ahead to check up on Charlie. They'll work with the guys on the GPS tracking."

Quay was still running with his lights and sirens on while pushing his truck to speeds over eighty. He really wished he could make that cabin before Charlie got there.

"You know, I had another thought. Maybe the guys in the air can follow at enough distance to not be heard by Charlie. I don't want to spook him. They can work with the local spotters, too. The sheriffs and highway patrols can relay his position on the scanners as he goes by. Charlie will be expecting that. He won't expect them to chase him, because he knows that they'll figure it's too dangerous. We can use the scanners to share that information. We can play him along a little

228

while. I don't think he'll realize that we'll be tracking him without their help. I'm guessing he's been out of the loop too long to keep up with the latest technology. At some point, he'll try to lose the local spotters. When he does that, we can follow him without him knowing what we're up to."

"Okay, sounds good," answered John. "If we're not so close on his tail, he may ease up on the speed. It'll be safer for Sam, at least until he gets to where he wants to go."

"So give them another call. Let's have the office set it up with the various departments to use cell phones instead of the scanners for our real plans. We can have them patch us in by phone. Let's use the scanner to distract and mislead Charlie into thinking we're just using the highway patrol and locals as spotters. If we lose sight of him, so much the better. It'll give him a false sense of security. Maybe we can set up some fake scanner calls, too. See what you can do, John. And also," he paused, thinking for a second, "see if we can patch a direct link with my cell phone to the chopper pilots."

"Got it. I'll call. You just handle the driving there." John dialed the office and explained the plan. Dispatch assured him they would get on it right away. They would get a system going within minutes. The highway patrol cars could sit on top of overpasses in visible locations. They'd be able to spot Charlie and pinpoint his location and relay it without pursuit.

Five minutes later, John and Quay heard the repetitive *thwomp, thwomp, thwomp* of helicopter rotor blades echoing overhead. Two state patrol choppers dipped down and hovered briefly ahead of them to say hello and let them know they'd gotten the clearance for their plan. They were new, white Bell helicopters that could take up to four passengers.

"God, they're huge," John said. "If nothing else, they can intimidate!"

Cars ahead and behind them pulled over and stopped. People were obviously confused and worried. People were peering up out of their car windows at the big, white birds. Truckers had pulled over and climbed out of their cabs to get a better look. The choppers were so close they could see the pilots inside.

The two big birds lifted off in unison like white clouds of thunder. Within seconds, their rotors made only a distant rumble. With luck, they'd be able to stay above the clouds, silencing their echoing rotors while zeroing in on Charlie's truck using the radar and the GPS tracking.

Boogie called back with the cell phone number of each of the pilots in the choppers. That would also give them an advantage. Now they could keep informed of Charlie's whereabouts without having to use the dispatch or the scanner.

Quay dropped his speed and settled into a steady eighty miles per hour. He kept his bubble on top to help clear the way for them, but he doused the siren. They had more time now. They'd moved beyond most of the traffic from the Cities and were coming up on Hinckley. Hinckley was a town with a history that included fur trading in the 1800s and a fire that had wiped out the town. Now it was home to a large casino that pulled in the resort crowds from several surrounding lakes. It was far enough north of the Cities that traffic was considerably lighter here. It would be even less once they passed Hinckley.

John glanced over at his brother. Quay had suddenly become silent. It was obvious Quay was still worried about what Charlie would do to Sam when he got to his cabin. John guessed Quay was reviewing everything Charlie had said. He was afraid Quay would begin reliving the last two years, and every iota of his guilt would return.

"Quay? Do you want me to drive? Give you some time to think?" John finally asked.

"No. That's okay. I'm okay, John." He paused. "But, you know, I just can't figure it out. Why did Charlie just go off on me? We hadn't given him enough information to make him believe he was done for. He could have talked his way out of it. Everything we had was circumstantial. He had to know that. He's got enough police background to know that.

"And you know, actually, I'd even forgotten Charlie Frank was the man in charge of security at Cameron. Karen never talked about him. He wasn't a big deal. As far as I knew, he was never considered a suspect. I didn't learn he was the security chief until after Karen was murdered. But it didn't click as being important. I wasn't allowed in on the investigation of Karen's murder. I've never had any other reason to go over to Cameron BioTech."

"Yeah, I agree," John nodded. "But maybe he was expecting you to show up."

"Why? What set him off? Am I part of his problem? Was he just trying to pull me into an investigation? Was that his motive? And if so, I want to know fucking why!" Quay's voice rose as he pounded the steering wheel in frustration. "For someone who supposedly just has a grudge against a former coworker, this whole deal is fairly weird. All I did was answer questions in an IA investigation about him. I didn't convict him!"

"So you got any ideas? Let's walk through it."

Quay was momentarily distracted as he braked behind a motorist who was refusing to give way. He moved into the left lane, got behind another slowpoke, and honked at the young kid in the beater ahead of him. The kid sped up and pulled into the right lane. He flipped an angry hand signal at Quay as they passed.

"Punk!" Quay muttered as he stepped it back up to his cruising speed.

"Let's ask ourselves the questions," he continued, back on track again. "John, how do you think Charlie Frank is connected to Ernie Elson and SPARTA? More importantly, how is everything connected to Karen's murder?"

John took over. "Charlie himself suggested that all of this was connected. But I just don't get it. Where's the money coming from to finance the SPARTA activities and protesting? There's got to be money behind it. If that's what happened, why are they doing it? Why does someone want them protesting? What's the benefit? Negative attention for Cameron BioTech? Why? And how is Charlie Frank involved? That's the big question."

Quay shook his head. He spit out a tasteless piece of bubblegum, tossed it into his ashtray overflowing with wrappers, and popped in a fresh piece of bubblegum. John noted the ashtray filled with a disgusting pink mass of chewed gum and wrappers. It was almost as bad as cigarette butts, he thought, but not quite. However, he wasn't about to complain to Quay now. Quay's driving was still steady, but he noticed Quay seemed to be driving on autopilot. Even though he was now cruising at a slower speed between seventy and eighty miles per hour, he was still dodging cars as they pulled into the right lane out of his way. But he wasn't talking. He had gone deep into memories and speculation.

After several more minutes of driving in silence, John had a new idea. "I don't know, Quay. I don't know the answers. What I do know is that we've got to get Charlie. He's got all the answers.

"So how about this, Quay? Can we get one of those choppers to set down somewhere up the road and pick us up? If we could, I could have one of my men meet us near Lutsen with a car. We could take it from there, head to Charlie's cabin, and be at the cabin waiting for him. Or, better yet, if we can find a clearing, we could drop in close to his cabin. We've got the location. We're pretty sure that his plan is to go there. He doesn't know that we know about the place. One of the choppers could still keep him pinpointed and let us know when he was pulling in. If he veers off, our men up there could pick up the tail. Either way, we'd have him. What do you think? It might give us a break."

"I just pray to God that's where he's heading," answered Quay. "If we do that, we want to be sure he's not going to turn off before there. Can we do it and pick up the car north of Lutsen after we're sure he's heading to his place? Will that give us enough time? Then we could be more certain of his direction."

"I'll check with the chopper pilots. We'll see what we can do."

Quay sped on, blowing huge pink bubbles and popping them in staccato bursts. He still wasn't willing to turn off his flashing lights. Time was critical, even if they knew where Charlie was taking Sam. Once Charlie got to that cabin, Sam's life was in even more jeopardy. Charlie would be holding the upper hand there, because he knew the territory. And he wouldn't need Sam anymore. He'd probably kill her rather than have the extra baggage slow him down. There was no choice. They had to be there first.

Chapter 24

John talked intently with the chopper pilot for more than ten minutes as Quay listened to one side of the conversation. They made arrangements for the final leg of their sprint to Charlie's cabin. Their plan was coming together. After agreeing that the best place to meet with the chopper would be a small airstrip outside of Barnum just south of Duluth, Quay and John planned to turn off 35W onto a county road to meet one of the helicopters. Per their plan, the other helicopter would continue tracking Charlie and Sam.

Boogie used the BCA's influence to verify the location of Charlie's cabin. He'd also managed to get a satellite view of the property. He transmitted that to the chopper pilots.

From Barnum, John and Quay could be flown to Charlie's cabin, which they now knew was west of Temperance River near the Boundary Waters. John's deputies would arrange for a car near the location if they needed it. Then they'd stay back until John and Quay were in place. They agreed to move in to block the exits after Charlie arrived with Sam.

So everything was in place. One pilot would stop for Quay and John. The second helicopter pilot would continue following Charlie. That pilot would be able to keep up with Charlie's travels by using his GPS. Staying high and out of range, he would continue to pinpoint Charlie's location without Charlie's knowledge. They agreed that if Charlie stopped anywhere before he reached the cabin, they would use the heat imaging radar to follow Charlie and Sam. One way or another, they had him. The trick now would be to surprise him and free Sam unharmed.

Quay took the exit at Barnum and headed west. He knew it would really be a race now! They had been on the road for almost an hour and a half. They needed to make up time. Charlie had at least a half-hour to forty-five-minute lead given the speed he was traveling. Quay turned off three miles later onto a small gravel road leading through the pine trees. They'd been told the road led to a small landing strip hidden by trees. The chopper waiting for them with blades now slowly rotating was a welcome sight. Quay parked his truck close to the tree line while John called Boogie to let him know where they'd left it. Hopefully, they wouldn't need it. Someone would come up and pick it up in the next few hours.

Quay and John pulled their guns from their storage boxes and hauled their Kevlar vests from the rear of Quay's truck. They ducked under the whining blades to the open door of the chopper. The pilot reached out an arm to lift them up.

"Hi, guys. I'm Mike," the pilot shouted above the whine of the chopper blades. "Welcome aboard. I'll be your chauffeur today."

John and Quay introduced themselves and settled into seats. Quay climbed into the front seat in the cockpit while John squeezed into the rear seat. The chopper began to lift off as soon as they were aboard. Quay inspected the complex bank of red and black LCD gauges in front of him. He listened intently as Mike explained the SRC or Search Radar Control display.

"Where are we heading? You got a location for me?" Mike looked at Quay as he began programming his computers.

"Yeah, we've got it. We're going to patch you into our man at BCA headquarters via cell phone. We don't want our perp listening in, so we're not using the radio. Our guy can give you coordinates. He's also got the GPS location you filed on Charlie Frank. Our tech guy's name is Boogie. He'll be our go-between."

Mike laughed. "And I'm supposed to take a guy with a name like that seriously?"

"He's one of the best tech guys in the country. Don't let his name fool you. He's no slouch," said Quay.

Quay punched in Boogie's direct number on his cell and handed the phone to Mike. As Mike listened to Boogie, he began punching the coordinates into his onboard computer system. The helicopter automatically began making adjustments in direction as they lifted off.

"I just sent the info to my partner in the other chopper. He'll continue to use the GPS to stay on top of the guy, but he'll have this, too, just in case. So, we can move on ahead. Give you a surprise advantage. Ready?"

Quay nodded and busied himself with a new piece of bubblegum. He carefully wrapped his old piece of gum in the wrapper and placed the fresh piece in his mouth. As he began chewing with renewed dedication, Mike watched him shaking his head slightly with puzzlement.

Within minutes, they were airborne over Duluth and turning inland away from the sun-sparkled, teal-blue body of water beneath them. Quay and John surveyed the disappearing maze of streets and buildings, replaced with a carpet of trees that became thicker with each mile. Splotches of greens, browns, and occasional blues of open water flew by. Occasionally, the trees would part to reveal a small building or cabin nestled among the trees. Small dirt roads wound through the trees, looking like velvet brown ribbons connecting buildings. The overall effect was that of a dot-to-dot puzzle, thought Quay.

"How soon will we be there?" Quay asked, looking at his watch. It was after noon already. He hated sounding like a little kid who'd just climbed into the family vacation vehicle, but Charlie Frank was a loose cannon. Who knew what he was going to do once he got to his cabin? Who knew what he'd do with or to Sam? What's more, Quay was still was trying to comprehend Charlie's mysterious reaction to their appearance at Cameron. This whole thing didn't make sense. His accusations against Quay sounded paranoiac. Could Charlie have fallen that far off the deep end? What was Charlie Frank afraid of? What was he into? There had to be something else that was driving him.

Quay was fairly certain that Charlie Frank was just a small part of a much larger picture. That said, none of this was good. This was part of a larger operation, more than a case of a couple murders ordered by a crazy, vengeful former cop.

First of all, Quay didn't think Charlie Frank had ever been that smart. That fact alone made him increasingly afraid that there was enormous danger for everyone involved with this case. And given what he already knew, he surmised that the motivation involved a very high-stake operation revolving around the research at Cameron and the money it could generate. As always, it boiled down to the money. He had to get to Charlie. If he could get Charlie to fill in some of the blanks, he would be able to piece it all together.

His first order of business, though, was to make sure Sam was safe. He couldn't afford to have Sam on his conscience, too, in addition to Karen. Besides, when he really got down to it, right now it was all about Sam. He hadn't really admitted it to himself until now. But now he knew he had to face it. He was beginning to care for Samantha Atwood as more than a partner. She had become a part of his life. Karen was no longer here. He missed Karen, and she'd always be a part of his heart, but Sam was beginning to fill the void left by Karen. He enjoyed Sam's company. He felt at ease with her. He was beginning to realize she was good for him. Now he was afraid he might lose her too, just like he lost Karen. She could be ripped away by some merciless, crazy creep. He had to stop this maniac if he wanted a chance at starting a life again—maybe a life with Sam.

Mike interrupted Quay's moment of reflection. "I think I can have you there in a little over thirty minutes. We can do up to ninety knots with these birds. Then we'll find a place to put you down. We also need to check with my partner, Will, in the other chopper, to see how far back down the road Charlie is. Do you have the necessary stuff to handle this guy? Or are you going to want some air support?"

"I won't know until we have him in sight," answered Quay. "We've got our gear and the handguns but nothing else. We're going to have to win by wits with this guy. He's a former cop. I'd definitely like to have you stand by. If we can get into the cabin, we might be able to surprise him and take him without any trouble. Then we'll need someone to pick us up. He's got some questions to answer. There isn't time to waste. We're going to need to get information out of him. After we nab him, we might take him back to John's office near Lutsen." He turned to John. "Do you have a place a chopper can land by the station there?"

239

"Sure we do," answered John. "I've got a place nearby where we set down helicopters when they come in. We could have Mike stand by there, so he'll be at a distance but close enough to come in quickly if we need him. We would be able to call him when it's all clear, and he can drop in for the pickup if we've got a clearing, or we'll all meet up at the station. One way or another, it's going to work, Quay."

Mike indicated they were coming up on the cabin's GPS location. All eyes began scouring the earth below for a clearing in the trees or a road that was wide enough to allow the big bird to settle down.

Good fortune smiled as an opening appeared about a mile north of the cabin. The leafy mat of the white pines and birch separated, and a patch of green grass appeared as if a small table had been specially cleared for them. A creek bubbled along one side of the hidden glen and disappeared into the trees. Quay spotted a doe standing at the edge of the creek. She paused, ears pricked up, looking up at the intrusion, and bounded away into the woods.

"Okay, Mike, let's have you drop us off in that little open area. We'll hook up with you again if we need you after we tackle Charlie. We'll want you to stay within range. We will keep you in the loop. Advise John's guys to move in to close the exit after Charlie comes in."

"That sounds like a plan," Mike answered and began dropping the helicopter into the glade. As Mike circled the opening, Quay pointed out the cabin in the distance.

"Mike, can you circle over the cabin area before you take us down? Do you think we have time?" asked Quay.

"Sure can. It'll just take a minute," answered Mike.

From the air, they could see that the cabin appeared to be a log A-frame centered in a cleared acre of land. A wide, natural stone chimney crawled up one side of the cabin, jutting out above the roof. The rear of the cabin faced a small lake. A full wall of floor-to-ceiling windows wrapped around the back of the cabin. Below the windows, a long cedar deck walked off to a screen porch spanning half of the cabin's rear wall. John pointed out a rough dirt drive edged with a cedar-chip walking path. The path created a dark, whimsical thread leading to the lake. Trees had been cleared around the area closest to the cabin. White pines and thick, dark underbrush lined the perimeter of the lot.

Two log outbuildings nestled next to each other off to the north side of the main cabin. One building appeared to be a boathouse close to the edge of the lake, and the other was the size of a small guesthouse. A quick survey of the area indicated that there was no other cabin around the lake. Quay estimated the lake itself covered about fifteen acres at the most. A dock stretched out several yards into the water from the cedar path on the shore. A speedboat on a boatlift nestled next to one side of the dock. A large canopied pontoon boat sat moored on the opposite side.

"Whew! That's quite a piece of property for a single, retired cop's salary," observed John.

Mike gave an appreciative whistle. "Yeah! That's an understatement. I'd have to accumulate a few years' salary to afford a place like that. It looks like the buildings are fairly new, too."

Quay agreed. "There's no doubt Charlie's had a little monetary help along the way to be able to afford this place. I'm hoping he'll be able to answer a few of our questions. We just need to catch him alive."

Mike lifted the copter away, circling up again, and then headed for their chosen landing spot. With an expertise born of experience, he set the chopper down in the small clearing among the trees. The brothers quickly jumped out the open door, landing with arms full of their gear. Mike hollered out, "Good luck! See ya fellas soon," as he lifted off.

Quay and John ducked away from the wash of the rotors and pulled their Kevlar vests loosely over their shoulders, tacitly agreeing that the forty-pound vest was easier to wear than to carry. They pocketed their service revolvers and set off at a quick pace in the direction of Charlie's place.

Quay was glad that he'd worn his casual clothes this morning. The boots he wore made the trek easier. John, at the last minute, had taken off his sports jacket, tossing it into the back of Quay's truck, and grabbed the sweatshirt he'd brought along that morning. He was glad he had it. But his dress shoes weren't quite the right gear for this trek. He found himself slipping every few steps on the moist mat of pine needles, and because of his shoes, he struggled to keep up with Quay. It was a good thing it wasn't hot, he thought. The air in the woods was cool and brisk even though the sun was shining.

However, although it was cool, the brothers quickly encountered another form of discomfort. Black clouds of mosquitoes had quickly discovered them and were swarming around their heads, arms, and torsos. The fifteen-minute hike through the woods was now marked by a barrage of irritating, buzzing pinpricks on every naked expanse of skin. By the time they finally arrived at the cabin clearing, Quay was swatting with both arms to chase them from his face and head. The effort was only effective for a moment.

"It's no wonder they call these mosquitoes the Minnesota state bird," complained Quay. "My God, these things could carry a person away. Why didn't we think to grab the bug spray? I had some in the truck. And how come they always swarm me and bite me more than you?"

"Good blood, brother," laughed John. "And I really didn't plan on doing a hike through the woods when we left this morning. Maybe Charlie's got some mosquito spray inside that cabin." As they pushed through the last gauntlet of underbrush, he said, "Didn't we put in those camouflage net hoods? We could use those to ward off the mosquitoes."

"Yeah, I think we stuffed them in the pockets of the vests. We can grab them in a minute. I want to get a good look at this place first."

They broke out into the clearing and approached the log A-frame with caution. Both men now secured their service revolvers in shoulder holsters for quick retrieval. At the last minute, Quay also placed his personal revolver in his waistband. Listening intently and checking the outbuildings as they came through, they observed no vehicles or any indication of other people on the property.

"So far, so good," Quay noted in a hushed tone. "Let's see if we can find a way inside. We should have a little time." Scanning the perimeter of the clearing, he led the way to the porch at the front of the cabin.

"That could be a problem," observed John, pointing to the edge of a window covered with a lace of spider webs. "Look here." John was indicating a black wire traveling from the foundation of the building up to the window. "Looks like he's got some sort of security hooked up. Or else it's a booby trap. We'll need to disable it or at least get a call in to the security company to allow us in. Can we get a clearance that quickly?"

"Probably not," answered Quay. "I hadn't thought about the possibility of security out here. If we break through without clearing it, the security company will notify Charlie. There goes our advantage of surprise." He leaned forward, scrutinizing the wire. "He must have something in there he really doesn't want anyone messing with."

John was peering through a wide window on the other side of the porch when Quay's phone interrupted them with a piercing shriek.

Quay lurched and answered quickly, stopping the unnatural clamor.

"Yeah, what's up?"

He paused for a minute and then looked toward the dirt drive winding through the woods and leading toward the cabin.

"Okay. Got it. Thanks."

Hanging up, he turned to John. "Will, the guy in the other chopper, says we don't have much time. Charlie is about thirty miles away. God, he made good time. He must have been flying. It took him less than four hours. We've got to establish a place to hide. We need to have an observation point. Then maybe we can ambush him when he gets Sam out of the pickup. There's not enough time to get into the cabin. He's got to believe we're not here yet. He won't be as cautious if he thinks he's alone."

John began scanning the property to the side and behind the cabin. Tall, thick trees stood watch over the entire property.

"How about we take cover in that stand of trees opposite this front porch. We'd have a clear shot if we need to take it. It's not too far away, so we could rush him if we need to."

Quay looked over at the direction John was pointing.

"Right, I don't want any shots fired if we can help it, John. We need to take Charlie in with no injuries. He's got a lot to tell us. We can't afford to have a dead suspect. And Sam needs to get out of there safely. I think I can guess what he's going to do. Let's establish a position further to the rear of the cabin, back toward the lake. We can still see him pull in the drive. He'll be out of sight for a minute if he enters the cabin. But he'll have to come out to park the pickup. I'm guessing he'll want that truck out of sight. We can grab Charlie first, then retrieve Sam."

"Sounds good," agreed John. "But we gotta move. If he's nearing the cabin, we've got to get out of sight now."

"Yeah, I agree. Let's head that way. But I want to take a second to look at those buildings, too."

They left the porch and hurried toward the lake, following the cedar path they'd seen from the air. The outbuilding that looked like a boathouse was further to the right of them. It had large double doors facing the lake. A latch secured by a padlock held the doors closed. Two windows on the side toward them had been covered with some sort of paper or black paint. Quay scratched at

245

the window but discovered the paint was on the inside. The padlock over the latched doors looked weak.

The other building, between the boathouse and the woods, appeared to be a small guesthouse matching the log A-frame design of the main house. The little guesthouse was nestled back into the woods so that only its front looked out from the woods toward the main cabin. The door to the little A-frame was centered in the front over simple wooden steps. One curtained window looked out the side toward the lake. A small opening in the trees and brush had been cleared in front of the side window to allow a view of the lake. It appeared to be big enough for only one room.

John walked up the steps and tried the door. He turned to Quay and shook his head. Quay was guessing, actually hoping, that Charlie might stow Sam in that guesthouse so he'd be free to move about in the cabin. He probably wouldn't stay long, though. It was obvious this was just a stopping off place. Charlie would have plans to get out of the country. Quay figured he had money stashed in some offshore account. He just needed to get to it. All the more reason to nab him here!

Agreeing that they'd seen enough, they sprinted twenty yards to the brush that edged the property and dove into the cover of the pines. They chose a position halfway between the cabin and the guesthouse. They crouched and pulled the camouflage netting over their heads. Within minutes after settling into the dense undergrowth beneath the stand of white pines, Quay and John watched Charlie's black Avalanche power up the driveway toward the cabin, followed by an ominous cloud of brown dust. The pickup slowed as it neared the cabin and crept slowly forward. It was clear that Charlie was looking for signs of an ambush. Quay and John hunkered down lower, making no movement or sound.

Evidently feeling secure enough that there was no one around, Charlie pulled his pickup up near the front right of the cabin. The front of his vehicle pointed directly at Quay and John. Stopping within feet of the long front porch, he shut off the engine and again waited, surveying the area.

Quay froze and held his breath. He hoped they were blending in with the trees and underbrush. The Kevlar vests were heavy, but they had both agreed they were a necessary evil. They weren't sure what Charlie would do or how far he would go. The key was to remain hidden from Charlie's sharp eyes.

At least, Quay thought sardonically, the net hoods protected them from the buzzing mosquitoes. The damp, woody smell of the forest floor hung in the air. Squirrels rustled through the leaves. Birds flitted from tree to tree. A woodpecker attacked a tree nearby with a machine gun rat-a-tat. Mother Nature was doing a good job of covering their intrusion. In the distance, Quay thought he heard the whirring echo of the chopper. That was good. Maybe, if Charlie heard it, he would think they weren't here yet, or better yet, hadn't found him.

The pickup remained silent and still, a quiet, lifeless, menacing object. Quay could see Charlie's outline as he remained motionless behind the wheel of the pickup. There was no sign of Sam. Quay began to worry.

Abruptly, Charlie opened the pickup door, leaned his head out, and hesitated, once again sweeping the perimeter of the lot around the cabin. Quay and John could see he was listening and looking for any nuance

247

that might indicate a disturbance or unwelcome intruder. They breathed a sigh of relief when the pickup door sprang fully open and Charlie climbed out. They watched as he skirted the front of the pickup, using his remote key set to unlock the passenger door.

After yanking the passenger door open, he roughly grabbed at a bundle inside on the floor. The bundle came tumbling out of the door and landed in a heap on the ground. The crumpled pile of legs and arms twisted around a tan Sherpa jacket, and a groan emerged from the heap. Then it unfolded slowly. A disheveled Sam began flexing and stretching her limbs. Quay realized he'd been holding his breath. He exhaled, relieved to see that Sam was alive. Her groans increased with each movement, carrying across the property. Auburn hair fell in long, twisted strands over her face. Quay could see that her cheek had been scraped, but otherwise, she appeared to be unhurt. She stretched upright, raising and flexing her arms. She was barefoot and leaned over, rubbing her legs and feet.

Quay's knuckles turned white as he gripped the Glock he'd slipped from his holster. He aimed directly at Charlie's chest. He wanted nothing more than to get a shot off at that madman. Then it'd be over.

But he knew that would be a huge mistake. He needed Charlie alive. John placed a hand on Quay's arm in silent warning. Quay lowered the gun. Charlie had a lot of answers to a lot of questions. Quay had to keep a clear head. This wasn't the time to let his emotions rule.

They watched as Charlie leaned forward, grabbing Sam by the back of her belt and pulling her upright like a limp puppet. In one fluid motion, Sam heaved herself straight up while throwing her head back.

The back of her head smashed into Charlie's forehead with a loud thud. In what was almost a synchronized dance movement, she turned to the side, leaped into the air, and kicked her long legs out in an attempt to catch Charlie at the knees. However, Charlie was prepared and sidestepped in an agile move that belied his size. At the same time, he instinctively reached out and wrapped a handful of her long hair around his fist as he steadied himself. He shook his head to clear the blood now trickling into his eyes from the cut on his forehead. He bellowed with rage.

"Listen, bitch, you could have a short lifespan at this rate." He twisted his fistful of her hair and gave it an extra yank, pulling her face close so she could see the insanity behind his eyes.

"You need to play it nice, or I'll make you hurt until I decide what to do with you. You can choose, pain or no pain."

"Go screw yourself! I don't care what you do," Sam retorted. "You can't get away. They'll get you."

"Oh my, aren't we tough? You just keep on believing that if it makes you feel better. But I'm a lot smarter than your boyfriend, Quay Thompson," Charlie crowed. "I know how he and his cop brother are tracking us. It won't be long before they're here. They thought they were so smart using those highway patrol spotters. They didn't count on the fact that I had a scanner, too. But they won't get here in time. I'm still way ahead of them."

Sam twisted anxiously to wriggle out of Charlie's grip. Her weak ankle twisted again, and she winced with pain. Rocks buried in the dirt drive ground into her bare feet. Charlie pulled her closer, twisting her arms behind her as he clamped on handcuffs he'd pulled from his jacket pocket.

"I've had my escape planned for more than a year," he explained in raspy braggadocio. He held her with one hand while opening the rear door of his truck. Reaching in, he retrieved a black duffle bag. With the bag in one hand and Sam secured in his other arm, he began dragging Sam toward the dock.

"You and I are going to take a very short ride in my little speed boat now. Bet you've been longing to go for another ride with me. I promise this will be your last ride. When your *friends* arrive to look for us, they'll waste time looking in the cabin and outbuildings first. After they finally realize we're not here, it'll be too late. They won't know where we've gone. And you want to know my little secret?" He leaned toward her ear and continued in a raspy stage whisper. "I own this entire lake. That's part of what they won't know. They discovered the cabin. I heard that on the scanner. They'll be here before too long. But they won't get the whole picture." His paunchy belly shook as he laughed at his secret advantage. "The lake's ownership is listed under another name. They can't track it to me. They won't look beyond the cabin. Besides," he continued in a tone of feigned seriousness, "I've got a special plan for them. I've covered all the contingencies. I was always a good cop, you see? They just never gave me the credit I deserved. And I've even got a special plan for us on the other side of the lake."

Charlie was raving on excitedly now, waving one arm toward the lake and boasting about his plans as he pushed Sam along in front of him. He'd pulled his gun out of the pickup and was using it to steer Sam. Sam

250

pushed back against the muzzle, trying to slow him.

"If you were such a good cop," she said, "how do you think we connected you to these murders? You can't be that good. You have to know you can't succeed," she countered as she made another attempt to lurch away from him. "As a 'good cop,' you also have to have learned somewhere along the line that crime doesn't pay. They'll get you eventually. How can you possibly outrun them, Charlie? You know better than anyone how your police buddies work."

"Huh! Police buddies. Some buddies! Yeah, you bet I do." He laughed savagely. He grabbed the collar of her jacket and pulled her against him, jabbing the gun into her side. "Your friends will find their own surprise when they try to get into my cabin. They *will* try to get in, you know. They'll have to try. They'll try to get in, and they'll think they'll find all this evidence in the cabin to convict me. But they'll never know what happened. Because—kaboom! It will be the last you and I'll ever see of that SOB ... that is, if I let you watch. No one, *no one*, will ever know what happened to me. They'll find the pickup, spend days looking for our bodies. Quay Thompson will be gone, and so will I. I'll have my revenge, pure and sweet. I'll have his wife, his girlfriend, and his life. And best of all, I'll be free!" He shouted the last words to the sky.

He was cackling now as he dragged her down the path leading to the dock. Quay and John watched in horror as Sam stumbled along, ineffectually fighting against Charlie. They had been able to hear a good share of his loud, wild ranting. It was enough to make Quay's gut twist into a knot. The woods had provided a nice acoustical wall for Charlie's insane boasts. His hysterical

251

words bounced back from the lake in repetitive echoes. Charlie was right in one respect; this was something they hadn't considered.

John turned to Quay and whispered, "Well, what do you think? It's almost as if Charlie knows we're here and wants us to hear the entire conversation."

"Let him go," answered Quay. He barely moved his lips as he responded. His voice had become a low growl. Every muscle in his body was tensed. Every fiber of his being was ordering him to jump out, chase after Charlie, and tackle him before he reached the boat. He wanted to pound him into oblivion. Hell, he just wanted to kill the man—right now! But he couldn't take a chance with Sam's life.

"He's just posturing for Sam. He doesn't know a thing. Let's let him think he's escaping. I don't want to blow up the cabin, but we might have to, to make him believe he's killed us. Or we can let it go and let him wonder if we're onto him or not. I think I want to know exactly what he's got over on the other side. Let's call the chopper boys and ask them to take a look. Maybe they can do that from a high enough altitude that it won't alert Charlie to our presence yet. We'll decide about the cabin before we move. Then we can circle around to the other side of the lake."

Quay and John hunkered down again and continued to watch as Charlie dragged the unwilling Sam down the dock and tossed her into the speedboat. She stood as if to jump. Charlie drew his gun from his pocket and crashed the butt of it across Sam's head. She crumpled limply onto the floor of the boat.

Quay lurched up from his covered nest in the brush. John grabbed his arm, wrenching him back before

252

he could attract Charlie's attention. Settling back into cover, Quay groaned softly. His eyes bore into the hull of the small speedboat, willing Sam to move. Charlie maliciously shoved her body aside as he stepped over her and climbed into the driver's seat. He leaned toward the dock and pushed a button to lower the boatlift. Once in the water, the boat began to drift. The motor sputtered to life, then purred as the boat began to slide out into the still water. It turned and powered slowly out of the small bay. Quay and John listened to the motor's echo fading away to the opposite shore.

It was a beautiful fall day. The clear, blue water of the lake was sparkling with the reflection of the greens, browns, and reds of the pines, cedars, and maples. Quay looked out over the lake and watched as a majestic eagle made a swoop to the lake, skimming the surface and soaring away with a small fish secured in its talons. Quay stood, stretching his legs and moving away from their covered lair.

"God's country. Isn't it ironic? All this beauty surrounding such ugliness." He let out a humorless chuckle. He looked at John, and John could see the pain in his eyes. "Normally we would say this is the ultimate place for relaxing," Quay continued. He looked after the boat as it edged across the lake. "You and I'd be on a lake up here on a fall day, soaking up the scenery, drinking a few brews, catching our quota of fish." He looked at his watch. It was now early afternoon. It felt like it should be midnight. He was exhausted. This day that had begun innocently enough had become fraught with frustration, tension, and terror.

Quay took a deep breath, recaptured his strength, and felt driven to move. Charlie was far enough away now. They could begin their counterattack.

Chapter 25

Quay ripped off his net hood, turned to John with an intent stare, and then began walking.

"Going to Plan B," he said over his shoulder. "Call Mike. See if they can get that chopper moving. We need a location. We need to know what we're heading into."

John stood up, pulled off his hood, and stuffed the wad of net into his pocket as he exchanged it for his cell phone. He was waiting for someone to answer as he fell into step a few paces behind Quay.

Quay hiked steadily on the grassy path up to the cabin while yanking at the Velcro strips of his Kevlar vest. The vest wasn't necessary anymore. He began a silent replay in his mind of all the events of the last week: Annie Bell's body on the shore of Lake Superior, Ernie Elson and Annie, Jesse and James's revelation about SPARTA's involvement with Cameron BioTech, and now Charlie Frank's bizarre reaction and the ensuing chase. He tried to connect the dots, but there were so many missing pieces. Boogie had been following up on the information stolen from Cameron. Somehow that had to be a part of this entire situation. And finally, there was Charlie's odd comment about his retaliation with Karen. What was up with that? This just didn't make sense.

John interrupted Quay's musing.

"Quay! I got Mike. He's on the way. We've got to decide our next move." He moved forward to join Quay on the path.

"Yeah. I know."

Quay climbed up the steps at the front of the main cabin. He began searching for the wires that indicated some kind of a booby trap. He walked across the length of the front porch, looking in the windows as he did so. He was kneeling in front of the door, examining the lock, when John came up behind him. A distant rumble signaled the approach of the helicopter.

"Find anything?"

"Yeah, maybe. It looks like there are some trip wires here around the door. See these?" He pointed to fine wires attached to the side of the doorframe. "It's a good thing we didn't mess with the security wires. If we'd gone in, we would have met just the fate Charlie hoped for."

John's phone produced a soft ring again. Quay listened in on the one-sided conversation.

When John ended the call, Quay was waiting anxiously for an answer.

"It was Mike, right? What'd he have to say?"

"Yeah. That was Mike. His chopper was what we heard a minute ago. He's way up there, but he did get a fair look around the other side of the lake, he said. He says there's a small cabin, more like a shack, tucked in the trees on the opposite shore around a bend across from this cabin. He says it looks deserted, but he couldn't get close enough to get a really good look. He wanted to stay up away as much as he could so as not to alert Charlie."

"Good. That's where Charlie's headed. We'll let Charlie go there. But we have to figure out his plan from there."

"Mike also said it looks like there's an old four-wheeler parked next to the shack. And there's another four-wheeler about half a mile back up the trail north of the cabin."

"Huh. Well, that must be his plan then," Quay said. He began running through a scenario. "He'll use the four-wheeler to go through the back woods to escape. He probably has plans to ride that to another vehicle he has stashed somewhere. But why the second four-wheeler? I don't get it. If he uses the four-wheeler and then picks up another vehicle, he'll be able to get away and cross the border undetected. And you can bet the plan doesn't include taking Sam with him! Damn! Why is there another four-wheeler up the trail? I don't like that. Is someone else hooked into this?"

"Who knows? He's probably not planning on taking Sam along, though. But how are we going to stop him, Quay? What do you want to do? Do we have a plan?"

"Hell no. This is getting more complicated by the minute. We've got to move. We can't lose any more time. First, let's see if Mike or Will can find the vehicle Charlie may have stashed up the road. Have them call Boogie and get information on all vehicles owned by Charlie. Then we'll know what we're looking for, and maybe they can get to it first and take that one out.

"While they're doing that, let's get busy and try to flush Charlie out of that shack before he gets away. Somehow we've got to make him worry a little. We don't want him to panic. We don't want him to use Sam for protection, and we don't want him to hurt her. We'll have to finesse him. Let's have the guys keep an eye from the air when we get close. If Charlie takes off, he can track Charlie as he leaves. At that point, it won't matter what Charlie knows or thinks he knows."

John was nodding while tapping in numbers on his cell phone.

Quay continued, "I guess we'll have to circle around the lake or get over there somehow without Charlie seeing us. I hope he doesn't plan on leaving the shack right away. He's going to need a breather. At least, we can hope. It's time to get word to your deputies, John. We need a crew out here to clear the booby traps Charlie left for us at his cabin. When this is all over, we'll need to get inside. I have a feeling there might be a lot of answers about Cameron BioTech in there for us."

"Okay, I've already got a call in to Mike on that. Do you want my guys to just drive up now, or do you want to wait?"

"Let's just have them get to the cabin here and be on standby. Better have an EMT on hand, too, just in case. Bring a bomb squad up here to take care of the cabin. Tell them not to enter the cabin until we give the all clear. We can have them go in as soon as Sam is secure and Charlie's on his way."

"Sounds right. Now what do you have in mind for our buddy Charlie?"

Quay wasn't listening to John. An icy hand was wrapping around his head, its fingers slowly choking him. He felt his skin tighten, making the hair on his arms and neck stand up. Comprehension combined with haunting fear. He looked out over the small lake, watching as deep shades of green and gold crept out from the shore toward the center of the lake, reaching it in long, unfriendly shadows. Charlie's motor continued to rumble its way across the lake. He could no longer see the boat. Charlie had rounded a corner.

The vague thump of the helicopter echoed in the distance. The lake had become still and eerily glassy. The

258

air was changing; an ominous silence hovered. Then came another rumble in the distance. Quay's anxiety was confirmed. The sound he'd thought was the helicopter in the distance was not the rumble of the chopper's rotors, but instead was the rumble of an approaching thunderstorm. And it was coming in fast. That explained the change in the air. He'd instinctively known a storm was looming but hadn't recognized it right away.

He looked at his watch. Almost three. The sun was already dropping in the afternoon sky behind dark clouds. The day had gotten away from them. The storm created an added problem. Charlie was escaping with Sam in tow. They needed more time. They were going to lose daylight even faster now that a storm was coming.

For a moment, he felt himself once again become a bystander watching the day's events flicker past him in slow motion. He felt helpless. He was tired. He knew John was, too. And everyone was looking to him for the magic solution.

"Quay?" John asked. "What is it?"

"John, we're running out of time. By the time we get around the lake to that cabin, we're going to be in the middle of a thunderstorm. It's going to get dark earlier than normal. Charlie can take off on that four-wheeler in the dark and follow any path he wants. We won't have much success tracking him at night."

John's phone erupted with several shrill beeps.

"Yes!" John impatiently answered. "Really? Okay, hold position. Let me talk to Quay."

"What's up?" Quay asked.

"We've got another problem. Mike did a high fly over and ran a heat sensing radar around the shack. There's somebody already by that shack over there.

Either Charlie has a partner or he has uninvited company!"

"Well, now. That throws another twist into the day's plan." Quay's face bore an anxious expression.

"And that's not all."

"Oh, great! There's more?"

"He says that's a big thunderhead coming in fast from the west. He and Will can't stay up there if there's a thunderstorm."

"John, just ask them to hold for about ten minutes if he can. We've got to check that boathouse."

Quay dropped his Kevlar vest on the porch and was already on the move, running to the small boathouse near the shore. The window facing the lakeside was painted over; however, he remembered seeing that the window on the other side was only clouded with layers of fine cobwebs and a film of dirt. He ran to that side and wiped a spot on the window to clean as much as he could. Cupping his hands around his eyes to shield the light, he peered into the dark interior. As he'd hoped, there was a small canoe hanging off to one side. He turned toward John, who was just joining him at the window.

"John! I think we have an answer. Tell Will to take off. Ask Mike if he can find a spot up the road to land and wait out the storm for us."

John stripped off his vest and threw it in the brush next to the building. He was on the phone with Mike, speaking with urgency.

"Yeah, Mike. Can you just hold on the ground? We'll get back to you. Thanks, buddy!" John's voice reflected his newfound assurance.

Quay continued his inspection of the door and windows of the boathouse. There were no trip wires here.

He looked and felt around the edge of the door and the side window. Charlie hadn't taken the time to secure this building. Quay signaled John, and they began throwing their combined weight against the boathouse door.

The double garage doors were old, with rusting hinges. The doors would normally swing out, but there was a latch with a padlock across the doors. The screws holding the latch in place began to loosen. Finally, Quay was able to grab the latch with his hands, kick the door, and pull it away from the stressed wood. John wrenched the other door open.

Musty, dank air greeted them. With a joint effort, they quickly lifted the canoe from its braces on the wall of the boathouse. It was a small, green fiberglass Coleman canoe. The color had faded. Gray water markings covered the bottom and reached a third of the way up the sides. Two metal seats provided bracing inside. The paddles looked new and rested under the seats.

Racing in tandem with their burden, they brought the canoe to the water. John leaped into the front. Quay took the rear. They'd canoed together many times. Old habits returned unbidden. The brothers working in tandem glided rapidly through the placid water. The storm was nearing now. Lightning flashed from a wall of black thunderheads in the distance. The sky was turning a yellow-green beneath the clouds. That meant hail. Quay was certain the wind would pick up soon. There wasn't time to think about it. They had to outrun the storm and get to the other side of the lake before it hit.

"What'd you find out from Mike? Can he find a place to wait it out?" Quay paddled fiercely while interrogating his brother.

261

"He said he'd look around. He might be able to take it to a county road and set up flares to stop traffic. He'll call us when he's set."

"Okay, let's let him worry about that. We need to set up a plan. Do you have any guesses about the other person in the shack?"

"Quay, I don't know. But Mike might have had some insight on that, too. Remember he said he saw a small ATV in the middle of a clearing about two miles north of here? Maybe it's just someone who decided to drop in, you think? Could it be that Charlie has a partner? Or is it just a coincidence? Some hunters come back and forth up here like that. It could be nothing.

"We can wish it's nothing. I know there are a few hermits up here who live in the back woods. They don't want to be bothered by civilization. They don't have a real place to live. So they become 'borrowers.' They don't consider it to be trespassing. They just break into an old, unused place that looks like it's pretty well isolated, and they hole up for the winter."

John was speaking in ragged bursts, interrupted with deep gasps for breaths.

"How do they get their supplies?" asked Quay.

"Usually they'll either own a four wheeler, or they'll borrow one and use it to get into town every so often. My guess is that if Charlie doesn't have a partner, he's got an uninvited guest."

"That will be a nice surprise for him. It'll throw a wrench into the works for him."

"Not only that, but I also know these guys usually aren't too friendly to anyone approaching. They have a stash of weapons, and they'll use them to protect themselves."

"Oh great! But if he has a partner, a helicopter could be his other method of escape!" Quay was really wishing he had a cigarette. He didn't have any bubblegum left. He could use anything about now. And besides that, he was discovering just how out of shape he had become. This rowing was hard work! His shoulders and upper arms were burning. The storm was closing in. A stranger was in the shack where Charlie was taking Sam. And he was playing catch up. It just seemed to be getting worse and worse! His breathing became more labored with each stroke, a combination of exertion and expectations.

The wind was beginning to pick up. At least it wasn't coming directly at them, which made the paddling somewhat easier. They were skimming across the lake. From the rear of the canoe, Quay guided them closer to the shoreline. When the storm hit, they agreed they might be safer if they were close to the shore. The water would be calmer there, and the trees next to the lake could provide some shelter. And in addition, it would be more difficult for them to be spotted if Charlie were looking for them. At least they were on the best side of the lake with this approaching storm.

Quay was beginning to see the silhouetted outlines of the shack. Barely visible was a small dock in front of the property with the motorboat tied next to it. He spotted a dirt path winding its way from the shore through the trees back to the shack. A thin line of smoke wafted from an old stovepipe chimney of the shack. The whole of the building wasn't much bigger than a tool shed. The small shed looked like it had been put together haphazardly with rotting barn boards. A window had been placed on the front wall at an awkward angle adjacent to the door. In an inane moment of distraction, Quay wondered how that little shack would even have room for a stove. And what's more, how could it be safe to burn a fire in that small space?

Chapter 26

Darkness settled in early with the nearing storm. Charlie Frank dragged his struggling hostage up the rocky path toward the shack. He'd spotted the smoke from the chimney as he neared the shore. What the hell was that? No one was supposed to even know about his hunting shack. He'd cut the motor within sight of the shack and drifted up to shore to dock the boat. Managing this wildcat of a woman would be a problem. He decided he'd have to stash her in the brush along the path. Then he'd investigate his shack.

There was a small niche in the stand of trees just off the side of the path. Charlie dragged a struggling Sam over to a low pine and pushed her down. He'd gagged her mouth with the sleeve torn off an old flannel shirt he'd kept in the boat. Now, Charlie looked at her and smiled. She wasn't going to be a problem. He'd cuffed her hands behind her. She glared at him from her position under the tree. He'd brought a small chain from the storage bin under the seat in the boat. He deftly looped the chain through the handcuffs, working it around the base of the tree and back through the cuffs again. He secured the chain with the clasp, locking it into the handcuffs. Sam continued to look up at him, glowering. She tried to speak, but only dark, angry mumbles came through the gag.

"Be still, now. I'm going to check out the shack. You'll be fine right here." He smiled as he looked down at her, but it was an insidious smile that left her with a chill of hopelessness.

Charlie patted her on the head and moved around the tree to the path.

The wind whistled through the tops of the cedars. Branches creaked as they bent under the force of the rising wind. Charlie crept up the path, keeping his eyes on the shack, looking for any sign of movement. Abruptly he stopped, ducked behind a tree, and swept the perimeter. He dug his pistol from his pocket. This just wasn't part of the plan, he thought.

Crack! A gunshot echoed. Charlie instinctively ducked. What the hell?

He ducked into the shelter of the trees, peeking out to get some sort of view of the shooter. Then a gruff voice called out, "Whatcha lookin' for, Charlie? You don't need to come sneaking up here. It's your place, isn't it? But I think I'll do what you'd do. I'll shoot ya first and ask questions later. What do ya think about that, Mr. Manager?"

The reference to Manager caught Charlie by surprise. Who was this guy? He felt a twist in his gut. He flashed to the wrecked pickup truck and heavy, gray dust swirling over the scene of the accident. No! It couldn't be. Ernie Elson was dead. He'd made sure of that. Charlie was angry and frightened now. He decided to bluff his way through.

"I want you off my property! Who the hell are you? You're trespassing on my property. Who do you think you are? Put that gun away before I shoot you for trespassing!"

Now the gruff voice had a body. A tall, slender man appeared around the corner of the shack. His booted, denim-clad legs braced in a confident stance while long, dark, wild hair blew around his face. He glared at Charlie from black-rimmed glasses.

"Elson?" Charlie couldn't hide his shock. "Elson, what are you doing here? You're dead," he stammered, then corrected himself. "I heard you were dead! How'd you get here? How'd you find this place?"

"Why yes, I am supposed to be dead," Ernie Elson answered calmly. "But as you can see, I'm just as alive as you are. Just thought I'd pay you a courtesy visit, Mr. Manager." He was talking in a conversational tone, but the expression on his face was one of hatred.

"Stop calling me that. You're crazy. What are you doing?" Charlie paused to watch Elson pull something from behind his back.

"I came to mete out punishment. We need to settle a score."

Charlie flinched. "What are you talking about? Settling a score? What's the matter with you? You still working on the SPARTA payroll?"

"I know who you are, Charlie. You're my infamous Manager. You're the one who set up all the incidents at Cameron BioTech. You're the one who 'donated' money to SPARTA to carry out all the protests. You're also the one who tried to kill me after I eliminated one of your potential problems. You never appreciated my intelligence, did you, Mr. Frank?"

Charlie stared speechless at Ernie.

"You thought I was just a whacko you could use to your own ends. Just what were your ends, Charlie?"

Charlie continued to stare at Ernie in silence.

"You see," continued Ernie, "I was smarter than you gave me credit for. I figured out that maybe you were just a pawn yourself in someone else's game. You don't have enough intelligence to organize the schemes at Cameron that you were setting up. And it was a big game, wasn't it, Charlie? I'm guessing you were getting paid big bucks to stir things up at Cameron. And it wasn't just because you were upset about the genome research at Cameron, was it?"

"You have no idea," Charlie began.

"Oh yes, I do!" Ernie snapped. "I have a very good idea. You were hired to discredit Cameron BioTech, weren't you, Ernie? And you used SPARTA to start your game. Only you didn't figure that we at SPARTA were serious about what we believed, unlike you. You just wanted the money. What else did you want, Mr. Frank? Mr. Manager? Tell me, why did you kill that woman from Cameron and turn the cameras on us? Was there another motive? You see, that was your mistake. I had to really think about that one." He paused a moment for effect. Charlie waited silently now.

"In your first move to discredit Cameron, you also discredited SPARTA by killing an innocent woman. I didn't forget that, Charlie. And if I could have discovered who you were, we'd have had a meeting a long time ago. It just all came together after you attempted to kill me. I saw you that day. I got your license tag, you old fool."

The looming storm was beginning a wind-driven drizzle down around them. They were so entrenched in their conversation they didn't notice the bolts of lightning striking near them.

"Look, you don't need to do this," Charlie reasoned as he spoke above the wind. "You've got it all wrong. I'll pay you good money. We just need to leave here. They're going to be looking for me here." Charlie was getting more than anxious now. Time was slipping away, and so was his advantage.

"Oh, I don't think so, Charlie. At least they aren't going to find you alive."

Ernie Elson took an old M-1 rifle from behind him and began to raise it to his shoulder as he finished speaking. Charlie saw it and made a desperate rush at the crazed Ernie. Charlie ran headlong into his midsection as Ernie clung to the rifle. Ernie staggered with the blow but managed to keep his balance. He raised the rifle above his head and twisted, connecting the butt of the rifle with the side of Charlie's head while slamming Charlie aside. Regaining his balance, Ernie watched as Charlie stumbled and fell grotesquely into a heap behind him.

Chapter 27

Just minutes before Charlie encountered Ernie, Quay and John pulled their canoe onto the shore. The storm was moving in, and they had rowed furiously to get to land ahead of the storm. Rain was just beginning to hit the shore when Quay flew out of the canoe before John had fully beached it.

"I'm going for Sam," Quay said above the storm. Quay was already running up the path before he'd finished telling John what he was planning. He shoved heavy, wet branches aside on each side of the trail. Spray from the rebounding branches showered his body. Water dripping from his head matted his blond hair in loose clumps. Each branch sprayed him with more droplets as he pushed on up the trail. The mixture of rocks, leaves, pine needles, and water on the path made it even more difficult for him to gain secure footing. Slipping, he struggled to stay upright on the path. It was almost completely dark now due to the storm. He had no flashlight. He wouldn't have used one if he had one. He still knew the importance of keeping their arrival a surprise. He had to count on his eyes' ability to adjust to the darkness.

He stopped to scan the perimeter of the path.

That was when he heard it. It was a moan or groan. It seemed to come above the whistle of the rain and the wind in the trees. Where had it come from?

There it was again. It had to be Sam! Charlie must have abandoned her here. He wouldn't have wanted the extra burden if he thought someone was in the shack, he reasoned. She was just ahead of him. He pushed on up the path, rounding a slight curve. There seemed to be an opening in the brush on

270

the right. Quay pushed into the branches, ignoring the thorns cutting into his arms. Sam was there in the patch of brush, struggling to stand. Her arms were stretched behind her around the trunk of a tree. Her hair was hanging in limp reddish-brown ropes. Soggy strands clung to her face.

Quay removed the gag from her mouth while whispering to her in soothing tones.

"Thank God, you're all right. My God, Sam, I was so worried. It's all right; I'm here. I've got you. You're okay." He was reassuring himself as much as Sam. He knelt to release the cuffs binding her to the chain and the tree.

"Good thing he used standard issue cuffs, Sam," he said reassuringly, trying to ease her tension.

Then his questions came in staccato bursts, giving her no time for a response. "Are you really okay? Did he hurt you? What did he do to you? I'll kill that sonofabitch if he hurt one hair on your head. We saw him with you at the cabin, Sam. We were there. Did you know?" Sam could only nod or shake her head. She was still trying to get enough moisture in her mouth to get her voice back.

"I'm okay, Quay," she choked out in a dry whisper. "He didn't really hurt me that much."

Disconnecting the chain linked through the cuffs, Quay pulled Sam up toward him. Her unsteady legs caused her to stumble. She clutched Quay's arms and looked into his rain-soaked face. For one brief moment, the storm was gone. Quay stopped to stare into Sam's eyes and leaned down to place a gentle kiss on Sam's cheek. Then he wrapped his arms around her, squeezing her in a bear hug while kissing the top of her head.

"I've never been so glad to see anyone in my entire life," he murmured.

She pulled away and looked steadily into his eyes.

"We've got to talk about a few things after this is finished." Quay's voice was husky.

She nodded. She was trembling slightly, but she wasn't sure if it was from the rain, her terror, or Quay's sudden display of tenderness. She swallowed, shook herself loose, and returned to business.

"I'm really okay, Quay. We've got to get him. We can't let him get away. He's pure crazy!" She was regaining her strength. She was also regaining her anger.

"I know. But we've go to take him alive. He's got some questions to answer. Can you walk?"

"Yeah. You go on ahead. I'll try to move around and cover the back perimeter. Where's John?"

Quay couldn't hide his admiration. She truly was extraordinary. She'd just been through a harrowing kidnapping, and yet here she was acting as if nothing had happened. She was a pure professional, focused on the capture.

He smiled as he explained, "John's coming along behind me. He'll be my backup. Here, take my gun. I've got my personal revolver along, too." He reached behind him and retrieved the small thirty-eight revolver from his waistband. "You circle around if you can." He looked at her bare feet.

"I can do it. Don't worry about me."

Sam turned abruptly at a snap behind her only to see John walking up the path to join them. He broke into a huge smile upon seeing Sam standing next to Quay.

"It's a relief to see you, Sam," he said.

She smiled and nodded. "Good to see you, too—believe me."

Suddenly, angry voices echoed above the storm. The sounds were coming from farther up the path near the shack.

"Let's finish this," Quay urged.

The three of them looked at one another and in silent agreement headed up the path for the shack. John fanned off to the left on a small trail, and Sam pushed through the brush on the right, choosing her path carefully with her bare feet. Quay jogged up the path straight on.

With one exploding crash of thunder, hard pellets of hail and piercing rain slashed through the trees. The storm had begun in earnest. Lightning flashed everywhere. Exploding cracks of thunder followed on the heels of each lightning strike.

Quay could hear Charlie pleading with someone. John, who was still in sight of Quay, turned to motion to Quay that he was in place and ready. Quay nodded and hoped Sam had gotten around the shack. They couldn't wait. It sounded like someone was threatening to kill Charlie. It was time.

Chapter 28

Charlie stared in disbelief at Ernie Elson and cringed. This guy was an absolute nutcase. Talk about your crazy scientist. This do-gooder, Ernie Elson, was going to ruin his plans. How had this crazy lunatic survived? He should be dead!

Elson was turning and crouching slightly now while pointing his rifle at Charlie's chest. Rain was pelting both of them with combined pinpricks of icy hail. They stood six feet apart, separated by white-gray sheets of the North Country thunderstorm.

"You don't want to shoot me, Ernie." Charlie's voice was pleading above the roar of the storm. He hoped he could distract Ernie long enough to make a break away. He stood slowly and circled to the side of Ernie as he spoke, so that his back was closer to the shack. Ernie turned, following Charlie's movement, fully facing him now.

"Look, we can help each other. I've got loads of cash. We can each disappear," Charlie reasoned.

"I don't think you ever wanted to help me." Ernie's tone became taunting as he added, "Mister Manager!" His face twisted into an angry sneer. "You wanted to use me. You wanted me to destroy Cameron BioTech for you. You had no interest in SPARTA or what we could accomplish. You are a lying, scum of the earth, sonofabitch!" His voice had risen in a wild crescendo.

"No! I only—"

Suddenly a shot rang out from behind them.

Charlie shrank, falling over the rotting wood of the steps leading into the shack.

Ernie ducked and whirled toward the sound, holding his rifle in front of   him.

Quay called out, "Too bad, Charlie. You, too, Elson. You're both done. You've got nowhere to go now!" Quay had fired a warning shot into the air above their heads, hoping to distract them and gain an advantage.

Then John's voice called out from the woods to their left. "Ernie Elson, throw that gun down. We've got you covered. You can't get away."

Ernie Elson froze. Squinting through the streaking rain, Ernie lowered his rifle when he saw the two men approaching him. A flash of recognition lit his eyes.

"My God! You're that guy from the BCA who was at my house earlier this week. I know you!" He looked at Quay and then looked past him to John.

Charlie used the distraction to sidle backward.

"Who's that guy? One of your back-up buddies?" asked Ernie, pointing to John with his rifle.

"You could say that," Quay answered. "He's my brother. Now it's time you gave up the rifle, Ernie. You don't want to add anything more to your list of mistakes."

"Yeah, right! Where were you guys when this maniac tried to kill me? You need to take care of him!"

"We will, Ernie. But we need you to cooperate. Put your gun down now. We don't want anyone to be hurt," Quay responded, using his best soothing tone.

Ernie looked from Quay to John and slowly lowered the rifle. His shoulders slumped, his head dropped. He gave every appearance of a beaten man.

"You have to get down on the ground, Ernie."

"Well, isn't that just sweet?" Ernie said as he sagged to the ground. Ernie knew the routine. He'd seen it on television a hundred times. "Now, what? You guys don't have anything on me, except the fact that I don't like this guy, Charlie. You need to get him. He's the one who tried to kill me. He's got a lot he can tell you about Cameron BioTech."

Quay sprung forward and gingerly removed the rifle from Ernie's hands. John clasped cuffs on Ernie's wrists.

"We know, Ernie. We can talk about that later, after we get back to the sheriff's office. You can just sit here and soak up the rain for a little bit." Quay turned to John.

"Will you call the guys and see who can get in here to give us a hand? I'm going to follow Charlie. He just scrambled behind the building. He can't get too far. Sam's around there. She may be able to stop him."

Quay was just sprinting around the corner of the shack when another shot rang out. Then Sam's voice called out.

Charlie had used Ernie's distraction to cover his getaway. When Charlie had neared the corner of the shack, he was able to jump up, turn, and sprint toward the back—but he abruptly stopped in confusion. His getaway four-wheeler was gone! Someone had moved it.

"Damn you, Elson," he raged above the storm.

The moment's hesitation cost him.

"Charlie, stop! Now!" It was Sam's voice. He recognized the voice of that whiny bitch. He turned away from her voice and began to run. Sam's gun spat, and Charlie felt white-hot pain searing through his right knee.

The impact of the shot whirled Charlie's body as his knee buckled with a scorching pain that surged up his leg. He bellowed in anger and crumpled into a muddy puddle on the ground. Looking around, his eyes focused through the rain to see Sam Atwood standing next to a massive cedar tree with her gun still aimed at him. The rain had plastered her hair to her head. She was standing barefoot, legs braced, her arms stretched out in front of her with a gun aimed steadily at him. Her clothes were caked with mud, leaves, and pine needles. Then he watched as a broad, confident smile spread across her face.

"Too late, Charlie," she crooned. "For such a good cop, guess you were a little too slow."

Quay rounded the side of the shack just in time to see Sam leaning down to yank Charlie's arms behind him and push him over onto his stomach. Charlie's face was pinched up in a mask of pain. He bellowed out a shriek of rage and pain.

Quay slowed as he heard Sam chiding Charlie, knowing she was in control. She was good. There was no doubt about it. He smiled a relieved grin as he looked at her and then at Charlie. Sam glanced up at the same moment to see Quay round the corner of the shack at a run and then quickly slow down as he hear her. He pulled cuffs from his pocket and tossed them to Sam. He couldn't resist taunting Charlie one last time.

"It must be a little awkward to be taken down by a woman, huh, Charlie? A big guy like you who runs the show. Must be really embarrassing."

Charlie looked up at Quay and glared.

"Funny," Quay added, "I bet you'd like to flip me the bird if you could. But now, Charlie, you can't even do that. You're just a lame duck. Worthless. How's that feel? You just got bested by a woman." He smiled, looked at

277

Sam, and then back to Charlie. Sam gave Charlie a final shove back to the ground and then turned to Quay. She rewarded him with a satisfied grin.

"Still trying to prove you're as good as a man, huh, Sam?" His nonchalant demeanor couldn't hide his pride.

"Yeah! And you're damn glad I'm your partner, Thompson!"

He couldn't help but laugh. His tension was spent. Relief surged through him as he took two full strides to Sam and embraced her in a bear hug.

"Yeah! You're right. I am damn glad."

Quay and Sam lifted Charlie together, each grabbing an arm. He was dead weight with the injured knee. They each hooked an arm through an elbow and dragged him along as he hobbled on one foot. He groaned and cursed as they rounded the corner of the cabin and dropped him to the ground in front of John.

"That guy is pure crazy," Ernie Elson sputtered to John. "He tried to kill me!"

"Sure he did. We know all about it," answered John. "It's over now. We'll get everything sorted out in a bit. We need to get help."

John placed the call to his deputies just as the storm began to let up. His deputies would come around the lake on ATVs. They'd pick them up and return them to Charlie's cabin. A couple BCA fellows had picked up Quay's truck in Barnum and were bringing it to meet them at the cabin. John, Quay, and Sam could take Quay's vehicle up to the sheriff's office. John's deputies would take care of the rest. Then they could go to his place and get cleaned up. It sure would feel good to get out of the wet clothes, he thought.

Quay pulled out his phone and called Mike with the helicopter. He gave him the all clear and thanked him for his service. Quay knew the BCA would hand out an appropriate reward for his help.

The storm had begun to wane down to a few fine sprinkles. The air smelled fresh. The scent of wet pine hung in the air. Birds began to return to the air, and a rustle of life returned to the woods.

"God, I could use a cigarette!" Quay complained.

With a twinkle in her eye, Sam reached into the pocket of her jacket, cupped something in her hand, and held it out to Quay. As she opened her fingers, he saw a square, pink packet of bubblegum.

"You are something else!" he said as he took the gum. "Where'd you get this?"

"I grabbed a couple packs when we left your office this morning. Thought you might need some extra stress relievers sometime today."

"Yeah, I guess I sure did! You mean you managed to keep that in your pocket through this entire ordeal?"

"Mmm-hmmm." She nodded, smiling. "I really didn't have much to do when I was riding with Charlie except try to get comfortable on the floor of that cab!" She gave Charlie a slight kick with her toe and relished his groan.

"Well, we're both glad you're okay," said John as he reached around and gave her a small hug. "You had us really worried."

"Ah, not me! I knew she could take care of herself." Quay grinned.

"Yeah, right! You were sweating bullets about her, and you know it," said John as he gave Quay a shove.

279

Sam watched the two of them and knew the play was for her benefit, but also that it was their way of releasing the tension. It had been a tough day, and it wasn't over yet.

Chapter 29

Sunni Hyun hurriedly gathered files and thumb drives and fled the research lab. The office was buzzing with news of Charlie Frank. He had been captured somewhere north of Duluth. The information spread like wildfire through the building. Charlie had a cabin in the back woods up near Lake Superior. Now she couldn't afford to sit and wait. There was no time to waste. Her operation at Cameron BioTech had come to an end. She had to disappear. Charlie Frank would spill everything.

She'd thought Charlie's plan to hire Ernie Elson and use SPARTA to tarnish Cameron's image had been a questionable idea in the first place. Now it had ended right in his lap. He'd assured her that he could handle everything. He wanted the money. She tried to persuade him that they shouldn't bring anyone else in on the plan. He wouldn't listen and assured her over and over that he knew what he was doing. He'd treated her like a child. Or maybe worse, he'd treated her like a weak female.

Sunni had lost control of him shortly after Karen Thompson's murder. It had been a plan for discrediting Cameron. Investors would flee in light of the bad publicity drawn by a murder. Unfortunately, that hadn't worked out very well, either. The North Korean operatives had been furious when it happened. But she tried to assure them that Thompson's death would work to their advantage, explaining that they could use the murder of one of Cameron's people to demonstrate the danger of Cameron's research. Americans wouldn't like what they read about their research. The media in America had been so easy to manipulate, she thought. Her goal and that of her masters was simply to destroy Cameron's credibility.

Still, they believed this American Charlie Frank was out of control. They questioned her and demanded she pull in the reins on Frank. Charlie insisted everything would be all right. Since then, it had been a yearlong battle to keep him in line. She'd set up plans that would work to their advantage. Charlie's only job had been to carry out her plans.

The original strategy of the North Korean research facility had been to distort and reshape Cameron's image in America. They surmised that if they could destroy their top global competitor, it would leave the genome research field wide open for them. That meant millions, possibly even billions of dollars in the hands of Hang Sun Research. What a boon it would be to their country and their leader. It would also rob the States of the economy boost they desperately needed. The United States was in a fearful economic crisis. Another company biting the dust and the loss of more jobs would make international news. It might be the last straw for the Americans. In turn, the North Korean labs would own total control of genome research for years to come.

Charlie Frank was but a small part of that plan. Now he had let his impulsiveness destroy the entire future of Hang Sun Research. They weren't going to be happy, Sunni thought. It would be better if he died.

Charlie's attempt to kill Ernie Elson was another mistake. What baffled Sunni was how Charlie thought he could have pulled that killing off without drawing more unnecessary attention to SPARTA. SPARTA had been meant to be a pawn, nothing more. Charlie Frank had botched the entire plan. He had drawn too much attention to their agenda of destroying Cameron's credibility. Someone was destined to figure it all out. And now they had. Quay Thompson had arrived on the scene. For some reason, Charlie Frank, her uber-confident operations man, had gone ballistic when he realized Thompson was there.

She feared what Charlie could reveal about the interests of Hang Sun Research and their motives. She hadn't told him much, but he had deduced a lot. It was imperative that Charlie be silenced. It was time to withdraw and cut the losses. There would be another way, another time to destroy Cameron BioTech. She would develop a new plan to share with her bosses. But first, she had to clean up the mess with Charlie Frank.

Sunni stopped by the front desk to check out with Hal, Cameron's security officer, before she left. Hal proudly shared the latest information he had received on the "Charlie Frank case." He'd just gotten word, he said, that Charlie Frank had been taken into custody and was going to be transferred to the BCA headquarters here in the Cities. Hal said they told him they planned to detain him there long enough to finish some preliminary questioning.

Then Hal dropped the information that hit Sunni like a blast of ice water. Hal told her that the BCA detective, Quay Thompson, and that woman, his partner Sam Atwood, had called, and they would be stopping by Cameron to interview people as soon as they finished with Charlie. That could be as soon as tomorrow morning.

She had to move quickly. She made excuses to Hal and left early for the day. Sunni lived close enough to the Cameron Research Labs. She could clear out any incriminating evidence, pop all the information from the hard drive of her laptop into a couple thumb drives, and be ready to leave in no more than an hour. She'd wipe the hard drive and ditch the laptop somewhere. That shouldn't be a problem. She could gather up her passport and get a quick flight out to somewhere—anywhere. She just needed to get a head start.

Chapter 30

Charlie's gray Lexus sedan was discovered late that afternoon fifteen miles from his cabin. It had been parked at a small resort close to the boundary waters. They discovered he'd rented a cabin at the resort last weekend, but the owners claimed they hadn't seen him since he left to do some portaging in the area. It was evident he'd been making his escape plans for quite a while. He'd thought it all out. Then Quay and Sam's visit had freaked him out. He'd overreacted. That had been only one of his mistakes.

Two Cook County deputies had helped the EMTs load Charlie into the ambulance that took him to the hospital in Grand Marais. His leg was set and immobilized. He was going to have to remain in the hospital for at least twenty-four hours. That was fine with Quay. It would make it easier to question him.

It was early evening by the time Quay and John returned to the jail to see their prisoner, Ernie Elson.

Quay, Sam, and John had taken a couple hours to get cleaned up at John's house. Sharon had put together a quick, warm meal for them. Quay had called headquarters, delivering a report of the day's events, and then he'd enjoyed a few minutes' distraction playing with his niece and nephew.

They had all agreed that it would be best for Sam to stay at John's home that evening and spend time relaxing with John's family. She was exhausted. Her ordeal over, she had taken a shower and finally collapsed into a deep sleep in John's guest bedroom. With Sam secure, Quay and John decided they'd pay a visit to Ernie Elson first.

285

Elson had been taken directly to the sheriff's office, where he demanded to talk to whoever was in charge. Quay and John led his interrogation. Ernie quickly denied his own culpability. He was eager to talk about Charlie Frank. However, Ernie's confession filled in very few blanks. He repeatedly asserted that he had been manipulated and used by Charlie Frank. The fact that he murdered Annie Bell seemed to have little meaning to him. He chose to dismiss her murder.

"She was a former student," Ernie explained easily to John and Quay. "She wanted to be close to me. You know how kids are these days. It's not always the teachers who initiate the affairs, you know. I just couldn't get her to leave me alone."

"Sure, Ernie. Now tell us how it happened that you murdered her," Quay urged.

"Well it wasn't really like that. You see, she joined SPARTA mostly because of me. She worshipped me." Ernie smiled, his ego dictating his statements.

John encouraged him. "Yes, we've heard that, Ernie. So she had a thing for you. One of those student-teacher crushes, huh?"

"Yeah, that's right." He ran his hand through his long, black hair, pulling it out of his eyes. His beard had become grisly and tangled. His dark eyes sunk into his face with dark circles beneath them.

"She was an eager SPARTA member, because I was the president of SPARTA. When I spurned her advances at the SPARTA conference that weekend, she attacked me. She came to my cabin that last night and threw herself at me. I tried to push her away, you know? She fell back awkwardly and hit her head against the chair in the room." He looked down, shaking his head. "I tried to break her fall but wasn't able to. She just lay there. I thought, at first, she was unconscious. But when I tried to revive her, I discovered she was dead."

"So you're saying it was accidental. Is that right?" Quay leaned forward, looking intently into Ernie's eyes.

Ernie returned his gaze, looking directly at Quay. "Yes, that's what I'm saying. I didn't try to kill her. It was an accident that happened when she came at me."

"Well that's very interesting, Ernie." Quay paused a moment. "You see, Annie's autopsy showed the marks of your hands on her neck. Did you accidentally grab her by the neck when she came at you? And then, did you just accidentally twist her neck? And snap it? Wasn't that what you did, Ernie?" Quay's voice rose as he leaned into Ernie's face.

Ernie bent away from Quay. He looked to John for help, and seeing none, looked down at the floor.

"I need an answer, Ernie. Wasn't that what you did?"

"I think I need a lawyer."

Then after a long pause, he finally spoke again. Ernie's voice was resigned, defeated, and small. "Yes, you got it right. That was what happened. She found out that I had been getting paid by Cameron to create the protests and disrupt their work. She didn't mind the protests. She just didn't like that I was getting paid. She thought it sounded like a conspiracy. She said that was a breach of everything she believed in. She attacked me that night. I had to stop her. I knew she would go public if I didn't. I couldn't allow her to destroy me and to destroy SPARTA. SPARTA's work is important."

John looked at Quay. Quay sighed and turned away from the table.

287

"Let's get this signed, sealed, and delivered. John, you'll have to keep him here for the BCA, so we can get back to him when we have more questions. I know we'll have more to ask him. We need to get all the facts about his connections to Charlie."

"We can do that, Quay. I'll have the boys take care of it right away."

Quay turned back to Ernie.

"Oh, just one more question, Ernie. How'd you get up here to Charlie's place? How did you put that all together?

Ernie smiled now. He brushed his beard, slicked his hair back once more, and began his story anew. He was eager to relate how Charlie had tried to kill him. He proudly explained how he had managed to track Charlie down to his job at Cameron BioTech using the license plates, and then he'd used the Internet to locate Charlie's properties. He'd really had to do some digging, but he found it. That day, he'd driven to Cameron Research to confront Charlie. He'd seen them, he explained, as they flew out of the parking lot, racing after Charlie.

"I was in Nam, you know? So I had a little knowledge of helicopters and planes from my time over there. When I got back, I got my pilot's license."

"So, you flew up there?" prodded Quay.

"I have a small plane that I store at the Crystal Airport. Not many people know about it. After I saw you guys leave, I turned around and headed for the airport."

"How did you know he'd go up to his cabin?"

"Well, I didn't. But I figured that'd be the place I'd head to. It's close to the Canadian border, and Charlie was in big trouble if he was taking off like that."

"So you flew up there?"

"Sure, I flew up there and managed to land at a small landing strip by Lutsen. They let me rent a four-wheeler near there, and I used that to get over to the cabin using GPS. I saw the cabin and decided to explore the perimeter of the lake since I had the time. I found the shack and Charlie's four-wheel ATV over there across the lake. He had a bunch of stuff stashed in the shack. He even had that old rifle there with the ammo. It was clear he was getting ready to split. It was a no-brainer at that point. I just waited him out."

"You're a resourceful man, Ernie, there's no doubt. Too bad you didn't use your smarts to better the world." Quay paused. "I've got one other question for you, Ernie. This one is very important, so be sure you think about it before you answer."

Ernie nodded, looking up at Quay.

"Were you there with the SPARTA group at Cameron the day Karen Thompson was murdered?" Quay waited, holding his breath.

Ernie stared at him for a moment, and then sudden realization hit.

"Thompson? Your name's Thomson, right? Is that what this is all about? Are you related to that woman?"

"She was my wife, Ernie. Now let's have the answer. Were you there with SPARTA that day?"

"Yeah, we were all there. I'd been instructed by my Manager—you know, Charlie Frank—to be there for the press conference that day. We were supposed to make a lot of noise in front of the cameras. You know, make sure our presence was noticed."

Then a panicked expression slid into Ernie's eyes.

"Oh, no. You don't think I did it? No way. I didn't know anything about that. I absolutely didn't have anything to do with that. That had to have been Charlie! That was just the start of my problems with the whole thing. I was angry because SPARTA was being investigated about that sniper. Charlie, uh, my Manager, sent me a message that he didn't know anything about it, either. Claimed he was just as surprised as we were. But I never believed him. I always thought he knew something about it."

"How did you talk to Charlie? How'd you get your directions and your money?" asked John.

"We always e-mailed. He'd send an e-mail to my school account. There was never any sender address. It was always just from 'The Manager.' I got my money in an envelope. He always left it under the seat of the pickup while I was in class. I never saw him. I just left the door of the pickup unlocked for him on certain days. The money was always there."

"So you never knew who Charlie was until just recently after he tried to kill you. Is that right?"

"That's the truth! There's no way I could have possibly been involved with that murder. All of us from SPARTA were standing at the back of the crowd that day. All of us. All your investigators accounted for every one of us that day. We didn't do it! I didn't do it!"

"Well, we appreciate your help here, Ernie," Quay said as he stood up, stretching his lanky frame. "You're going to do some time in the jail here for a few days to start with. We'll probably have a few more questions for you tomorrow." Quay absently pulled a piece of bubblegum out of his shirt pocket, unwrapped it, and popped the pink piece in his mouth. He turned to his brother. "Sheriff, let's go visit our man Charlie."

Quay pulled his jacket off the chair back, slung it over his shoulder, and headed toward the door. As they left the interrogation room, John signaled his deputies to take care of Elson and followed Quay out the door. Ernie Elson closed his eyes and slowly bowed his head to the table.

Chapter 31

The two brothers—one lanky with short, dark hair, one taller with tousled, blond hair—strode confidently into the lobby of the Grand Marais Hospital. The combination of the shower and subsequent interrogation of Ernie Elson had refreshed Quay.

Earlier at John's house, Quay had carefully shampooed and combed his hair out of his eyes. He'd borrowed a deep purple Viking's cap from John and slapped it on his head. Indignant blond curls sprouted out in awkward angles around his ears. He'd borrowed a clean flannel shirt from John to throw on over his gray T-shirt. The green plaid shirt hung loosely over pants that still looked like he'd camped out in them. At this point, he didn't care what he looked like.

Tonight he was going to finally learn the truth about Karen's murder. He knew Charlie Frank had the answers. Charlie had announced to him this morning that he'd had a hand in Karen's murder. He would finally be able to bring closure to his anguish and guilt, and most importantly, Karen could rest in peace. His confident stride demonstrated his hope and determination.

The hospital lobby was quiet. It was past visiting hours. John and Quay approached the reception desk, flashed their badges, and asked for Charlie Frank's room.

Charlie had been settled into a secure room on the third floor. Quay and John took the elevator to the third floor in silence. The nurse at the third-floor desk eagerly shared information about Charlie's knee surgery. The bullet from Sam's gun had smashed Charlie's kneecap. The surgeons had removed the bullet and had immobilized his leg. They couldn't do surgery until the swelling went down. Then there would have to be several follow-up surgeries to completely repair the knee.

A guard sat quietly on alert outside Charlie's door.

Quay pushed open the door to Charlie's room and looked in at the huge man lying on his back in the hospital bed. A small lamp was lit on the wall next to the bed. His leg was slightly elevated in a contraption that looked like the twisted wires of an acrobat's trapeze. Charlie's eyes were closed, but they opened in a droopy-lidded look at the sound of the door opening. A look of recognition and fear flashed across his face as Quay pushed into the room to stand next to the bed.

"Good evening, Charlie."

Charlie looked away.

"We need to talk," said Quay. "You aren't going anywhere for a while. You've got nothing more to gain. Now it's time to wipe the slate clean. You and I both know that prison isn't a very nice place for a cop. You talk to us now, and things might go easier."

Charlie closed his eyes and again turned his head to the wall.

"Charlie, we need some answers. Tonight is the time to clear it up. Sam's okay. You didn't seriously hurt her. That's in your favor. We just need to know what was going on at Cameron. We know that you were being paid. We need to know who was running you and why."

"I'm not talking to you, Thompson. I'm not ever talking to you!"

"Then talk to John. I don't care. Talk to him."

"I'm not talking to any Thompson. You're both wasting your time. Get the hell out of here and leave me alone."

Another ten minutes passed as Quay and John tried unsuccessfully to convince Charlie to talk. Their questions echoed back at them from the sterile white walls. Charlie Frank was determined not to talk.

Quay and John left Charlie's hospital room late that night. Quay slumped into the seat of John's truck and rode back to John's place in silence. He was defeated. It seemed there was nothing more they could do. John understood Quay's emptiness and suggested they try to get a good night's sleep and try again in the morning. The morning light might give them some inspiration. They'd get the answers tomorrow.

The morning sunlight filtered through the blinds onto Quay's bed. The blankets revealed a bed that remained unused. The exhausted man sat in the rocker next to the window, staring out at the woods behind the house. The night had closed in about him, a dark, inky blot on his soul. He'd searched through that soul for answers. He'd decided he was not going to walk away from this until it was settled. He'd finally constructed a plan.

During the night, he reviewed everything he had learned that week. He'd known Charlie Frank before when they'd worked together in the police department. He thought he knew what had driven him then. Charlie was an angry man for more than one reason. Years ago, his wife had cheated on him and had finally left him for another man. Fortunately, they'd had no kids. Or maybe that was unfortunate. He might have been a different man if he'd had kids who counted on him. Probably due to his anger issues, he'd also been passed over several times for promotions in the department. Then there'd been that investigation. Charlie had been on the take, he was sure of it. He wondered what else Charlie had been into. After all his failures, Charlie must have thought he needed to redeem himself. Someone else must have known about Charlie's miserable life and used it to get to Charlie.

As Quay reviewed what he knew about Charlie, Quay came to the realization that he could use that weakness of Charlie's to get the answers he needed. However, he also knew that Charlie hated him; Charlie would never talk to him or help him. Charlie Frank considered Quay Thompson to be his archenemy.

But there was another possibility. Charlie might talk to Sam. She'd been his victim. She'd no doubt developed somewhat of a bond with him. She might be able to use that captor/victim identity to establish enough of a relationship with him to get him to trust her. Sam said he'd talked to her all the way to Duluth. He'd bragged about what he'd done. Maybe she could get more out of him now.

Sam was dressed and enjoying breakfast with John's kids in the kitchen when Quay joined them. It was a comfortable scene, with Adam and Alli chatting and joking with Sam. They were happily sharing the latest stupid puns they'd learned at school from friends. Sam's eyes twinkled as she pushed her hair behind her ears. She leaned forward and gave Adam a high five. Sharon was leaning against the kitchen counter, enjoying her children's adoption of Sam as a friend.

Quay pulled out a chair and joined the group at the table. Sam glanced up at him. He looked more haggard today than he had yesterday, if that was possible. He was wearing the same clothes he'd left in last night. She smiled at him, reached into her pocket, and pulled out a pink packet of bubblegum. She squeezed his hand as she placed it there.

"You doing okay this morning, Quay?" she asked.

"Well, I guess I've been better, and I've been worse."

Sharon busied herself dishing up a warm breakfast for him. Adam and Alli looked at their uncle and were quieted. They sensed his disquiet.

"John told us that Charlie's refusing to talk. What are we going to do? We've got to get some answers soon. Something has to be going down at Cameron since all this happened yesterday."

"I agree. I think I came up with an idea last night. I think we can get Charlie to talk, if you're willing to give us a hand."

"Sure," Sam was quick to assure Quay. "I'll do anything we need to do."

"Well, let's get you up there to visit with him. He thinks he knows you. He's developed some kind of relationship with you. He felt in control when he had you captive. Maybe we can use that to get him to talk."

Sam was already on her feet.

"I'll get my self cleaned up a bit. Sharon, can I borrow some of your makeup?"

"Sure, let me show where I keep my makeup. You use whatever you need."

Sharon and Sam disappeared up the stairway. Quay patted Adam on the back and gave Alli a quick hug, saying good-bye as he walked toward the front door.

Quay waited in his truck for Sam. He was anxious to get going. Sam came striding out the front door looking like she was walking down a model's runway. She'd borrowed a colorful, loose shift dress from Sharon. Fortunately, she and Sharon were about the same size. She'd also borrowed a pair of matching pink flats. Her hair was pulled up into a deep auburn, twisted knot on top of her head. Quay was amazed at the transformation. She looked innocent, fresh, and wonderful.

As they rode to the hospital, Quay shared everything he knew about Charlie with Sam. They discussed how Sam would approach her visit with Charlie. Quay felt it was important that she play upon Charlie's ego. But he reminded her that they also had to remember that Charlie was no dummy. He'd recognize that she was manipulating him if she didn't play it right. Sam assured Quay that she could do it.

"I know how important this is to you, personally, Quay. I'll get it out of him. We'll do it right, too. We'll get it all recorded, and he'll go down for it. Don't worry. By the end of today, you'll have your answers."

"I hope so. I thought that yesterday. Guess it doesn't always go the way you think it will."

"This time it will, Quay. Chew your gum and relax! Let me do the work this time." She smiled at him and jumped out when he pulled up to the hospital door.

Chapter 32

Sam tapped lightly at Charlie's door before hesitantly pushing it open.

"Charlie?"

Charlie's turned to look at her, and she saw a flash of appreciation cross his face before his features rearranged to anger.

"What are you doing here? You here to gloat, too? Your boyfriend, Thompson, was here last night. I told him I wasn't talking to him."

Sam ignored his reference to Quay.

"No, Charlie. I came to see you," Sam said softly. "I wanted to see if you were all right. I shot you. I'm sorry about the knee. You just didn't give me any choice, you know. I think you'd have done the same thing if you'd been in my place. You know how it is."

"Yeah, you're probably right. I know you were just doing the job." Charlie warmed to her inclusion of him in the profession. "That's what we were trained to do, right?"

"That's right. You know," she paused, looking intently at Charlie, "we got to know each other on that ride to Duluth." Charlie shifted restlessly, looking away to find his water glass. "You told me a few things about yourself, Charlie."

Sam was nearly holding her breath. Realizing what she was doing, she forced herself to breathe normally.

Charlie eyed her suspiciously as he sipped his water. It was clear he wasn't sure about her. He wasn't going to buy this so readily. She had been his captive just hours before. Now she was here professing empathy.

Sam knew she needed to reassure him before she could ask for any answers. Assuming Charlie's silence meant acceptance, she continued, "I know you've had a rough time, Charlie. I also know you think you got a raw deal from the police department because of Quay."

Charlie erupted. "That sonofabitch ruined my life. He's deserved everything he got."

"What do you mean? You said that before, but you never explained it to me," Sam asked innocently. "I don't understand. Tell me about him."

"He's a rat. You watch out for him. He'll turn his back on anyone, even you, to get what he wants. All he wants is to climb up the ladder."

When he paused, Sam intuitively remained quiet.

"He'll look like a fool when I get done with him. He's lost his wife, and he'll be discredited with the BCA because it's too late for him to do anything about Cameron BioTech. No one will want him on a case anymore. He'll be proven to be an incompetent cop. They'll discover he just puts on a good front. Your partner is gonna be done."

"I understand. Truly I do, but, Charlie, you have so much talent. But in this case, you've let your need for revenge guide you. Look what you've done. My God, Charlie, you've put together what appears to be a massive conspiracy to destroy Cameron. How does that make you feel? How'd you do it?"

"Ha," Charlie laughed. "I had more power than you could ever believe. I was an operative for people outside of this country who had more money than they knew what to do with, which they paid me, by the way—" Charlie abruptly stopped, looked at Sam, and realized he had said too much.

299

Sam seized the opportunity to cajole Charlie to tell her the entire story.

"Charlie," she began softly. "You know what I'm here for. You've got to tell your story. Let people know what's gone down. They paid you, but now where are they? Don't let them get away without showing them what you're really capable of, Charlie."

Charlie yanked on his bed sheet, pulling it up to his chin. His demeanor softened. His eyes glistened. He rubbed a meaty palm over his face and back across the top of his head. Fine wisps of hair stood askew after the motion. The simple motion left the weary weakness of Charlie Frank exposed.

"Yeah. I know what you're here for. Let's get to it."

Sam sighed and began.

"Charlie Frank, you have the right to ..."

Charlie interrupted Sam, waving her off. "Never mind. I know the routine. It won't do any good to have a lawyer here."

Sam stepped to the door and motioned to the guard. Charlie looked away as the guard entered the room. He would be the third party who listened as a witness. Sam placed her phone on the bedside table, setting it to record.

Charlie began to tell the story for them in measured detail. He explained how a North Korean researcher by the name of Sunni Hyun, who worked at Cameron, had contacted him. How he'd been paid thousands of dollars over a period of three years. How his assignment had been to destroy the credibility of Cameron BioTech using his position inside the building. As a security guard, he had full control of the building.

He'd hired Ernie Elson from SPARTA to organize the protests outside the facility and develop a distorted image of Cameron's research for the media. He explained how he had searched out and paid Ernie Elson to maintain that constant protestor's presence and voice against Cameron.

He explained that Sunni Hyun had demanded that he allow her to filter out research information from Cameron to her control overseas. He turned a blind eye to her visits to research data departments. Overall, he said his job had been mainly to disrupt operations and provide opportunities for Sunni to get into the research data library.

"Where or who was Sunni Hyun's control, Charlie? Did you ever find that out? You were surely clever enough to discover who you were dealing with," Sam said. Charlie's ego responded to Sam's clever stroking.

"Yeah, I found out," Charlie assured her. "I'm pretty good with tech stuff. I traced some of the stuff she e-mailed out. She used that research library at Cameron to send it out. It went to a connection with a research facility in North Korea."

"So, you're saying a research facility in North Korea was trying to disrupt work at Cameron?" Sam was confused.

"That's right. This genome research stuff has the potential to be worth millions, maybe even billions of dollars if they can identify the sources of cancer, diabetes, cell regeneration, and hundreds of diseases. The cloning capabilities alone will allow them to clone new organs, I guess. I don't understand all of it. The Cameron CEO says the company that controls that stuff can patent the new treatments that are developed as a result of the studies and research. Some North Korean company wanted that money."

Charlie paused to take another drink of his water. He shifted in the bed, rearranged his injured leg, and continued.

"And that company didn't want to share it with a company in the U.S. Cameron BioTech was way ahead of all the other research facilities in the U.S. So the Korean facility had to shut them down."

"My God, Charlie!" Sam was stunned at the magnitude of his story. "And you discovered this after Sunni hired you as an operative?"

"Yeah! I discovered all of it. And I was doing fine until I decided to stop them. I couldn't keep doing it. After Ernie Elson e-mailed me that he'd killed the girl, and they ordered me to take Ernie Elson out of the picture before you got to him, I realized I had to get out. I'm not a murderer." He paused, reflecting. "I really thought the accident had killed him. I didn't want to do it. Sunni said they were going to ruin my reputation and then kill me. I had no choice." Charlie looked at Sam with pleading eyes.

Sam took in the look, patted his hand, and urged him to continue. "So what was the deal with the break-in at Cameron? Did you stage that?"

"Yeah, I did. I thought that if I could make Cameron aware that something was going on, they'd catch Sunni Hyun on their own."

"But then Quay Thompson showed up, and that wasn't what you wanted, was it? You didn't want him to mess it up. Is that right?"

"That's about right. When he showed up, I knew that everything was going to collapse, and I'd be the one blamed. Because of Thompson again. Instead of an innocent bystander, he was going to nail me again. I couldn't let him take me down again. I thought if I could escape, there'd be enough of a follow-up that you'd find out about North Korea anyway. I could get away, with no damage done. You gotta know, Sam, you weren't going to be hurt. I was never going to hurt you. I just had to scare you. Scare Thompson off."

"I understand, Charlie." Sam grabbed his hand and squeezed it. It was a gesture that was part sympathy and part professional encouragement. She had to keep him talking.

"You didn't seriously hurt me, Charlie." Sam was trying her best to sound sincere. She continued, encouraging him, "I understand you were trying to stop a desperate situation. It was your only way out, wasn't it?"

The hospital room grew still. Sterile pans clinked in the hallway as nurses went about their duties.

Sam wanted to urge Charlie to continue his confession. She knew she had to get the answer to one more question before they were done. Then they could wrap it all up.

"Charlie ..." Sam hesitated, took a deep breath, and pushed forward. "I know you didn't want to hurt anyone. You say you're not a murderer. But there's one more unanswered question. What about Karen Thompson? Didn't you kill her to get revenge on Quay? Was that what really happened that day?"

"Hell, no!" Charlie's voice boomed with renewed strength. He pulled himself up, shifting to look directly at her. "I wanted to hurt him, but I didn't shoot his wife. I

303

was as shocked as anyone when that went down."

"You didn't do it?" Sam was confused.

"No! God no! I think it was Sunni who did it. I think she used that press conference to rev up her attack on Cameron. I saw her coming down from the upstairs labs right after it happened. I didn't dare say anything. I had to pretend no one was there. She was good. No one even had a clue that she'd been there. Everyone thought she'd been working at her station in the lab that day."

"So why did you tell Quay and me that you 'took care of his wife'?"

"I just wanted to torment him, ya know? I hate that guy. That man ruined my life. And I thought you'd tell him after it was all over. I heard about how broken up he was after she was killed. It drove him crazy that they never found out who did it. It felt good to see him suffer some, like he'd made me suffer."

"You really, really hate Quay Thompson, don't you, Charlie?" Sam asked.

"Huh. Yeah, I have to admit that I do." Charlie nodded and looked down at his hands folded in his lap. "I know I hurt him. I know it was wrong. Now I'm the one who's going to suffer. That ought to make him happy."

"If you hated him so much, Charlie, how can we believe that you weren't the one to kill his wife?"

"All you have to do is find Sunni Hyun. Search her place. She's probably still got the gun. It'll all check out. I'm not lying, Sam. I'm telling you the truth, one cop to another." He looked at her with a grim smile.

Sam sighed, looked at the guard, and nodded. He left the room, leaving her alone with Charlie. She ran her hand through her hair, wiped her eyes, and stood to leave.

"Thank you, Charlie. Thank you. You get that knee taken care of. We'll take care of you. You won't be forgotten. You've been a big help. That's going to go well for you. We'll try to work out something. Quay will help. You'll find out he's not really the bad guy. He'll speak for you. I'm going to see if we can catch Sunni Hyun. We're going to have to call in the big boys for this one. Get some rest."

She patted Charlie's shoulder as he wiped tears from his eyes. Grabbing her phone and stopping the recording, she turned quickly, left the room, and hurried to find Quay. They had the answers they needed.

Epilogue

Quay was leaning against the desk in the hospital lobby when Sam came out of the elevator. Her relief was evident as she sprinted across the lobby and grabbed his hands, pulling him close to her.

"It's over, Quay. We've got our answers. It's over."

Sam clung to Quay and began to laugh with relief. Her green eyes sparkled as she looked into his. "You'd better sit down. We've got it all!"

They huddled together in two chairs in the corner of the hospital lobby while Sam related Charlie's story.

Quay listened intently, head bowed, while Sam told him everything Charlie had revealed, especially the part about Karen. When she was done, he sat back and quietly processed what she'd told him. Sam studied Quay as lines of worry slowly faded from his face and turned into lines of relief.

"Well, partner," he began as he pulled another of his ever-present pieces of bubblegum from his pocket, "I guess this one's finally finished for us. Let's get the call into headquarters. They're going to have to notify the FBI and the State Department and get to work on Sunni Hyun. Hopefully, we're not too late."

They walked out into the sunlight. Quay stopped as they approached his truck and pulled Sam toward him. He wrapped his arms around her, holding her tightly against him.

"Thank you, Sam," he whispered in her ear. "Thank you."

She returned his hug with a firm squeeze and brushed his whisker-stubbled cheek with a kiss.

"You've got your life back. Now that the story of Karen's murder is solved, you've got your redemption. Now let's get on with it, okay?" she said.

"I'm think I'm ready, Sam. I'm finally ready."

Quay looked over her shoulder out toward the lake. It truly was a beautiful day in the North Country. After the rain, the leaves on the trees had become brighter, with more brilliant oranges, reds, and yellows. Lake Superior glistened with peacock colors in the distance, its waves waltzing toward the shore in white ribbons. He realized he hadn't noticed how truly beautiful it was until today. He turned Sam toward his truck, blew a large pink bubble, popped it, and pulled it into his mouth. Life was good.

Made in the USA
Middletown, DE
10 September 2022

10190582R00170